THE
WHISPERER

Lucinda Hare

Book One of the Dragonsdome Chronicles

lucinda@dragonsdome.co.uk
http://www.dragonsdome.co.uk/
http://thedragonwhispererdiaries.blogspot.co.uk/

Published by Thistleburr Publishing
www.thirstleburr.co.uk

The Dragon Whisperer
Thistleburr Publishing, ISBN: 978-0-9574718-8-7

The Dragonsdome Chronicles

The Dragon Whisperer
Flight to Dragon Isle
Dragon Lords Rising
The Stealth Dragon Services
Dark Dragon Dreams

* * *

The Fifth Dimension

The Sorcerers Glen

* * *

Catastrophe ~ A Scottish Wildcat's Tail
*

Haggis ~ A Blind Cat's Tail
*

Falling for Autumn: Child & Adult Colouring Book
Seadragon Songs of the Sea: Child & Adult Colouring
Book

PRAISE for *The Dragonsdome Chronicles*

My 15 year old son picked up the first book in this series and was hooked over a year ago. He got me to read it and I was hooked too. *Amazon review*

I hold my hands up. I am a 62 year old woman who loves dragons. I have just finished all 4 books in this series in less than a week. What a ride I was taken on. This is not a children's book. It is quite frankly a superb fantasy adventure for all ages and the film rights need to be snapped up. All I can say is 'Thank you, Lucinda'. You have made an old woman feel young again even if just in my imagination. *Amazon review*

I'm not sure whether I'll be able to convey with words what I felt reading The Dragon Whisperer and Flight To Dragon Isle. The books were so irresistibly wonderful that I've read them back to back one after the other in a couple of days. I felt like I was ten again and that the universe was just a big adventure waiting to be discovered. *Caroline, from Goodreads*

I think The Dragon Whisperer is the best book I have ever read. (I have read a lot of books – in our house we have about twelve thousand) I think the way the words are written sounds like magic. *Rachel, aged 14*

'One of the most captivating new books to be published for 8+ for some time . . . It made me laugh, cry and remember exactly what's so special about the time when you or your child live in hope of finding a dragon of your own.'
Amanda Craig The Sunday Times

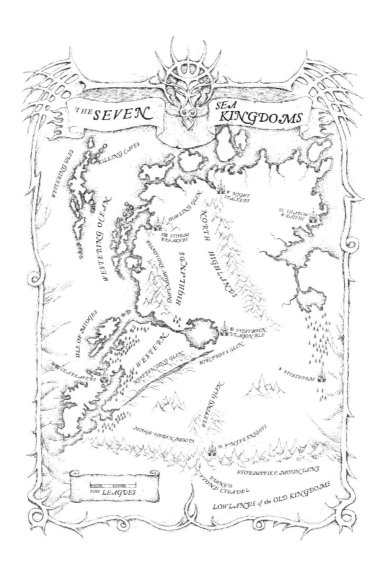

THE SEVEN SEA KINGDOMS

WESTERING ISLES

KILLING CAVES

WESTERING OCEAN

NORTH HIGHLANDS

NIGHT STALKERS

SHADOW WRAITHS

HOWLING GLEN

XII STORM BREAKERS

FIRESTONE MOUNTAINS

WESTERN HIGHLANDS

ISLE OF MIDGES

WAVEBREAKERS

WESTERN DRAGON GLEN

FIRESTORN DRAGON ISLE

SORCERER'S GLEN

FIRESTORM

WEEPING GLEN

MIDGE RIDDEN MOOTS

IX WINTER KNIGHTS

FORKED STONE CITADEL

STORMSTIKE MOUNTAINS

LOWLANDS of the OLD KINGDOMS

100 LEAGUES

iv

THE DRAGON WHISPERER

PROLOGUE

The beacon on the castle's topmost tower could barely be seen through the driving snow. The dwarf, shading his eyes against the storm, beat the gusting flames away from his frozen cloak and went back down into the courtyard to wait.

Cocooned by his heavy bearskin, he was beginning to drowse when the snow falling about him suddenly danced and whirled. The wind howled, the blast almost forcing him from his feet. The dwarf blinked, brushing layers of snow from his heavy, beetled brows. He looked skyward. Within the high inner bailey walls, the air shimmered and sparkled like frost. The fallen snow in front of him was crunched flat, as if by a great weight.

Towering above him, black against the blizzard, stood a great dragon; a chill mist rose from its heaving flanks. A young man, scaled and spiked in the same armour as his dragon, dismounted swiftly.

'The time has come?' he demanded.

'My Lord Earl' – the dwarf went down on bended knee – 'the midwives say it will be soon.'

The Dragon Lord turned to his dragon, Stormcracker, whose great black nose was nuzzling against his shoulder. 'Wait for me, Stormcracker,' he said as he strode into the castle, followed by the dwarf.

Outside, the wind veered round to the south, driving the heavy clouds from the sky to reveal the rising twin moons. As silence settled, a storm of wild dragons appeared overhead. Snow slid down the steep gabled roof of the ancient castle as one landed, its talons gripping a stone gargoyle. Soon it was joined by another, and yet another, until every roof and chimney, every tower and battlement was crowded with them. Then the dragons lifted their heads and sang.

The unearthly sound shivered through the air, raising goose pimples on the flesh of the young man, who paced a dimly lit chamber below. Swiftly the song rose beyond the range of human hearing. In the Sorcerers Glen a pack of wolves hunting elk stopped in their tracks and turned towards the distant castle. A hibernating bear snuffled restlessly in its den; high above its cave on the lower slopes of the Sleeping Wizard Mountain, a sheet of snow broke away with a loud crack to tumble down the side.

The bells tolled midnight and the day slipped into midwinter. Barely had the last chime died when a cry cut through the air; a child's cry, clear, robust, bursting with new life.

The young man turned towards the opening door, the dwarf a few steps behind him. The midwife came out of the birthing chamber, a bundle wrapped in her arms. Beyond her the man could see a woman in the great four-poster bed, lying silent and unmoving against the damask pillows.

'My lord' – the midwife curtsied, holding out the crying babe – 'you have a daughter.'

'Her mother?' Anxiety made his voice rough. 'Is her mother well?'

'She is well, my lord, but she is sleeping. It was a difficult birth. She will need to rest. The apothecary attends her.'

The tension seemed to slide from the man's broad

shoulders. Taking the child, he looked down into tawny eyes that mirrored his own. He smiled, puckering the edge of the newly healed scar that ran ragged from forehead to chin.

The midwife hesitated. 'You are taking the babe to safety, my lord?'

The man nodded. 'To Dragonsdome. None must learn the child's true heritage.'

'We are all sworn in service to our lady, my lord. You need not fear. None here will betray her or the babe.'

In a moment the young man was gone, the fur-wrapped baby in his arms, the dwarf following in his footsteps.

Out in the courtyard he stopped abruptly in his tracks. The wild dragons perched around the castle battlements were all looking down intently. Neither man nor dwarf had ever witnessed such a thing. All was eerily silent, as if the whole world were holding its breath.

The dwarf looked down at the child and gasped. Eyes that had been tawny in candlelight now glowed in the near dark, a bright inhuman gold. 'My Lord Earl!' There was superstitious awe in his voice.

Curious, the man bent over the child and drew a ragged breath that stung the back of his throat. He raised his head to look up to where great golden eyes considered them and their tiny burden.

Then Stormcracker's armoured head reached down to inspect the infant girl. Her crying fell silent and she gurgled with pleasure, her tiny fists brushing against the velvety muzzle of the giant above her.

Greetings, little one . . .

The dragon's deep singsong cadence rumbled in the babe's head as she held out her arms to embrace the dazzling creature – utterly strange and yet strangely familiar.

Greetings, Dancing with Dragons . . . His blue tongue rasped across her skin like hot sandpaper. *Come, little one . . .*

Slowly the great spiked tail that had dealt death to countless hobgoblins uncoiled and slid forwards to twine around the tiny child, lifting her gently from her father's unresisting arms. The man stood, stunned, for a moment, before a rare smile lit his handsome face. Running lightly between his dragon's great spinal plates, the black-armoured Earl mounted swiftly and settled into his pilot's chair, taking his daughter back into his arms. The dwarf settled into his familiar position behind him, buckled against one of the dragon's spine plates, his double-headed axe resting between his boots.

'Come, now.' Wrapping cloak and arms around his daughter, the man gathered up the reins of his stallion. 'To Dragonsdome.'

The Imperial Black dragon rose silently into the night sky. Barely had they crested the castle battlements when the dragon's outline rippled and they were gone, the downdraught from the wings obliterating their tracks in the snow as if they had never existed.

Chapter One
The Battledragon Roosts

This is going to hurt . . . Quenelda warned as the dragon's head gently butted against her, his hot breath licking around her. She spoke in her head, where only dragons could hear.

Pain is nothing, Dancing with Dragons, the Sabretooth dragon boasted, baring his yellowing fangs. *I am strong. Have I not survived more battles than you have years?*

Yes – Quenelda smiled – *you have . . .*

From her perch on the dragon's scaled foreleg, the skinny girl jumped lightly down and stepped onto the circular metal gantry outside the roost. Sweeping the mane of blonde hair from her face, she called out confidently to the dwarf who straddled the dragon's broken tail.

'He's ready.'

'Hmmm...' Tangnost Bearhugger, dwarf dragonmaster to the Earl Rufus DeWinter, grunted doubtfully as he took the strain. 'Now!' he bellowed over his shoulder, his deep gravelly voice muffled by his helmet visor. 'By the One Earth, pull!'

Behind him, a nervous apprentice obediently pulled down on the pulley chains for all he was worth. The greased wheels creaked, the links rattled, the chain was cranked upwards tooth by tooth. Slowly, inch by grudging inch, the winch that cradled the Sabretooth dragon's stubby tail lifted it from the ground, exposing the compound fracture.

The dwarf gritted his teeth. His sweating hands were slipping inside his heavy gauntlets. Shifting his grip, he grunted, then heaved with all his considerable strength. There was a loud crack as the broken bone slid into place, followed immediately by the dragon's bellow of pain.

Tangnost ducked instinctively as white-hot fire licked around him, searching hungrily for a chink in his soot-streaked roost armour. Dragonfire from the angry Sabretooth, known as Two Gulps and You're Gone, blazed around the roost, and then, with a roar and a rattle, escaped through a series of pipes and chimneys into the cold dawn air. As the flame died, the walls of the battleroost glowed cherry-red in the gloom. Glazed bricks pinked as they started to cool.

The job was finally done. Tangnost sucked in an incautious breath of relief – and immediately wished he hadn't. Even filtered through his heavy mask, the supercharged air seared the back of his throat and made his one eye water. He coughed and shook his head at his own folly.

Badly injured battledragons were, as a rule, put down immediately. And quite right too, the dwarf thought ruefully. Healing any injured animal was fraught with difficulties, but nursing a bad-tempered, carnivorous battledragon that was trained to flame, disembowel or decapitate wasn't good for the nerves. Even nerves like his, tempered by eighty years of experience, sixty-five of them on the battlefield before a hobgoblin cleaver invalided him out. It was downright madness, even if that battledragon cost five thousand golden guineas and had taken five long years to train.

Everyone knew that; everyone except a certain young lady dressed in an oversized leather jerkin, patched boy's breeches and heavy flying boots, with a stubborn set to her jaw and determination in her tawny eyes. Already back in the baking-hot roost, Quenelda was now casually scratching the battledragon under the chin as if he were a kitten! Tangnost wondered briefly if she had any idea what they had just achieved and how dangerous it had been.

How does your tail feel, Two Gulps and You're Gone? Quenelda asked politely, completely ignoring the terrified apprentice, who was quaking in his boots.

It throbs, Dancing with Dragons . . . Two Gulps admitted, milky smoke still curling indignantly from his nostrils.

But the sharp pain in your tail . . . ?

It lessens – but it feels hot, and it itches so.

I will tell One-Eye. Keep the weight off your injuries while we tend you.

The battledragon breathed out in soft acknowledgement and turned his scaled head back towards the dwarf and the apprentice tending his tail. His tri-forked red tongue flicked out to taste the air.

I am hungry, Dancing with Dragons, he complained. As if in response, his third stomach grumbled. It sounded like a volcano about to erupt . . . or a dragon preparing to flame. The dwarf took an involuntary step backwards, and with a shriek his young apprentice fled the roost.

Tangnost found himself gazing into two flared nostrils the size of furnace doors. Wisps of steam curled lazily up with the threat of worse things to come. Beyond them, the Sabretooth's reptilian red eyes watched the dwarf's every move with unhealthy interest. A gobbet of corrosive saliva dripped from between yellowed teeth and onto the metal decking, where it sizzled.

Tangnost froze. Sabretooths were notoriously highly strung. They killed at the slightest provocation, and usually could only be handled by the master with whom they had bonded, or by those esquires who had raised them from the egg. An injured Sabretooth was twice as dangerous.

Unaware of Tangnost's dark thoughts, Quenelda slid off the dragon's foreleg and fondly slapped an armoured scale.

No! No! You are not to eat them! She scolded, as she moved round to join her father's dragonmaster. *Or any other Wingless Ones who care for you here at Dragonsdome. We have to bind your tail now and splint it to keep the break in place, but the worst is over. We'll feed you again before we go. Rest well, Two Gulps and You're Gone.*

Rest well, Dancing with Dragons.

The battledragon settled into his stony nest, massive shoulder scales reverberating as he started to purr contentedly.

Judging it safe to remove his helmet, Tangnost wiped the sweat from his brow with the back of his gauntlet and looked into eyes that held a depth of knowledge far in excess of their eleven years.

Quenelda grinned back at his sticky discomfort, at the craggy face dominated by a patch where a hobgoblin arrow had stolen an eye. The strong jaw and broken nose were framed by shoulder-length hair, bound at the right temple in a single warrior's braid after the fashion of his clan. Of all her father's retainers, Quenelda loved the near-legendary dragonmaster best. With the Earl constantly away at war, commanding the elite Stealth Dragon Services, or SDS, Tangnost was the closest she had to a parent. No matter how busy he was, the dragonmaster always made time for her, answering her endless questions with patience and humour, listening with keen interest to her views, as if a young child's opinion truly mattered to him.

As she grew older he often allowed her to accompany him when doing his rounds, especially on difficult cases like this one. And if he was a tough, demanding teacher, he was always fair, and had a gruff heart buried somewhere beneath his armour. The apprentices and even the esquires might be frightened by the one-eyed dwarf, but Tangnost was nonetheless a hero-figure to them; his exploits during his years in the SDS Bonecracker commandos the stuff of fireside tales. And like Quenelda and her father, the Earl Rufus, Tangnost passionately loved the dragons and other creatures in his care.

'I think that's the worst of it over, but the wound . . .' Quenelda shrugged off her heavy, sweat-soaked jerkin, letting it fall to the floor. 'Two Gulps says it is burning him, Tangnost! What does that mean?' She rolled up the sleeves of her finely embroidered shirt, leaving sooty fingerprints on it.

'That is the poison beginning to spread.' Tangnost effortlessly slipped into his familiar role as tutor to the Earl's young daughter. 'We need to ensure the wound doesn't fester. See this streak of darker blue, threading beneath the scales, then fanning out from the break like the tendrils of a tree root?'

Quenelda nodded, listening to his every word.

'Smell it,' the dwarf ordered.

Frowning, Quenelda leaned forward and cautiously sucked in the hot air. She wrinkled her nose in disgust.

'What do you smell?'

'It's sweet, sickly . . . like rotting fruit.'

Tangnost nodded. 'That is the start of infection. That is why the wound feels hot to him, why he is so difficult to handle. Hobgoblin weapons are filthy and many are poisoned. It makes us fear them all the more if we suddenly drop dead weeks after a battle. If we don't treat this now and it spreads, Two Gulps risks losing his tail to gangrene. Then he won't be able to balance, won't be able to run, let alone fight. Here' – the dwarf selected a heavy ceramic apothecary's pot from a low shelf, removed the lid and held it out to Quenelda – 'what's in this, lass?'

Quenelda dipped a finger in and sniffed. She screwed her face up as she thought, testing the grainy texture between her fingers. 'Mandrake . . . barkloam . . . moonlight . . . a hint of appleweed?'

Tangnost gruffly nodded his approval. 'Yes.' Why not push her a little further? he thought. 'Why this combination?'

She didn't hesitate. 'Barkloam to help the wound close and heal. Mandrake to draw out the infection. Moonlight for energy, and ground appleweed bark to lessen the pain.'

'Good.' The dragonmaster nodded, quietly satisfied. 'Good.'

Ever since Tangnost could remember, Quenelda had taken every opportunity to watch him and his roostmasters at work. Slipping away from her nanny and tutors, she would suddenly appear in the roost, sitting quietly, eyes bright with concentration, listening and watching intently as they instructed esquires in dragonlore and dragonhandling. With his five sons all dead in the war, Tangnost loved her like the daughter he'd never had from the moment he first held her.

Once, when she was still a babe, she had disappeared from the nursery. A frantic search of Dragonsdome's vast stables, roosts and paddocks had found her asleep in the battleroosts, curled up beneath the protective wing of her father's battledragon, Stormcracker Thundercloud III. She seemed to have no fear of these deadly creatures, no fear of flying, and they had never harmed so much as a hair on her head.

Before long, Quenelda started to explain how the dragons were feeling, even what they were thinking. Well, the roostmasters had smiled indulgently – lots of young children pretended to talk to animals; they were always having made-up conversations with imaginary friends, and so they didn't pay much attention. But the Earl and his dragonmaster did.

When she was barely five years old Quenelda had warned that Nightmare Nemesis had dreadful indigestion in her third stomach due to eating one half-rotten hobgoblin too many; the roostmistress had ignored her, and the resultant flatulent explosion had flattened half the maternity roosts. Then, when she was seven, she knew that Sunset Spitfire had a fractured trapsom even though the surgeon had declared her fit. The injured battledragon had lived up to her name and reputation when she turned on the dragonsmith who was grafting on a new scale and toasted him and his two apprentices, leaving three piles of ashes and three greasy stains on the floor that took months to scrub off.

Soon Dragonsdome's roostmasters and dragonsmiths began to pay attention when Quenelda chose to share her insights with them. There was no question about it – the young girl had a way with dragons. Only Tangnost, the Earl's dragonmaster, knew just how great that gift might be, but he kept his thoughts entirely to himself.

'Tangnost?' Quenelda impatiently tugged the dwarf's long battle-braid, a childhood habit. She was looking at him quizzically.

'Harrumph.' Tangnost coughed, embarrassed at being caught daydreaming. He put the pot down at Quenelda's feet, careful to hide his excitement. If he was right . . .

'Apply this thickly,' he said gruffly, mind racing. 'You know the drill.' As Quenelda bent to her task, the dragonmaster turned to his young apprentice, inwardly cursing the fact that they were so short-handed he had to resort to untrained and untried youngsters.

'Helmet off,' he barked, making the nervous gnome jump. 'Make yourself useful! Now, Root lad, bring a bucket of tar and a ladle from the cauldron. And make sure it's hot, mind.'

'Sir! Yes, sir!' Root jumped to his assigned task.

'Don't dawdle!' Tangnost growled as the stocky young gnome finally staggered up with a bucket of bubbling tar. 'We haven't got all day. On with it, lad, on with it! Let's see if you've learned anything of dragonhandling in your first season at Dragonsdome. Mind that tar!' he warned as the bucket slopped over the rim to splash his boots. 'It's hot! If you're going to scout like your father, my lad, you've still got a lot to learn about dragons. Now' – he held the boy's gaze for a moment – 'take it slowly, like I've shown you.'

'Sir! Yes, s-s—' Root croaked. His mouth was so dry with fear he couldn't even swallow, and he was beginning to sweat heavily beneath the cumbersome armour.

Root's father was one of the Earl's best scouts. It was a dangerous profession – tracking the hobgoblin war bands – but one that brought great honour and privilege. It meant that Root, his only son, had been given an apprenticeship at Dragonsdome. Few commoners could expect an apprenticeship under the tutelage of one of the greatest dragonmasters of the age. He must not – Root gritted his teeth – he would not let his father down. He would not betray the fact that he was afraid of dragons; dreadfully afraid. But he couldn't help wishing he had been allowed to follow a more traditional family career, such as a rat-catcher's apprentice.

It wasn't enough that they weren't in front of the dragon, in front of foot-long fangs and a walking blast furnace. No, Root found little comfort in tending the dragon's tail. When he was four he had seen a man-at-arms decapitated by one casual flick of a spurred tail when he got too close to a battledragon. The dwarf's head had bounced five times before coming to rest at Root's feet.

Root's heart fluttered. The air was so hot and his throat was parched. Sweat ran in rivulets down the inside of his roost armour, pooling in his boots. He felt faint. He took off a gauntlet to wipe the sweat from his eyes. Hand shaking, trying to shut out the memory, Root dipped the brush back into the tar. The shell beads strung round his wrist rattled with nerves as he raised the dripping brush.

Quenelda watched impatiently as the gnome boy painted on the hot tar. He was so slow! And he was doing such a bad job. The tips of his beaded hair braids were actually hanging in the bucket! Why didn't the dragonmaster intervene? She could show the youth how it should be done.

'Quenelda' – Tangnost turned to go, his armour clanking – 'I just want to check on a Case of Bad Indigestion. Keep an eye on the lad. Once the tar is on, call me and we'll get the splint on.'

Nerves made Root clumsy. He was making a bad job of it and he knew it. He glanced up at the Earl's daughter, her hair tucked behind her small pointed ears. She was always so haughty, and right now she was frowning at him, her lips pursed in their usual thin line of disapproval, just waiting for him to make a mistake so she could show him how it was supposed to be done. And why did she not have any roost armour on? Was she not afraid of being burned by the bad-tempered battledragon?

The great bells of the Dragonsdome belfry struck the Hour of the Strutting Cockerel. Outside, a cockerel obligingly cleared its throat and prepared to announce a new day. They had worked through the entire night! No wonder nerves were fraying.

Quenelda sighed loudly and started to tap her foot with impatience, making the buckles on her flying boots jingle. The uneven rhythm grated on Root's nerves. Picking up on her impatience, Two Gulps and You're Gone twitched his tail.

Root froze. Tar dripped on the floor.

He glanced at Quenelda's back as she moved forwards to soothe the dragon. She was so confident. Even her aristocratic voice made Root jump.

As if she could read his very thoughts, Quenelda sighed loudly and turned back to him. 'Oh, do get a move on,' she said loudly, raising her eyes skyward in exasperation.

Root flinched, dropping the brush into the bucket. Boiling hot tar splashed on his unprotected hand, burning it badly. He muffled a cry.

'Quick!' The Earl's daughter swiftly guided the youth round the dragon towards the water trough. Keeping a firm hold on his armour, she plunged his arm into the freezing water up to his elbow.

'W-what are you doing?' Root was almost weeping with pain.

'If you're going to work with battledragons,' Quenelda said sharply, 'you had better learn how to treat burns. Cold water will stop the burning. Keep your hand in there.'

She opened one of the small pouches on her flying belt and withdrew a small glass pot. 'Hand,' she ordered him brusquely.

Trying not to show the pain, Root held it out.

'Tsk,' Quenelda clucked with disapproval. 'You shouldn't have taken your gauntlet off. Surely you know that by now?'

The back and fingers of Root's left hand were raw and angry. The blistered skin was already peeling off. The cold water had indeed taken the edge off the pain as she had promised. The sticky green paste was soothing, although it did nothing to cool Root's flaming cheeks. He gritted his teeth. Why must she always treat him like a child?

'This should take the heat out of it.' Quenelda spread the ointment on thickly, then cut a strip from the dragon's bandages with her sickle-shaped flying knife and wrapped Root's hand carefully.

'Make sure you go to the hospital barracks and get this checked tomorrow.' She returned the salve to its pouch. 'It should heal quickly. This ointment is terrific for scale re-growth. B—'

'Scale re-growth?' Root squeaked before he could stop himself, looking at his hand in horror. He didn't want to grow any scales!

'But' – Quenelda ignored his interruption – 'make sure you keep the wound clean or it may become infected.'

'Th-thanks, Lady Qu-Quenelda . . .' Root stuttered his clumsy thanks, but she was already turning away when footsteps clanged on the gantry outside.

'Why isn't the tar on yet?' Tangnost bellowed, making them both jump. Quenelda and Root shared a brief awkward smile before turning back to the injured dragon.

Half an hour later the dragonmaster ran his eye approvingly over the neat cast-iron splint that held the dragon's tail rigidly in the sling, and declared himself quietly satisfied. Inwardly he could barely keep his excitement in check. He had taken a great risk, not just with his reputation but with his life. A gamble, many would say if they knew the truth of it, but the Earl's daughter had never yet let him down, and he had not made his decision lightly.

'Guard Quenelda with your life. Teach her everything you know,' the Earl had commanded when he made Tangnost dragonmaster. 'As if she were my son and heir and destined for Dragon Isle. But do so secretly, so that none may remark upon it. The dragons love and protect her. They witnessed her birth. Who yet knows what that may mean?'

And so he had quietly taught her as he had taught the Earl, and had watched as she outstripped her father's achievements at the same age. He had all the pride of a father for a daughter. Were she the Earl's first born and a boy, she would be leaving for Dragon Isle. Instead, everyone thought her triumphs were his own, and it was far safer that way.

His thoughts turned back to the battledragon. What an achievement! Assuming they dealt with the infection of course . . .

As if sensing the dwarf's excitement, Two Gulps and You're Gone uncoiled his long neck and turned his head to inspect their work, lamplight softly glinting off his red and yellow patterned scales.

Thor's Hammer! Tangnost swallowed dryly as a rush of adrenaline punched through his bloodstream. How could Quenelda be so utterly certain the injured dragon would not reduce them all to pyramids of ashes if she could not truly talk to him? Until now he had not honestly believed it possible, had not dared to believe the child could actually talk to these great creatures, could whisper to them.

After all, others could talk to dragons after a fashion; he himself could pick up vague images and sense strong emotions in his mind, as could all dragonsmiths and dragonmasters. SDS Dragon Lords bonded with their dragons and thus flew as one creature, but that was the result of years of work together. But now . . . but now he believed it possible. What else might the young girl be capable of in time?

The consequences for the war would be far-reaching. Battledragons were dying faster than they could be replaced. Imperial Blacks only bred once every seven years; Sabretooths laid a single egg. Ever since the death of the old Earl, the hobgoblins had swarmed in ever greater numbers. If they could treat injured dragons and return them to the battlefront, the possibilities were endless! And the cradle that Quenelda had suggested for the injured dragon – he must talk to his cousin Odin on Dragon Isle to see if their forgemasters could construct something . . .

'Is it done, Tangnost?' Quenelda stretched as gracefully as a cat and took a long drink from her leather water flask, then offered it to the dwarf.

Tangnost nodded. 'We're done.' He gratefully took a deep draught and poured more water over his neck to cool himself. His ancestors came from the acrid dessert mountains of the Old Kingdoms, so he did not suffer in the battleroosts as others did – but still, it had been a long, sweltering night.

Wiping his moustache and returning the flask to Quenelda, he turned to his apprentice. 'Get to your hammock, lad. You look exhausted.' He frowned as he watched the miserable gnome stumble wearily down the steps and wished that, in the absence of the boy's father, he had more time to devote to his instruction.

A nearby dragon flamed, blasting a wall of hot air throughout the roosts. As the fire died back into semi-darkness, Quenelda rubbed her aching temples. The stench of sulphur and scale oil, added to the tiredness, was making her head throb. Two Gulps' three stomachs rumbled again, reminding her of her promise to him.

'He's hungry.'

Tangnost grinned. 'So I notice! That is a very good sign. Well, once that tail is mended he'll be able to hunt for himself again. Meantime we'll just have to build up his strength as best we can. Marwood?' he bellowed.

'Sir?' Setting down two half-cauldrons of coal, a groom ran over.

'Increase his feed: another elk and an extra cauldron of brimstone. We'll see how he's doing in a couple of days.'

'Sir! Yes, sir!'

Tangnost looked at the young girl in front of him. In the dim, flickering light of the wall torches he saw that Quenelda's sooty face was smeared with grease and ground brimstone dust, and her damp bedraggled hair was plastered to her as if she had been swimming in the moat. Grinning up at him, she looked more like a stable hand than an earl's daughter! And she stank! No wonder the grandly dressed young ladies at court looked upon her antics with scandalized horror!

Soaked in sweat within his filthy armour, Tangnost ran a calloused hand through long black hair now tinged with silver at the temples, and supposed he looked no better. He found himself smiling back wholeheartedly. Quenelda was so like her father in character – adventurous and strong-willed – and flying dragons was as natural to her as

19

breathing. It was no surprise that she was determined to follow his footsteps into the SDS. A breath-taking ambition, but one unlikely to succeed. No woman save those of royal blood had even set foot on Dragon Isle since the Academy's founding in the Century of the Canny Stoat, let alone taken to the skies on a battledragon.

Wearily, the pair descended to the middle gantry. Tangnost looked around and sighed. The never-ending Third Hobgoblin War had brutally culled the number of battledragons under his care. Since this year's spring campaign had begun, three more stalls in the Sabretooth roost now lay empty and silent. Those dragons and many of their flight crew would never be returning home. It was a toll that was increasing almost monthly.

Following the dragonmaster's resigned glance, Quenelda shivered with revulsion. It was widely known that hobgoblins enjoyed dragonmeat as a delicacy, and that dragonbones were highly prized as armour – they believed it made them invulnerable to sorcerer weapons and dragon attacks.

With a nod Tangnost turned off into the tack room to change the ceramic armour for his chain-mail hauberk, leather jerkin, studded boots and weaponry.

Head spinning with exhaustion, Quenelda stepped outside the battleroosts into the early dawn. Cold sharp air washed over her like a bucket of water, sending a delicious shiver up her spine. She raised her eyes to where the plump harvest moons shone gold in a rapidly lightening sky. By the time the twin sickles of the hunter's moons rose in two weeks' time, her father would be home.

She could barely contain her excitement.

When Tangnost first proposed that they treat an injured battledragon who had broken his tail and crushed his master to death when he crash-landed under hobgoblin attack, Quenelda had thought he was jesting. The agonized and grieving Sabretooth had flamed at anyone who came within fifty feet – until the Earl's dragonmaster arrived, Quenelda behind him. Then the battledragon had immediately calmed, allowing them close enough to inspect his injuries and wounds.

She was so lucky, Quenelda thought. The dwarf could do anything with dragons. No wonder Lord Hugo Mandrake, the Grand Master himself, had offered him a place when he had been invalided out of the Bonecrackers, but Tangnost had preferred to stay with his Earl at Dragonsdome, where his reputation as dragonmaster soon eclipsed his legendary feats on the battlefield.

And now this! Two Gulps and You're Gone would live to fight another battle. One of her father's favoured battledragons was going to return to the war. Not even Dragon Isle with their High Magic and Battle Mages had managed that! With Tangnost as her tutor, with her father the Commander of the SDS, surely now she could do what no other girl had ever done: win a coveted place at the elite SDS Battle Academy on Dragon Isle!

CHAPTER TWO
Bubble, Bubble, Toil and Trouble

Down in the castle dungeons beneath the dark waters of a sea loch, the growing light of day passed unnoticed. The only illumination down here came from a single smoking wall sconce that stank of sheep fat. Its feeble light was enough to reveal the outline of a black-robed figure, staff outstretched over a cauldron.

He was haloed by bruised purple-yellow flames that seemed to draw in the light rather than give any out. Strange symbols and fearsome creatures were woven into his hooded cloak, forming and re-forming on the shimmering fabric.

He paid no attention to the water that steadily dripped down from the stone chamber's vaulted roof. Nor did he notice the recently slain bodies of dwarfs still manacled to the prison walls. Instead, he eagerly watched the surface of the cauldron. The substance moved as sluggishly as pitch, yellow smoke curling thickly as sea haar.

Almost! Just one more ingredient.

The figure stepped away from the toxic brew, lifting the burning brand from its wall bracket. He picked his way across the slippery floor of the prison and into one of the endless caverns. The bone-cold air was sharp with salt; heavy chains rattled and clinked in the dark, and large shadows shifted grey against the black. He lifted the brand. Light danced and flickered and caught the reflection of dozens of eyes. Bright dragon eyes.

He studied the panicking dragons thoughtfully, ignoring the pitiful screams that rose up around him. His experiments were promising, although the cost in wasted dragons was very high. He had begun with these wild moor dragons long ago, a small hardy breed used to the cold winters of the far north. But they were herbivores and placid in temperament, so his experiments had only taken him so far. Soon he had needed fresh breeding stock. He needed carnivores.

Few still existed in the wild and they were well protected. Only in the deepest darkest dragoncoombs and on the highest mountain eyries did some still survive beyond the reach of bounty hunters.

And so across the highlands and islands pedigree beasts began to disappear from roosts and paddocks, but given the remote locations – and the relatively small numbers – so far no one had raised the alarm. With the Third Hobgoblin War about to enter its three-hundredth year, the Sorcerers Guild had other things to think about than missing dragons.

He was very selective, choosing only those with specific characteristics and temperaments. He always knew exactly which dragons he wanted and where to find them. The smaller dragons, Adders, Vipers and Wasps – he had experimented with them all, using Dark Maelstrom Magic to change and warp them to his needs, creating something new; something dark and violent; a dragon that might bear hobgoblins – and he called them Razorbacks. Soon, soon they would be tested in battle against the SDS. But there was one dragon which he could not touch, dare not touch – at least not yet: Imperial Blacks, the last of the noble dragons from the Elder Days.

Huge and immensely strong, Imperial Blacks had one

characteristic that no other living dragon now possessed: they had strong magic of their own. Alone of all living dragons they could create a cloak of invisibility, and as yet he had failed to penetrate that.

In the meantime he had another dragon, a cross between a Dale and an Adder, the only one to survive his experiments. It had the appearance and build of a herbivore, but the mind and heart of a carnivore. He had a special task in mind for it: to kill the Earl Rufus DeWinter, Commander of the SDS.

The dragons' hoarse screams brought him back to his immediate task. These specimens would not live much longer. Already sores encrusted their hide and their teeth had rotted; the corrosive brew he fed them was eating away at their flesh so that their scales had moulted and the dried skin beneath flaked away almost to the bone. Selecting one at random, he raised his short staff, both the symbol and the weapon of an Arch Mage. A blue bolt flashed brightly in the dark and the dragon fell senseless to the floor, provoking unearthly screams from its companions, who frantically tried to break their bonds.

Ignoring them, he drew a weapon from beneath his robes that gleamed with a cold light of its own. A hobgoblin blade made of whalebone. With a single stab he punctured an artery. Blood pumped weakly out into a dragonbone bowl, purple in the dark. Returning to his cauldron, he poured in the sluggish blood.

Hand trembling, eager now for the brew to feed his addiction, he lifted his staff, which began to tingle warmly in his hand. Dark runes and glyphs crawled along its length. Small flashes of silver and blue spiked out from the roiling cloud of black that hung around its carved head, then faded.

He spoke: harsh, strange words that warped the freezing air like molten glass. The brew seethed and turned a sickly bruised yellow. He dipped in a flask and drank hungrily. For a moment nothing happened. Then the power filled him, feeding him, and still he drank the black brew like a drug until its power pounded through his veins.

The price was high. His body, like a once magnificent oak, was rotten to the core, consumed by the corrosive magic and his relentless ambition. Ultimate payment lay in the future, but in the meantime the prize – in the shape of a crown – would surely soon be his.

It was time to fly. Royal couriers had reported that the SDS and their famous commander were due home before the moons waned. And he had to be at the Sorcerers Guild to formally welcome them, a traitor in their midst.

CHAPTER THREE
The Stealth Dragon Services

The Earl Rufus DeWinter, Commander of the SDS, frowned as he studied a sheaf of reports through red-rimmed eyes. His throbbing forehead was bruised and swollen purple where a hobgoblin mallet had landed a blow, almost cracking his helmet in two. He hadn't slept in days and the wound to his leg was a gnawing pain. His esquires stood ready to strip off the rest of his rusting, dented armour, and he longed for the bath house and rest, but first . . . first he wanted to study incoming dispatches from the east, where three regiments of the SDS were about to engage upwards of six trapped hobgoblin banners.

Accepting a mug of hot spiced wine from an esquire, the Earl moved restlessly towards the great map pegged to the wall and considered his strategy for the hundredth time, searching for a weakness in his plans, a flaw that he felt certain was there.

Like the points of a star, six great fortresses ringed and protected the Seven Sea Kingdoms, each home to a full SDS regiment. And at the kingdom's heart in the Sorcerers Glen lay Dragon Isle, the fortress island that had birthed the SDS so many thousands of years ago, and home to his First Born regiment. And there, drifting north-west of the kingdom on the cold ocean deeps, were the hundreds of islands that made up the Westering Isles, the hobgoblin breeding grounds.

The Earl Rufus ran his hand tiredly through tawny hair dirty with the grime and blood of two weeks' campaigning. A storm was gathering, he could feel it, and in more ways than one. These were unsettling times. Something had changed; he could sense it like the first scent of snow in the wind that heralded the early onset of winter.

In recent months the thirteen hobgoblin tribes had simultaneously struck dozens of coastal settlements, while venturing further inland than they ever had before to attack walled cities. Dozens of island communities had also been overrun, their inhabitants slaughtered. Unconfirmed rumours and sightings spoke of ravenous, twisted creatures that emerged from underground caverns at night to hunt. But most worrying of all, scouts had identified warriors from more than one hobgoblin tribe amongst the dead after recent clashes. Since they first rose from the seas millennia ago, the hobgoblin tribes had fought each other as viciously as they fought the Dragon Lords. It was their ultimate weakness. So why were they now uniting?

Many believed that the hobgoblins were simply desperate after one of the most cold and brutal years in living memory. But the Earl Rufus had his doubts. Instinct told him that a pattern was emerging from seeming chaos. But what did it mean?

Where once the elusive hobgoblins had slipped in and out of the sea under cover of darkness, now they laid a trail of devastation that a blind man could follow. Fishing settlements had been fired and crops burned, the choking black smoke betraying their presence from fifty leagues, almost an invitation to the SDS to catch them. The SDS found themselves fighting across the length and breadth of the highlands and islands, with supply trains stretched to the limit and bogged down in mud. Soon, if the weather worsened, the dragons would be unable to take to the air at all and the hobgoblins would have the upper hand.

The Earl Rufus frowned and rubbed his aching head. Individually each report was bad enough. Taken together, they suggested an emerging intelligence, the bare bones of a strategy. But who guided the hobgoblin tribes, and to what purpose? The Earl was suspicious of what he saw. From the onset he had been reluctant to draw in his two remaining regiments from the east, no matter how great and urgent the need. The co-ordinated attacks were all too . . . obvious, somehow. He feared treachery, so he sent his dragons north-east beyond the mountains, far from the most intense fighting.

It was just as well. Imperials on reconnaissance scrambled under a cloak of invisibility had reported vast numbers of hobgoblins moving by night and under cover of bad weather from loch to loch towards the unprotected eastern plains. Others were pushing upriver from the sea.

The attacks to the west were a ruse, an attempt to draw out the SDS far from their northern fortresses, leaving the densely populated eastern plains exposed and unguarded. Dragons and food enough to satisfy even the ravening hobgoblin hordes before they went into hibernation.

From his command headquarters on Dragon Isle the Earl Rufus had ordered the entire IV Nightstalker regiment forward from their base in the north in pursuit, with orders to drive the hobgoblins from their tunnels and coombs using all available Sabretooths and Vipers. The XIII Stormbreakers diverted half their strength eastwards from their fortress in the Howling Glen to cut off the hobgoblins' retreat to the sea, leaving only one mountain pass open to them. And beyond, on the open plains, the XX Shadowwraiths and IV Firestorm regiments were waiting. The trap would soon be sprung. At least sixty thousand hobgoblins would be forced to face the SDS in open battle and would die, leaving fewer of the creatures to breed and swarm the following spring. Why then was he still feeling so uneasy?

Perhaps because a mine in the Brimstone Mountains had been attacked barely two weeks before, swiftly followed by a second nearby and then a third. Their destruction left three fortresses, including Dragon Isle, critically short of brimstone for the coming winter. It was vital to secure supplies before winter closed in and made the journey impossible. Without brimstone their battledragons could not flame, and ultimately would die.

With his best commanders already in the field, preparing to engage the hobgoblins, the Earl had personally led the pursuit with five wings of Imperials from Dragon Isle, supported by Vampires from the Howling Glen regiment, leaving behind the heavier ground assault Sabretooths, Vipers and Adders. He had need of stealth and speed more than brute force. He had planned to catch them out in the open, confident he knew which mine they would attack next. But what was set to be a routine exercise nearly turned into a disaster.

A skirmish with a marauding war band of mercenaries unexpectedly delayed them. They were barely ten leagues distant when a blinding flash followed by a deafening explosion turned night into day and spewed fountains of rock and earth high into the air. The blast killed all his forward skirmishers instantly, and flattened surrounding woodland for fifty leagues. If he had not been delayed, his entire battlegroup would have died. Good fortune, the men said, that they had not been caught in the explosion. Good fortune that the hobgoblins were ignorant of how unstable and volatile brimstone was and had blown themselves to pieces.

And yet . . . the SDS Commander did not believe in coincidences. Without precious brimstone, battledragons would sicken and die. And although there was no proof, he believed it had been a trap, carefully planned and ruthlessly executed. If it had succeeded, it would have left the SDS demoralized, without their commander and with insufficient brimstone to see them through the winter. That a banner of ten thousand hobgoblins had also died meant nothing. The tribes could afford such a loss ten times over and not even notice it. And if it were indeed an ambush laid for him, might not the forthcoming engagement to the east be a similar trap?

Flying further north through appalling weather, the Earl had seen for himself the trails of destruction over five hundred leagues distant, all heading south and eastwards towards the densely populated farming plains. He had skimmed over glens and valleys where the hobgoblins had passed not a week since. They had been stripped of life, littered with the pale skeletons of elk and bear and wolf – of any creature not fast enough to flee the swarm. Why then had he turned Stormcracker and his Household Guard round to head south-west, back towards the fortress that straddled the high pass of the Howling Glen, the gateway to the south, and Dragon Isle, where the tribes had never before ventured?

THE DRAGON WHISPERER

Earl Rufus had ordered out patrols in every direction, but winter weather had closed in early. Thunder struck and torrential rain turned the roads and passes into dangerous quagmires, bogging down soldier and flightless dragon alike. Then the temperature dropped like a stone and water froze overnight. Howling blizzards made flying impossible. If the moons rose, they were hidden, and hobgoblin slime could only be seen by its pale light. One by one his patrols returned. They had reported little or no enemy activity in the high glens, moors and islands of the west. It was as if the hobgoblins had disappeared back into the sea. But dragons and men could only see so much. They could not penetrate the vast subterranean caves and coombs in the mountains and marshes that harboured and hid the hobgoblins. That was why the Earl needed his scouts. They had one of the most dangerous tasks of all, tracking the hobgoblins far beneath the ground. They too had departed three weeks since and had all returned but one: Bark Oakley.

The sun died in a blaze of red. A shifting ground mist drank up the last of the light in the Howling Glen as cold shadows and darkness pooled into one. High on the mountain peaks a bitter wind blew. As the first stars appeared, a small white dragon took off and floated slowly down the mountainside, a shifting shadow against the snow. A small figure sat easily astride the saddle. Mount and master landed below the snow line in a boulder-strewn ravine, close to where a torrential underground river poured out of the mountainside. Almost immediately the dragon took on the shades and hues of the boulder outcrop and faded from sight.

Bark Oakley, chief scout to the Earl Rufus, dismounted lightly and pushed back his heavy hood. He was dressed in a motley collection of furs, leather and rough cloth that made him hard to see even in the full light of noon. Countless pouches and strange pieces of equipment were attached to his bandolier and flying belt. The gnome's weather-beaten face was hidden behind a mask, glinting eyes narrowed thoughtfully as he studied the long glen laid out below him.

To the distant east the lights of the fortress twinkled in the dark. Somewhere to the west, snaking columns of infantry guarded a caravan of vital brimstone ore. They were strung out for over ten leagues along the military road that led from the moors through the glen towards the great fortress that straddled the high pass. Bark had passed above them two days since, close enough to see the huge wagons bogged down to the axles in the marshes, and their military escort of Vipers and Adders struggling to make headway in the waterlogged ground. It would take them at least another week to reach the safety of the fortress.

Overhead, a patrol of Vampires passed within hailing distance, but did not see him or his dragon. Like all scouting mounts, his beloved Moonshine Shadow was a Lesser Chameleon, a small, swift dragon who could blend into any background. Bark turned his attention back to the lower mountain slopes about him, studying the steep gorge intently for any sign of hobgoblins. He had been patiently searching the long glen for a week now and had found no trace of their elusive enemy, but the Earl's warning echoed in his head.

Find them, he had commanded. They have gone to ground. Something changes. Trust to your instinct, for I fear we are being misled as to their true intentions.

None had found coombs here in the Howling Glen, but that did not mean they did not exist. Time and time again the hobgoblins had disappeared below ground, confounding their pursuers. Bark's instinct told him they were here somewhere. For days now he had searched but found nothing. He touched a wooden talisman at his throat, a rough carving given to him last Yule by his son, Root. A smile touched his eyes. How he was longing to return to Dragonsdome to see how his young son was faring.

Far below, a giant elk and his herd started suddenly; steam rose from the stag's flared nostrils as he pawed uneasily at the cold ground. A young hind, barely into her third month, trembled with fear, her warning cry carrying in the still air. Motionless, Bark scanned the rocky outcrops and rubble below. He was downwind of the herd, so what had spooked them?

Then the first full moon rose from behind the mountain ridges and silver moonlight flooded the glen. He lifted his spyglass, letting it travel slowly across rocky outcrops and fields of shale and scree. There! Just a glint crisscrossing the jutting rocks of the gully below him, although already the water was washing them clean. Soon there would be no trace.

Skirting around huge boulders and wary of treacherous shifting shale, Bark moved stealthily and silently deeper into the ravine. He stooped to touch the gleaming slime, his fingers coming away sticky. Hobgoblins had been here very recently!

With a thumping heart Bark searched the gulley for a fissure or cave that would lead into the belly of the mountain. Casting about, he moved slowly down beside the thundering waterfall, closely examining the river bed.

'Ah!' He bent to scoop up a length of pale bone out of the hurtling snow-melt. It was hollowed out in the centre and carved with tribal whorls and dots; a broken hobgoblin blowpipe. He searched the ground and came across several spilled darts, careful not to touch their poison tips. The hobgoblins were here in the Howling Glen . . . somewhere.

Cautiously he edged further upwards into the dark mouth of the ravine, keeping the river to his left. Freezing mist hung in the air, coating him with icy pearls. The tip of the second moon rose slowly above the mountain peaks, constellations emerged overhead, yet still he could find no entrance into the mountain. The disappointment was bitter in his mouth. He did not want to let the Earl Rufus down.

Then realization hit him. There was one place he hadn't searched. Why had he not thought of it before? Bracing himself, he clambered over some boulders and into the waterfall.

'Ahhh!'

The shock of it made the gnome shudder and gasp. The ferocious power knocked him to his knees and soaked him in seconds. He scrambled forward, scuttling like a crab, trying to find refuge, searching for any grip on the slippery slabs of rock. Hobgoblin slime coated his hands and knees as he flailed like a leaping salmon trying to rise upstream. Water flooded over him, the weight of it almost lifting him off his feet. Gasping and spluttering, he was finally through and behind the curtain of water.

The sound of the river exploding from the mountain was deafening. Removing his mask, Bark knuckled water from his eyes and let them adjust to the gloom. Thin silvery moonlight seeped in from outside, just enough to see the thick slime that covered the floor of the jutting rock slab.

'So!' he exclaimed softly, pleased his instinct had not let him down. A darker fissure opened up in the rock face to his right, tall and wide enough for hobgoblins. Without hesitating he stepped through and into the mountain.

A rough curving passage descended rapidly into utter darkness. Slime stuck to the soles of his boots as he moved forward. The passageway branched. Unsheathing the knife strapped to his boot, Bark carved a shallow rune into the stone. He took a deep breath of stale air and continued on down the passage, softly, stealthy as a hunting lynx, ears alert to any unexpected sound, eyes searching the dark for traps.

The hobgoblins loathed the scouts who led the SDS into their secret lairs. Bark could not afford to be captured by the hobgoblins. If he was, he would not die an easy death. The hobgoblins loved their sport, and the Killing Caves of the Westering Isles were well named.

The thunder of the water gradually receded to a dull boom that vibrated through the rock. Discarded cattle bones littered the passageway, gnawed by sharp serrated teeth. The odd dragon scale gleamed coldly. Time and time again the passageway forked and then forked again, and at each junction in the bewildering maze of tunnels Bark scratched a rune to mark his route, blessing the acute night vision that took advantage of every scrap of available light and made gnomes such effective scouts below ground.

It grew colder and colder as he moved deeper into the mountain's heart. The sound of the waterfall receded into silence. Then at last a faint phosphorescent glow ghosted through the tunnels. Ahead, Bark found his way blocked by a rock fall. He bent down and touched the ground, examining it. No creature had passed this way for days, but he could smell the hobgoblins on the cold air that flowed up ahead. Returning, he chose another tunnel heading down in the same direction.

Suddenly a pit yawned in front of him. He stopped and listened. The sound of frothing, foaming water grew louder. Where there was water there were hobgoblins. Taking a metal peg and a small hammer from his belt, he unravelled a thin rope, secured it, and swiftly let himself down. The crash of water grew louder, then it was there in front of him, cascading down its hidden watercourse.

Sssssssssssssssssss . . . The sinister sound echoed softly through the passageways. It was no different to the whisper of wind through the heather, but the hairs on the back of Bark's neck stood up, sending shivers down his spine. Up ahead the faint glow, almost like moonlight, penetrated the darkness, and the repugnant stench of rotting fish reached his nostrils.

The water flume blocked his passage ahead, leaving a ragged crack to his left as the only other choice. He squeezed through. The roof above him began to slope down towards the floor so that he was soon forced to bend and then to crawl forward on all fours. Carefully he wriggled further into the black crevice, feeling his way with fingers that ached with cold. The green glow and the ghostly whispering grew stronger.

Finally Bark could go no further between the pressing slabs of rock, so he began to edge sideways. Breathing slowly through his mask, he let his heart rate slow before moving on. The sound of popping and slithering filled his ears. He was almost upon them!

Sssssssssssssssssssssss . . .

As he slid a few inches further, a great cavern yawned ahead of him; a river of hobgoblins poured through it. Bark could barely breathe for the smell of fish and rotting offal. Patiently he lurked in the shadows while his soaked clothing stiffened and his muscles cramped. Still the hobgoblins came on.

And they were all heavily armoured. Metal breastplates and skull helmets gleamed in the sickly cold light. Some wore fearsome face masks and armour carved from white bone. They all carried a fearsome array of weapons: spiked flails and maces, spiral swords, spears and bows. Bark shivered and shifted slightly. His cold muscles ached and trembled with tension. Even his boots, waxed with bear fat, were soaked through. And still the hobgoblins thronged past him.

Bark trembled with horror. This was no scouting party, or even a marauding war band; there must be a full banner, perhaps two or three. There was one last detail the Earl would want to know, but for that he needed to move closer. His heart was thumping loudly in his ears as he edged towards the lip of an outcrop. Slowly, so slowly, he inched out of the comforting shadows into the sickly green light.

Eyes narrowed to slits, he studied the hobgoblins' tattoos, the subtle difference in jewellery and weaponry that distinguished each of the thirteen tribes. Those who carried blowpipes with their deadly darts; others who fought only with nets and spears. He counted eight different tribes. The Earl's instinct had been right: the tribes had united – and was that their leader they were all swarming around? The huge, powerfully built hobgoblin in the centre of the cave?

'Galtekerion . . . Galtekerion . . . Galtekerion . . .' The hobgoblins hissed the name in unison, and the creature in their centre raised a webbed hand for silence.

'Prepare for our assault. We will catch the SDSsssss totally unawaresss in the Howling Glen passss Firssst our brothersss will lure out their troopsss by attacking the brimstone ore caravan, then we attack the fortress. Victory will be oursss!'

The cave erupted in violent hissing, the assembled hobgoblins stamping their feet in excitement at the prospect of the ambush.

Bark's heart beat hard in his chest. The SDS were soon to be under attack. 'The Earl! I must warn him!' he whispered under his breath.

Thump . . . thump . . .

He began to move backwards inch by inch, once more edging into the comforting darkness, forcing his cold aching muscles to respond. But his clothes were frozen to the rock! He tried not to panic, but his breath was coming out in gasps that bloomed in the cold. Something tore. Finally he was free! As he began to turn, he heard a loud sucking sound. Silhouetted against the cavern's glow a young Hobgoblin warrior crouched. It's head swayed from side to side as it drew in air over the sensitive glands in the roof of its mouth. Two glowing eyes turned to search the dark where Bark lay hidden.

The scout held his breath.

Sssssssssssssssssssssssss...

He heard its angry uncertain hiss, then a high pitched croak of excitement rattled from its throat. More young hobgoblins hopped onto the rocky outcrop where he had lain, snuffling and sniffing. Flails and spears were rattled on shields; the drums took up a different rhythm. The hunt was on! The time for stealth was over.

Frantically Bark scrabbled backwards. He wiggled along, fingers feeling the edges of the tunnel until it began to open up again.

Thump! Thump!

He stumbled to his feet, scraping his head against the roof as he did so. He touched his fingers to the warm stickiness that snaked down his face. His heart hammered in his chest. Blood! If the hobgoblins didn't already know where he was, they soon would. They were predators and could smell tiny particles of blood in air or water from a great distance. Once a frenzy came upon them they would stop at nothing to find him and rend him limb from limb. Bark ran. He barely paused at a junction, checked for his rune with frozen fingertips and sped along a second tunnel.

Behind him he heard the slap of webbed feet and the excited croaks of the hobgoblins.

He reached his rope. Flexing his fingers, frantically trying to regain some feeling, he reached up and began to haul himself up. He had barely reached the top and was pulling himself onto firm ground when frenzied croaks rose up beneath him. Swiftly he sliced through the rope: this would scarcely hold them back, but he had sorcerer weapons that would. He pulled a small spherical object the size of a walnut from one of his pouches and dropped it into the pit. He raced away, counting beneath his breath.

'One, two, three . . .' He put hands up to cover his ears and squeezed his eyes tight shut. There was a flash like lightning.

BOOM!

A second flash was followed by a second explosion.

BOOM!

Bark's ears popped. He waited until the brilliant light had faded. That would stop any warriors within fifty strides of the detonation, bursting their eardrums and ruining their night sight. Shaking his head, he sped on, but he was disoriented in the darkness, and when he came upon five tunnels branching from the path, he did not know which one to take to safety. Think! He closed his eyes, allowing his senses to reach out. Time to trust his instincts. Bark ran to each entrance until he felt a cold draught of fresh air blowing through one of them. Praying that he was not turning back into the path of the pursuing hobgoblins, he hurled himself through the narrow opening.

'Kkkkkrrrrooooakkk!'

The hobgoblins were right behind him. His heart leaped as he saw the ragged triangle of starlit sky. Freedom!

But they were almost upon him. Plucking another metal sphere from his bandolier, Bark let it fall. He heard it roll downwards towards the pursuing hobgoblins and waited for impact.

BOOM! The explosion blasted a wall of hot air up the passageway that punched him out of the mountain. Finally he was free, gulping in great lungfuls of clean night air. Where was he? The waterfall crashed down to his right. Moonshine Shadow must be just above him.

'Moonshine! Moonshine!' He called out to her, his voice thin in the vast silence of the night. Would she hear him above the crash and roar of the water?

In moments his dragon was swooping towards him. He was safe!

The dart took him in the neck, the pain exploding in his head. The shock forced him to his knees. Then ghostly figures rose from the rocks above and hopped towards him, croaking their excitement, their great bounds eating up the distance.

'Must escape . . . Must warn the Earl . . . Must warn . . .' Already he was feeling disorientated, his vision blurring at the edges. He stumbled, falling heavily. Sweat was pouring from his body now, and his movements were becoming jerky. He did not have much time. Gasping for air, he reached for his mount.

'Moonshine, hush . . .' Gathering up the reins, he lifted his foot to the stirrup, then doubled up in sudden agony as the first spasm took him. They would be upon him in moments.

Zzzzzzzzzzzing! Arrows and darts whizzed past, breaking into lethal shards as they ricocheted off the rocks.

'Steady there, girl.' The gnome gripped the pommel and dragged himself into the saddle as a dart lodged itself in the leather. Collapsing forwards, he wrapped his jerking arms around the slender neck. He was shaking uncontrollably, teeth rattling.

'C-c-come on, girl . . . g-g-got . . . got to warn . . . the Earl . . .'

With a snort the dragon took to the air, fear lending her strength. As she rose, her pigmentation changed to the dark hue of the sky and she faded from sight. Slowly gathering speed, they swept down the mountainside towards the fort – but not swiftly enough. Bolts and darts whistled through the air. One passed through the delicate membrane of the dragon's right wing and the second lodged close to her spine. She screamed, and for a breathtaking moment hung limply in the air; then she passed beyond the reach of the hobgoblins.

Bark could barely see the great fortress up ahead, the red-hot glow of the battleroosts beckoning him home one final time. He was cold again, so achingly cold and heavy that he felt as if he were cast from stone. Even breathing was becoming an effort as the poison spread through his veins. Sluggishly fumbling at his harness, he pulled out a flare and flung it upwards with all his strength. In seconds it exploded bright red, fading slowly, lighting the sky with its warning glow: Danger! Danger! Request immediate extraction! He hoped the SDS would find him quickly . . .

Three heavily armoured Vampires loomed out of the dark around him, but by then the wounded gnome and his dragon were spiralling down out of control. The rocky mountainside hurtled towards them. With nothing to break her fall, his mare slammed into the ground, throwing Bark heavily. He heard the crack as her neck broke, and screamed as his own leg splintered beneath him. Then darkness took him.

Bark opened his gummy eyes as he swam into consciousness. He heard voices, anxious, concerned, shapes looming out of the dark carrying flickering brands. The downdraught from a nearby dragon's wings blasted him. He groaned, his shattered leg trapped beneath the cooling body of his mount.

A voice cried in the rough tongue of the dwarfs, 'Over here. He's over here!'

His mouth opened but no words came out. His teeth chattered so hard a tooth fractured and still his jaw clamped down. He tried to grasp an arm, to tell them what was happening.

'It's the Earl's scout!'

'Move his mount. He's trapped . . . she's dead.'

'Pull the dart—'

'Nay, it's barbed.'

'It's also poisoned!'

'It's too late . . . To pull it would kill him now. He's lost a lot of blood. Tell the Earl . . . Move, man! Lift him onto my cloak.'

'Gently . . .' Another deeper voice cursed. 'Gently! Keep him warm. He's as cold as ice.'

He was lifted up and carried onto the back of an Imperial.

'You're safe.' A Bonecracker gruffly reached forward to cover the scout with his own heavy cloak. 'Hang on, Bark Oakley . . .'

Great wings lifted him smoothly up into the night sky. The stars spun silver as they sped over the high ramparts and into the fortress. Bark passed out again, awaking to find himself being laid on a pallet. Oil lamps glowed softly; all else was shadow.

Now he was burning, steam rising from his broken body. A damp cloth wiped his forehead.

'Bark? Can you hear me?' The physician's voice was distant, his cool finger on the erratic pulse at his neck. 'The Earl is coming. Hang on, Bark.'

Uneven footsteps drew closer, the crash of armour loud on the stone-flagged floor. A sentry saluted, fist thumping leather breastplate. Two strides, a jingle of spurs, and then the Earl was at his side.

'Bark . . .' The familiar voice, now rough with concern, came closer.

Bark tried to lift his head but his neck was not strong enough. His head lolled from side to side, blindly seeking the Earl. Taking the gnome's hand, the SDS Commander turned questioningly to his physician.

The old man shook his head. 'My lord . . .' The words held a weight of sorrow.

'My . . .' Bark summoned every last ounce of strength. Spittle foamed about his lips. 'M-m-my l-l . . . my l-lor—' A spasm took him so that he bucked and kicked, his spine straining. 'Y-you were right. Two banners . . .' His voice was growing fainter. 'Eight tribes, under one leader . . . Two banners . . .'

'One leader?' the Earl leaned forward intently.

'Yes my lord. Named Galtekerion. They h-h-have found a way through the mountains; even now . . . they are descending from the . . . ravines and gorges, gathering in the shadows. I think they will . . . attack the brimstone supply column.' The gnome sucked in a rasping breath. 'Eight t-t-tribes, my lord . . . B-b-but . . . this fortress . . . we are . . . their t-true target.' He groaned as his muscles spasmed again. His breath came in short gasps. 'Th-th-they . . . will draw m-more . . . of our forces out before falling on the fortress. They will attack just b-before dawn when we . . . when we . . .'

'Least expect them,' the Earl finished, looking at the tall armoured Dragon Lord who was waiting by the door for orders. If they succeeded, they would fire the unstable brimstone and take a fortress. It would be a double hammer blow for the SDS.

'Combat liftoff,' the Earl commanded. 'To arms immediately! I want all Imperials fully prepped, armed and cloaked within the hour. Now! Raise the dragonpads. Rouse the camp. We are under attack.'

His bugler ran from the tent. Urgent notes rang out, crystal clear in the silence. Scramble! Scramble! Scramble.

Bark heard orders being relayed, the shock and disbelief of answering voices. 'Shut the north portal, now! Send skirmishers to warn those guarding the brimstone caravan, and scramble the Vampires in support. All of them!'

In the barracks men-at-arms tumbled from hammocks to snatch up their chain mail, armour and weapons. Bonecrackers pounded out across the parade ground towards the dragonpads.

Bark heard the Earl give another order, but the words no longer made any sense to him. Again the bugler's urgent notes split the night. His jaw grated to one side. Darkness coiled and swirled about him, sucking him down into its depths. His legs thrashed and kicked.

'Hold him, gently now!' the Earl commanded.

Bark's strength suddenly flowed out of him. Now he could rest. The Earl was forewarned . . . A face floated before him. A tear spilled from his eye as he realized he would never see his son again. 'M-m-my s-s-s . . . R-R . . .'

The Earl leaned forward to hear the whisper.

Taking a breath was becoming harder and harder, as if a great weight lay on his chest. 'Root . . . my . . . son . . .' he tried again.

'Do not fear,' the Earl said, cradling Bark's head. 'He shall be brought into my household and taken care of. I swear it.'

'My lord . . .' The ghost of a smile was followed by a crack as Bark's spine broke and the air sighed from his lungs one final time.

The SDS Commander cursed, but there was no time for grief. Laying the head gently on the pallet, the Earl Rufus got to his feet. 'My helmet, my staff!' His esquires ran to where his armour and weaponry hung. His standard bearer unfurled his flag and followed his commander out to prepare for battle.

'Combat takeoff! Combat takeoff!'

'Go! Go! Go!'

'Up, Stormcracker!' the Earl Rufus urged his dragon, standing in his stirrups, battlestaff at the ready. 'Up, old friend!'

The great wings powered up and down. The Earl felt the shift of power beneath him as Stormcracker bunched his hind legs and raised his wings high. Steam bloomed from the great nostrils and pale purple flames licked along his tongue in eager anticipation of the battle to come. Around them, lighter, swifter dragons were already rising above the battlements and ramparts. Stormcracker sprang upwards, the great wings already on the downstroke.

Whumph . . .

Whumph . . .

The battledragon turned towards the west. All around the fortress, Imperials were rising up and dissolving into the night, thunder rolling from their wings.

That was when the first wave of hobgoblins rose up out of the gloom and their darts began to fall like black rain.

CHAPTER FOUR
Homecoming

Clang! Clang!

Quenelda woke with a start. A bell was ringing out across Dragonsdome. She blinked and rubbed the sleep from her eyes. What time was it? The fire in the hearth had died to an ember glow but no light yet showed behind the tapestried curtain.

Clang! Clang!

She cocked her head, listening. That wasn't the belfry ringing out the hour! That was the observatory bell! With a sudden eager smile she threw off the heavy fur bedcovers and sprang to the window, throwing the shutters open. Cold air and the deep voice of the bells rolled in.

Clang! Clang!

The beacon on Dragon Isle must have been lit! The SDS and her father were on their way home. Breaking the ice that had formed on the surface of the washing bowl, Quenelda plunged her hands into the water and splashed her face. Shivering, she hastily threw on warm clothing and a heavy cloak.

Collecting her flying belt and telescope, she ran along the great carved central stairway of Dragonsdome, skidded across the slate entrance hall and out past the Bonecrackers who guarded the huge oak doors. She bounded down the frost-crazed steps and turned to where the ancient keep lay hidden in the dark.

At the heart of Dragonsdome, a dozen saucer-shaped dragonpads eddied and drifted in the dark like deep-sea jellyfish bobbing in a current, the delicate struts of their landing decks, gantries and under-roosts picked out by winking light-sprites. And hanging beneath them, unseen in the dark, the great counter-weight pendulums and anchors. Somewhere up there her father's personal dragonpad was anchored and being prepared for his return. Quenelda headed towards it.

The sun was at its zenith when six squadrons of Imperial Black dragons, escorted by Vipers and Vampires, finally came into view, tattered battle banners rippling out behind him. At their apex flew the Earl Rufus DeWinter on Stormcracker Thundercloud III, his Household Guard in close V-formation behind him.

Quenelda watched the familiar rush and tumble below: people from all over the estate were converging on the keep. They raced against the swift shadows as wave after wave of dragons blotted out the sun overhead.

Dropping rapidly from three thousand feet above the sea loch, the dragons had slowed from a cruising speed of forty knots and were coming in from the west at nine knots. Cheers broke out, the sound rising thinly from the parade ground below.

Eight . . . seven . . . six . . . five knots . . .

Quenelda knew every move, every command, as if she were there landing with them. The dragons stalled one by one, their full wings capturing the wind like sails, sinews and tendons cracking with sudden tension.

Four knots . . .

Tails swept ten degrees to starboard to compensate for a gentle crosswind.

Three knots . . .

Spinal ruffs on Vipers fanned out, reducing their speed still further.

Two knots . . .

Hind legs swung forward beneath the dragons' bellies.

One knot . . .

Muscles bunched as they smoothly took up the immense weight transferred from the wings. Touchdown . . .

Boom . . .

Wings fully extended, spurred claws splayed, the Earl's huge Imperial Black executed a perfect landing, talons effortlessly gripping the decking mesh. A second later his front legs touched down. The SDS Commander's wingmen landed behind him, the dragonpads barely dipping as they absorbed the impact of one heavily armoured dragon after another.

Boom . . .

All around the keep, battledragons were coming in to land, the downbeat from their wings whipping the still air into swirling gusts followed by the heavy rumble of the landings. Quenelda watched enviously as battle-weary SDS pilots expertly guided their dragons onto the crowded pads one by one; imagining that she was up there with them, returning from a dangerous mission.

Boom . . .

Great sinews strained as wings came to rest unfurled, and commandos unstrapped themselves and dismounted down them.

Quenelda sprang forward with a cry. 'Papa! Papa!'

Dodging around the deck officer's half-hearted attempt to restrain her, she raced onto the landing deck, her feet pounding on the metal mesh. *Stormcracker! Stormcracker!* She called out.

The dragon's massive armoured head swung round at the sound of her voice as she hurtled up his outstretched wing, almost bowling the ground crew over in her haste.

Dancing with Dragons! Stormcracker Thundercloud III's singsong cadence filled her head, his golden eyes glittering. *It is good to see you again! May the wind always sail under your wings . . .* he silently greeted her.

Stormcracker! May you ride the stars for ever!

The tip of the dragon's black tongue rasped Quenelda with rough affection as she climbed up the last few girth-rungs to her father. All around, Bonecracker commandos, surgeons and dragonsmiths were dismounting wearily, many of them wounded. Dragons bearing the seriously injured were landing in the parade ground below, where the surgeons and apothecaries rushed forward with stretchers.

'Papa! Papa!'

Black pebbled armour sheathed the Earl from head to toe, moulded to the contours of his body like a second living skin. Horned and toothed in a mirror-image of Stormcracker, he looked half dragon, half man. At Quenelda's cry, the dragon's-head helmet swung towards her and spoke with the voice of a man.

'Goose!' The Earl stood up to greet his daughter.

With a cry of delight she hurtled into his open arms, hugging him fiercely. 'I've missed you so, Papa!'

He took her by the shoulders and held her away, smiling down at her. 'By the One Earth, it's good to see you! And I swear you've grown another three inches!'

Quenelda stood back, suddenly aware of the state her father was in. His armour was dirty, peppered with burn marks and scored with weapon strikes. The metallic smell of spent magic still lingered about him. With horror she realized that his pilot's chair had been damaged: the spell-charmed metal was buckled and charred. His staff, holstered on the saddle, was covered in soot.

'Oh, Papa!' She hugged her father again, grateful he was not badly injured.

'Goose!' the Earl protested. 'Let me take my helmet off.'

Quenelda smiled happily up at him, but as the rising helmet revealed her father's face, her response died in her throat, and she gasped with shock.

Her father's normally handsome face was gaunt, his skin the colour of cold candle-wax; his ragged scar stood out like a silver slug-trail beneath the soot and dirt. Bloodshot bruised eyes looked down at her through an unkempt mane of matted hair. A bloody bandage around his head oozed and more blood from a torn ear soaked into the scarf around his neck.

'Papa . . . ?' Quenelda reached out tentatively to touch his grimy cheek. Surely that wasn't grey that touched his temples? It must be mud. My father is unbeatable, she thought fiercely. My father is the Queen's Champion, and Lord Commander of the most feared regiments in the land!

He saw her concern. 'The hobgoblins attacked the fortress at the Howling Glen. It was a bloody fight, but we won. Come, Goose' – he gave his staff to an esquire, and stretched stiffly – 'let's go inside. My bones are aching from too many hours in the saddle. A hot bath and clean clothes would be—' But before he could finish speaking, the Earl collapsed.

Only then did Quenelda realise that the dark stain on his leg greave wasn't rust.

'Surgeon! Surgeon!' She cried in panic. 'My father is badly injured!'

CHAPTER FIVE
Two Gulps and You're Gone

Root stood shivering in his thin cloak, tired red-rimmed eyes still gazing anxiously skywards to where the dragonpads bobbed. Fear was gnawing at him like hunger, knotting his stomach with dread. There had been no dragons landing now since half past the Hour of the Stealthy Lynx. Griffins were still shuttling the badly wounded between the landing pads and the hospital barracks; Root had been there half a dozen times until a surgeon told him he was only getting in the way.

The wind was picking up, swirling dust around the parade ground. As yet another troop of battle-weary dwarf commandos headed for their families and their first hot food in days, Root stepped nervously into their path, desperation lending a quiver to his voice as he asked the same questions over and over again:

'M-my f-father . . . Are there any dragons overdue? Has anyone seen my father? Has anyone seen B-B-Bark Oakley? One of Earl Rufus DeWinter's scouts?'

The exhausted commandos shook their heads, most of them barely listening. Then a captain, his arm in a crude splint, stopped by the young gnome. Root couldn't tear his eyes away from the dwarf's ragged, rusty chain mail and dented axe. His desperate state frightened Root more than any words could.

'Ain't no one else coming home, lad,' the captain said, not unkindly. 'We're the last. We took heavy losses.'

Root stood there as if turned to stone.

The parade ground emptied.

Silence.

How long he stayed there he didn't know, mind blank, fists clenched. Shadows passed over the ground. Shading his eyes, heart thumping with sudden hope, Root looked up as a dragon swooped low overhead, but even he could see it was no battledragon. Escorted by four outriders, extravagantly attired, the white dragon flew the familiar banner of a red adder on black, the coat of arms of the Grand Master, who was coming to welcome the Earl home.

Pa was gone. He was all alone in the world. What would he do now? Root wondered. Where would he go? He couldn't think straight. He couldn't even move. The hobgoblins had once more killed his closest kin. He had been barely six years old when a banner had wiped out his village – he had been picking nuts and berries in the forest when the attack came, and was the sole survivor out of a hundred and fifty peaceful gnomes. Hearing the screams, he had hidden in the undergrowth and stayed there long after night and silence fell, too afraid to move. Finally, as dawn turned darkness to shades of grey, he had crept home to find his family lying like broken dolls in the ruins of their home. The SDS had found him three days later, filthy, starving and frozen, and had reunited him with his grieving father, stationed at Dragonsdome. But now the evil creatures had taken his father away too; what would become of him now?

'An escort flying with me? On my dragon?' Quenelda turned from the mullioned window high in Dragonsdome keep; she had been watching Root far below with idle curiosity. Now she looked at her father in open-mouthed disbelief. Tangnost bowed out of the chamber, a smile tugging the edges of his moustache.

'But why, Papa?'

The heavy doors shut with a click. She wondered what Tangnost had said to her father during the hour they had been closeted away together.

'I'm perfectly safe flying on my own. I don't need an escort, and you're home now. I'll be flying with you – won't I?'

A cauldron of hot water with cleansing herbs swathed the Earl in billowing clouds of fragrant steam so that she couldn't see his face properly. Bloody bandages and swabs lay discarded on the floor at his feet, stained like his leg with yellow iodine. The Earl had taken a hobgoblin bite to the calf and thigh at the turn of the new moons, and several new scars puckered his forearms and chest. Quenelda shivered. He and Stormcracker must have been utterly exhausted for the hobgoblins to get close enough to wound him.

'Goose—' The Earl winced as the old surgeon restitched the torn muscles of his leg, clucking and tutting like a mother hen at the mess the field doctors had made. 'I have a great deal of military and Guild business to see to – and yes, you may come with me sometimes – but not even you, my daughter, may set foot on Dragon Isle unless and until you are accepted as a cadet.' The Earl gratefully took a steaming goblet of mulled wine from a servant. 'And that cannot happen until you come of age in two years' time, if it ever happens. And, meantime' – he looked up at her – 'I'm sorry, Goose, but I must return to Dragon Isle just as soon as the Guild has met.'

'But why, Papa?' Quenelda's face fell. 'The SDS are standing down for the winter – aren't they?'

The Earl continued as if he hadn't heard her. 'You need an escort when you are out flying. Earth knows, I have tried to find a matron or goodwife to chaperone you.' He shook his head ruefully. 'But most women won't go near a dragon – certainly no woman of noble birth. And I know you can out-fly your escort and most anything else . . .' He smiled to take the sting out of his words. 'Oh, yes, I've heard how you take great delight in losing or humiliating every esquire Tangnost selects for you. This is why from now on you are taking one on your own dragon; that way you can't leave him behind. And this is also why, this time, I'm giving you someone who, unlike most other young men, would not be too proud to fly behind you; nor will he indulge your foolish escapades.'

'But, Papa! I don't need an—'

'Quenelda' – the Earl sighed in exasperation – 'my mind is made up. You're no longer a child. It's unheard of for a young lady to step out without a chaperone, let alone without an escort as befits her high rank. Let alone actually riding a dragon by herself . . . wearing breeches . . . and buckled leather boots.' He frowned. 'The war has made me into a poor father. Barely ever home, letting you run wild. When you were small it didn't matter, but you're a young lady now. Well,' he amended with a wry smile, 'you should be a young lady by now and should be chaperoned as befits your status. Most young ladies your age are already attending court.'

'But, Papa!' Quenelda knew how childish she sounded, and it only made her angrier. She almost stamped her foot in frustration. 'I'd die at court! Trussed up in corsets and dresses. Talking about fashion, endless ceremony . . . My brother Darcy loves that; he is always at court! I'd hate it. I know I would. I don't want to ever be a young lady!'

Fists held rigid at her sides, Quenelda glowered unseeingly at the wind vector maps and sky cloud charts that hung above the big map table in her father's study. She bit her tongue: she didn't want to mention the ugly speculation and gossip about her unknown mother that always ruined her visits to court.

'You don't want to be a young lady?' her father teased her. 'You already are. You were born the Lady Quenelda Katriona DeWinter. What do you want, then?'

'To become a Dragon Lord like you, Papa! To join the SDS and fly Imperial Blacks!'

The intensity of her reply took him aback.

'I thought . . .' Quenelda hesitated. 'Since Tangnost allowed me to help him treat Two Gulps, you might change your mind and let me apply to Dragon Isle now, before I come of age. I thought . . .'

'Goose . . .' The Earl eased himself into a high-backed chair by the fire, his injured leg stretched stiffly out before him. 'What Tangnost achieved with your help was truly incredible, and yes, that is bound to impress the Academy.' Far more than you know, he thought dryly. 'But' – he raised his hand to silence her protest – 'but,' he repeated sternly, 'even if the Academy decides to accept you, decides to accept a girl, there is a reason why you have to be of age before you may enter the Academy as a cadet. To become an SDS pilot or navigator you must first have mastered the rudiments of magic, runes and spells. All are required to study military history, master many weapons, dwarfish strategy and tactics, manoeuvring, weaponry, night flying, High Magic and Battle Magic – there is endless theory and exams.'

He paused to consider his daughter: her eyes were flashing fire like a wildcat at bay and the set of her jaw was fierce. His eyes narrowed. How she had grown. All angles like a half-grown colt. And her face . . . so like her mother's . . .

Earl Rufus held her gaze. 'You know how you detest study, detest discipline. How many times have you been flying when you should have been studying? Your tutors have all given up on you. They say you have the ability, but unless it has anything to do with dragons you don't have the discipline. You–'

'But–'

'– have yet to earn your first wand,' he cautioned. 'Let alone the staff of a Mage. And just because you can fly does not mean that you have the ability to fight. As the only girl you would have to prove yourself better than anyone else. Everyone will be watching you, thinking you were only accepted because you were my daughter. Tradition dies hard. Many would want you to fail.'

'But—'

'And there will be times,' he added gently, 'at the Academy, when you will not see a battledragon for months on end, let alone fly one! How do you think you would manage?'

'I'm certain I would pass!' Quenelda said desperately.

'All I need to learn is Battle Magic and how to fight. Mastering dragons is half the challenge and I can already do that. And then I'd be able to go to war with you, Papa, at your side. I'm nearly twelve. If I were your son and heir instead of Darcy, I could go to Dragon Isle now. It would be my right whatever my age!'

Seeing her father's disappointed frown at her brother's name, Quenelda paused. Although he was rarely at home and had little time for her when he was, she loved her handsome elder brother in his dashing uniform, but she could not understand why anyone would choose the Household Cavalry over the glory and tradition of Dragon Isle. Unicorns were beautiful creatures, and they had magic of a kind, but they could never compare with an Imperial Black like Stormcracker. And surely, exciting though it was, court ceremony could not compare with battle? Darcy's continued defiance in the face of his father's disapproval was baffling.

Sensing an advantage, Quenelda plunged on. 'Darcy joined the Queen's cavalry. He doesn't want to join the SDS. Let me fight by your side instead!'

It's my fault, the Earl thought. She's like me; she belongs up there in Open Sky and I have encouraged her. Pity that the child of my heart is not my heir, not a boy to follow my footsteps into the SDS. It would make things so simple. She could be taught far from prying eyes, one amongst many, until we learned the exact nature of her bond with dragons. Until she could take up her rightful place. None would question it. However, as the only girl, she would attract unwanted attention . . . But no, I would not swap my wild, passionate daughter for a dozen sons, and she has her own destiny to fulfil when the time comes . . .

The Earl gazed out of the window across Dragonsdome. A patrol was returning, swooping down towards the dragonpads below.

Should I keep her here at Dragonsdome – where no one will suspect her true heritage – under Tangnost's care, riding her dragons like a boy? he wondered. Or should I send her to the Queen's court, at least for now? For that is where her future will ultimately lie. But if I can now see a resemblance to her mother, others may also see it . . .

He frowned. So much was uncertain. The war against the hobgoblins had changed. The world was a far more dangerous place.

How do I prepare her for such perilous times? Nowhere is safe – only Dragon Isle. And I cannot yet take her there. She is too young, and until she masters magic it would be too dangerous . . .

'Goose,' he began, 'you cannot take the place of my son . . .'

He paused, sensing her disappointment in the sudden stiff set of her shoulders, the defiant line of her mouth, then came to a swift decision. Why not? I was barely older when I flew my first battledragon, although I was raised for war. Perhaps this way we will discover what she is truly capable of, and then perhaps the decision will be taken out of our hands. And Two Gulps will protect her against mischief . . .

'Quenelda, I know you can fly. But as I've said, there is a great deal more to becoming an SDS pilot than flying. Let us make a bargain, Goose.'

'Papa?' Quenelda was cautious.

'I shall not insist you attend court for a further year.'

She whooped with joy.

'But there are strings attached. Firstly—'

'Anything, Papa.' She was all smiles. Who knew what another year might bring? 'Anything.'

'Firstly, you resume your studies with your tutors. I will expect you to obtain your first wand by next midsummer. And I expect you to excel. Anything less will not do if you ever wish to attend Dragon Isle.'

Quenelda nodded glumly, not relishing the prospect of endless hours indoors with tutors as old and fusty as the books and scrolls they read.

'Secondly, for your protection . . .'

Quenelda gritted her teeth. He'd already told her she was to be saddled with another useless esquire.

Her father paused, wanting to enjoy the moment. 'I'm giving you Two Gulps and You're Gone.'

Quenelda's jaw dropped as his words registered. She stopped breathing.

'And thirdly—' he went on, pretending not to notice.

'Papa!' Quenelda jumped to her feet with fierce joy and rushed to embrace him, nearly knocking his injured leg. 'He's to be mine, Papa?' she asked as the apothecary glowered at her. 'Truly? A battledragon?'

'Yes, he is yours. Tangnost and I agree. You've nursed him through his injuries and you deserve this chance. Two Gulps can protect you better than ten score esquires and men-at-arms. But first you have to earn the right to fly him. Tangnost and I have agreed on tasks for you to undertake.

Only when you have completed them to his satisfaction will you be able to fly Two Gulps.'

'What tasks, Papa?' Quenelda was eager to begin. What if she could fly the battledragon to the royal jousts in two months' time? Her imagination raced away with her. How magnificent they would look. How—

'Patience, Goose!' The Earl put up a cautionary hand. 'These tasks will require great discipline. A battledragon will be unlike anything you have flown before. I know you have flown dragons some two years since, and have come out with me on Stormcracker since you were a babe, but you have never flown solo on a battledragon. It may look easy, but few fly them before earning their Mage's staff, and for good reason.

'Battlemounts are powerful, and take great skill and strength to control. You may think that because they are highly trained anyone may fly them, but they can be lethal in the wrong hands. Under Tangnost's guidance you may begin instruction with the senior esquires, but only when he gives the word can you fly Two Gulps. And I have a final task for you.'

Quenelda nodded eagerly,

'Flying comes naturally to you, as does dragonhandling. You are not so tolerant of those who struggle. You provoke those esquires assigned to you into foolish, even reckless behaviour. Oh, yes' – he looked at his daughter's guilty face – 'it is time you understood that for most, learning to fly is difficult. Even on Dragon Isle only a very few go on to fly Imperial Blacks. Many fail.'

Quenelda frowned. What had that to do with Two Gulps and her? She would never fail!

'There is a young boy about your age who will fly out with you as your esquire. His father, one of my best scouts, was killed by the hobgoblins two weeks ago.'

Quenelda nodded reluctantly, unsure where this was leading.

'I will introduce you to him shortly. You—'

There was a loud knock and a man-at-arms opened the door. 'My lord, the Grand Master is waiting.'

'One moment.' Getting awkwardly to his feet, the Earl turned to his daughter and kissed her lightly on the head. 'Quenelda, we'll talk further. I must attend to Guild business now. I'll send for you later.'

He nodded to the guard. 'Show him in, please.'

'My Lord Earl.' A tall, handsome man with long dark hair and piercing eyes strode into the room to grasp Quenelda's father by the arm and embrace him. 'Rufus' – Sir Hugo's voice was as rich and warming as his smile – 'it is good to see you home. We have all been most anxious for news.' He stood back to examine the bandages on the Earl's leg. 'You are injured!' he exclaimed with concern. 'Are the other rumours also true? You were attacked in the Howling Glen?'

'I'll live,' the Earl said grimly. 'But it hurts like the very devil. And yes, we have much to talk about before the Guild meet.'

The Grand Master became aware of another person in the room, realized it was Quenelda and instantly dismissed her. As she left the room, he and her father were already moving towards the sky charts and campaign maps scattered across the large oak table.

A frequent guest at Dragonsdome even in her father's absence, the Grand Master in his bright gold-stitched robes and distinctive five-pronged hat was a familiar sight to Quenelda. He was always interested in touring the battleroosts and talking with Tangnost over a leaf-filled pipe and a mug of heather ale; discussing pedigree and lineage, arguing the merits of one breed over another. And he had always taken a keen interest in his friend's son, Darcy, encouraging the youth's interest in the Household Cavalry and in tradition and ceremony. Over the coming midwinter festival he had promised one of his prize golden unicorn stallions to Dragonsdome to celebrate the boy's ceremony of knighthood, when Darcy became a man and knight of the realm. But Sir Hugo paid very little attention to Quenelda. After all, no one even knew who the girl's mother was and she was clearly of no importance. And he did not know about her extraordinary bond with the dragons . . .

Chapter Six
Lady Quenelda's Esquire

A great feast was already under way in the banqueting hall by the time Tangnost finally found Root huddled in a corner of the parade ground.

'There you are, Root,' he said gently. 'I've been looking everywhere for you.' The dragonmaster took in the gnome's tear-stained face and swollen eyes. 'They've told you, then?'

Root nodded wordlessly, afraid to say anything lest he start crying again.

'I'm sorry, lad.' Tangnost's oak-brown eye swam with sympathy. Helping the lad to his feet, he took him in a bone-crushing embrace, pressing him against his cold chain mail and tooled leather armour. Root clung to him and wept, the familiar smell of armour polish and leather oil in his nostrils.

It had all been so abrupt. The heart-thumping excitement; the people shoving and jostling for position to watch the dragons land; the cries of delight as husbands, fathers, brothers and sons dismounted into the welcoming arms of their families. The sudden dry-mouthed fear, like being punched in the gut, when he realized his father was never coming home.

'Your pa died bravely from a poisoned hobgoblin barb while out on reconnaissance . . . Hush, laddie . . .' The dwarf held him until his tears ran out, then gave him a hank of wool to dry his face. 'But he and his wounded mount managed to return to warn the Earl, and the ambush failed. He was a brave man and Earl Rufus will reward him by taking care of you. You needn't fear for your future. Now,' he continued, throwing his bearskin cloak around the shivering gnome and propelling him towards the kitchens, 'the Earl wants a word with you. But let's get some hot food into you first – you must be half frozen.'

'M-me?' Root stuttered, misery momentarily forgotten as adrenaline rushed through his veins. 'W-why? Why w-would the Earl want to see me?'

'He'll tell you himself, lad,' Tangnost said gruffly as he sat Root down and gave him a bowl of steaming porridge and a chunk of hot bread. 'Eat, lad, go on, eat!'

Root suddenly found he was starving, gulping the hot oats down so fast he scalded his tongue. Tangnost refilled his bowl from the great iron cauldron bubbling over the fire and found a spoonful of honey to sweeten it.

When Root had finished and some colour had returned to his cheeks, Tangnost pulled a few bits of straw out of his hair and said: 'Now, come along, lad. The Earl's a busy man. He don't like to be kept waiting and the feasting's already started.'

They crossed the dark parade ground and the crowded commons, then went through the tunnel that arched beneath the great inner bailey leading to the castle proper. Root had passed through the great arches flanked by the high watch towers when he had run errands for Tangnost. He had seen the warm yellow light spilling out through the mullioned windows, and the huge oak doors that lay behind the portcullis. But he had never once set foot inside.

Dragonsdome Mount was as magnificent as Root's imagination had painted it. At its heart lay the castle with its mighty milk-white keep. Over the centuries, successive generations had added to its splendour. Everywhere Root looked he saw cold suits of armour and dusty heraldic banners softened by the gleam of crystal and silver, carved wood and tapestries. The entrance hall was vast; intricately carved stone pillars soared up and up to a distant ceiling hidden in the shadows. It was thronged with servants, soldiers and hunting dogs.

Open-mouthed, Root allowed Tangnost to herd him gently upstairs. Music and laughter spilled out as they passed by the great hall, then on, up and up the great spiralling stairway to where the Earl's private chambers were, high in the keep.

At the door, two sentries uncrossed their pikes and grounded them. Tangnost's knuckles rapped loudly on the iron-studded door.

'Enter,' a deep voice commanded.

'Go on, lad, he's not going to eat you!' The dwarf ushered Root forward through the opening doors to a room lit with many candles.

'My Lord Earl.' Tangnost bowed, pulling Root down beside him. Heart thumping in trepidation, the gnome stole a look at the Earl Rufus.

He was seated on a high-backed chair beside the fire. Behind him, his daughter, Quenelda, stood looking out of the window. Her face half hidden by her long combed hair, she turned to scowl at Root. She had changed into clean clothes but, he thought, she could easily be mistaken for a boy in her dove-blue doublet, breeches and soft boots.

Tangnost's steadying hands rested reassuringly on the pale-faced gnome's shoulders. He propelled him forward another step. Root sniffed loudly. Wiping his face with the sleeve of his jerkin, he stared at the floor nervously.

The Earl Rufus gently explained to Root how his father had died in an engagement with the hobgoblins in the Howling Glen. Bark had discovered two hobgoblin banners beneath the mountains. Struck by a poisoned dart, he managed to reach the fortress to forewarn them of the attack. Because of his bravery the SDS had won against great odds. The Earl had pledged to take care of his son, and that meant that he, Root, was to be made an esquire and would begin his training immediately. Tangnost had made himself personally responsible for his basic training, after which Root would begin his duties as esquire to his daughter, the Lady Quenelda. Which meant she would teach him to fly dragons. If Root could master this, he would be appointed to Quenelda's own household as senior esquire, the first such appointment and a great privilege.

He, a lowly apprentice, to be made an esquire? It was unheard of. The sentry at the door shifted. The apothecary dropped his ladle into the cauldron and coughed to cover his embarrassment as he fished it out, giving a hastily smothered oath when he burned his fingers.

Only Tangnost seemed unsurprised, his mouth twitching into a smile that he wisely kept hidden beneath his moustache.

'L-Lady Quenelda?' Root squeaked in horror, the words out before he could stop them. They were more than matched by Quenelda's look of dismay as she took in her father's words and spun round to face him.

'Him?'

'My Lord Earl . . .' Foreseeing a tantrum, Tangnost bowed hastily, pressing the dazed Root down on one knee, then backing them both out of the door. The apothecary followed hastily, then his apprentice, who was struggling with the cauldron. The door had barely closed when Quenelda turned back to her father.

'A gnome?' she asked incredulously. 'An apprentice?'

Her father looked at her sharply. 'Is that a problem?'

'I've never heard of a gnome being made an esquire.'

'And I've never heard of a young girl who wears breeches and flies battledragons at the age of eleven years, have you?'

'But why an apprentice? Why him, Papa? He can't even fly! He barely knows one end of a dragon from the other. He . . .' She paused in the middle of listing Root's many deficiencies, suspicious that she had somehow fallen into a trap.

Her father looked at her keenly. 'Exactly, Goose. But he's going to. He's going to get the best tutor there is. You! You are going to teach him to fly dragons. That way, if he fails, you've only yourself to blame. You don't fly beyond Dragonsdome until you've taught him, and you don't fly Two Gulps until Tangnost is confident you can control the beast. Do we have a bargain, Goose?'

Outmanoeuvred, Quenelda glowered at him. 'Yes, Papa,' she muttered. 'We have a bargain.'

'Good. The lad can begin his training immediately. Well' – the Earl sighed wearily, wincing as he got to his feet – 'I must go down to the banquet and then I must attend to more Guild business. You have your own training to begin with the esquires, which will keep you busy until I return.'

Quenelda grimaced sourly as she left. This was not working out the way she had expected at all. A commoner as an esquire? Her esquire! And worse, she was responsible for training him. She didn't want to miss the winter joust – it was the most exciting festival of the year! But she needed Root if she was to leave Dragonsdome! It would be a difficult task: she had seen at first hand how hopeless he was with dragons. At this rate she would never fly Two Gulps into battle!

She kicked a pebble bad temperedly, barely wincing as it ricocheted off a sentry's armour to crack a window pane. 'A gnome for an esquire!' she muttered.

Not if she could help it.

CHAPTER SEVEN
The Stoner Manoeuvre

The next morning Quenelda was determined to banish all thoughts of Root from her mind. She hurried to the roosts to see her beloved Two Gulps and tell him that her father had given her permission to fly him one day.

We are to fight as one? The Sabretooth asked, milky smoke threading eagerly upwards from his snout in anticipation.

No. We are not going to fight. Well . . . Quenelda hesitated, sensing the dragon's wings droop with disappointment. *Not unless it's strictly necessary. Only if we have no choice . . .*

But someday?

Quenelda nodded. *We will fight together. I promise it. But* – she searched for a way to explain it – *I must shed my juvenile skin before I will be allowed to fight.*

Two Gulps seemed satisfied. *It is true. It is foolish to fight before you shed your first skin. Your scales will still be soft.*

My scales will still be soft, Quenelda agreed. *Now let me tend to your injuries. Then we will exercise . . .*

At that moment Tangnost appeared. 'I've finished my morning inspections,' he told her. 'I'm instructing the senior esquires this afternoon. I thought you might want to come along to watch. We're trying out a new battle manoeuvre . . .'

Quenelda's eyes lit up. 'Which one? The Stoner Manoeuvre?'

Tangnost grinned and nodded.

Quenelda eagerly walked over to one of the larger training areas, where a group of senior esquires were scattered around on the rough-hewn tiered seating, impatiently waiting for the Earl's dragonmaster. They were all youngest sons of noble families, learning the trade and art of warfare under the tutelage of Dragonsdome before applying to join the SDS, where they hoped to win fame and fortune.

Quenelda climbed up to sit behind a group of them. Her arrival was greeted with thinly veiled curiosity, whispers and furtive glances. They were unaware of the fact that, since she was small, Quenelda had always had exceptional hearing and eyesight. She tilted her head.

'. . . she has! She's been assisting Tangnost.'

'I heard she's been given the battledragon!'

'What? To fly?'

'No! Don't be ridiculous, she's only eleven!'

'And she's a girl to boot!'

'You don't say,' replied one sarcastically. 'A girl. Whoever would have guessed?'

'Show some respect – she can out-fly you any day of the week. No esquire can keep up with her. She's gone through six so far this year!'

'That's why she's here! To choose a new esquire. To watch us! To decide for herself who she wants!'

There were nods of agreement.

Quenelda snorted and looked at them all with a critical eye. Any one of them would be better than a wretched apprentice who didn't know one dragon from another.

Root, nervously awaiting his first training session and feeling her withering stare pass over him, tried to make himself as small as possible, and watched the training arena.

Bells jingled softly, and Quenelda looked up to where three dragons were tethered on roostpillars strung around the lip of the arena. By the size of their wings and length of their tails she realized the two Dales were elderly females. Tangnost favoured them for training because of their placid natures. The third was a whiskery old Viper stallion whose eyes were covered by a heavy leather hood with bells to keep him calm. Inexperienced esquires made careless mistakes, sometimes fatal ones. Trained battledragons, even elderly ones, rarely gave the unfortunate and the foolish a second chance.

'Right, lads,' Tangnost said. 'You have all studied dragon anatomy and handling, and practised a running mount on the wooden dragon. Today you get your chance to try combat takeoff on a dragon in flight; in other words, the Stoner Manoeuvre.'

A ripple of excitement spread out. His words were greeted with broad grins and nodding heads.

'Make no mistake . . .' The dwarf's eye raked them all fiercely. Smiles instantly vanished. One or two boys coughed. 'Forget the glamour. Forget about impressing the Earl's daughter.'

Quenelda grinned. A few esquires blushed and shuffled their feet sheepishly, as if the dragonmaster had read their minds. A few glanced over their shoulders to look at her.

'Your life may well depend on being able to master this manoeuvre and correctly identifying its corresponding bugle call,' Tangnost continued. 'So simply concentrate on getting it right! I know you can.'

There were enthusiastic nods of agreement.

Quenelda had watched countless combat takeoffs when patrols were scrambled; when the pilots and Bonecrackers had stormed up the outstretched wings of a stationary battledragon in preparation for immediate takeoff from the dragonpads. But she had never seen a combat takeoff with a dragon in flight – only in her imagination and in her dreams. Her eyes also lit up eagerly. Perhaps Tangnost was going to allow them to train with the old battledragon!

'As you all know' – the dwarf's voice interrupted her thoughts – 'the famous Stoner Manoeuvre was named after one of the Earl's ancestors, Earl Stoner DeWinter, who fought in the Second Hobgoblin War. His Sabretooth regiment was ambushed by night in the caves of the Dead End Glen. The dragons were tethered to the rocks outside when the hobgoblins swarmed through the cracks in the back of the caves. Calling his dragon to him, he alone escaped without saddle or bridle by mounting his famous battlemare Nebula Nemesis as she swept down the hillside. That kind of advanced training on battledragons is taught only on Dragon Isle once you have qualified as cadet. Here you work with Dales.'

There were a few disappointed faces, not least Quenelda's. They were not going to be allowed to train with the battledragon. She looked in resignation at the placid female dragons.

Sensing the air of disappointment, Tangnost smiled grimly. The esquires still had a great deal to learn. Even if they thought they knew it all, this lesson would teach them otherwise.

'Believe me,' he cautioned them, 'you are going to find

this exercise difficult enough on an elderly Dale, let alone a battledragon. Now . . .' The dragonmaster searched the stands, frowning. 'Root, where are you, boy?'

'Here, sir!'

Quenelda looked up in surprise to where her new esquire sat apart on the benches, clutching a large tri-horn. She hadn't even noticed him. His eyes were still swollen and puffy, but that didn't lessen her feeling of resentment.

Tangnost nodded, then called to the groom standing beside the nearest occupied roostpillar. 'Right, lad. Release the tether rope and wake her up.

Scrambling nimbly up the pegs inset into the stone roostpillar, the groom reached up and slipped off the dozing dragon's tether. Rheumy purple eyes snapped open and fixed him with a glare before the old mare switched her beady attention to the figures on the ground.

'EEEeeawkk! EEeeeweeekk!'

She let out the familiar keening cry of the Dale heard over the high moors, making Root jump up from his seat in fright. Quenelda shook her head as the nearest esquires openly laughed. The gnome was truly pathetic. How was she ever going to teach him to fly dragons if he behaved like this? A few heard her loud exaggerated sigh and followed her irritated glance with curiosity as the dwarf beckoned him forward.

'Remember' – Tangnost's one eye made contact with each of his young esquires in turn while he rested his hand on Root's shoulder – 'in the heat and chaos of battle, commanders often rely on their bugler. You will have to memorize each and every call on Dragon Isle, all five dozen of them.'

More groans rippled round the arena. Root's heart sank. Five dozen? He was struggling with just one.

'I know' – Tangnost held up a hand – 'I know you think it's boring, but you don't want to find yourself isolated from the rest of your troop by hobgoblins because you misheard the command. So we'll begin by putting the dragon through the exercise so you can judge her pace—'

'Or lack of it,' someone muttered sourly in front of Quenelda. 'That moth-eaten old hack isn't even going to get airborne! She's moulting!'

'– and let her get her wings warmed up. Remember the theory of flight dynamics, wing ratios and wind vectors. Let's see how much you've been paying attention to your roostmasters and tutors. Right, Root, ready with the bugle?'

The gnome nodded. He had been practising this one command in the stables until he was driven out by a barrage of brushes and a pail of mucky water. Tangnost had decided to break him into his training gently by giving him a task that he could manage despite his fear of dragons.

'Combat takeoff! Combat takeoff!' Tangnost bellowed suddenly, making the esquires on the benches jump.

Fumbling with nerves in front of Quenelda and the senior esquires, Root took a deep breath. A series of unsteady warbling notes that ended in a squawk earned him an exasperated glare from Quenelda and a sympathetic smile from a freckle-faced blue-eyed esquire before he managed to blow something akin to the right notes, even if they were a little feeble.

The old Dale was not impressed either. Her hearing

wasn't what it once was. She sat there blinking sleepily, forcing a red-faced Root to try again twice before she responded.

'EEEeeeawkkk!' With an irritable shake of her head, she spread her wings. After a few feeble flaps she rose a foot in the air . . .

Thump! She landed back on the roost pole with an audible thud – to a chorus of dismay from the esquires. A few scales fell to the ground.

The dragon made a second attempt. There was a collective intake of breath around the arena. Quenelda watched too, willing her to take to the air. Old bones creaked. The mare optimistically dipped down and up, wings half unfolded.

Down . . . up . . . down . . . up . . .

'That arthritic old bag of bones can't even fly!' one esquire muttered.

'Why can't we at least practise on a young leaf-eater that can?' his companion wondered. 'We'll just look stupid flying that old creature!'

Quenelda leaned forward and glared. 'Everyone knows why!' She hissed, making them jump. 'Everyone knows that there are no adult dragons to spare! They're all needed to support the war.'

Red-faced, the esquires hung their heads.

Fly, Eldest Grandmother, Quenelda urged the old dragon, using the formal speech of the Elder folk. *Fly* . . .

Perhaps all the dragon had been waiting for was some encouragement. With a triumphant squawk she launched herself into the air. It was touch and go as she dropped five feet before her frantic flapping saved her from collision with the stands. Slowly gaining height, she circled once above the arena before gliding down towards Tangnost.

'When?' he bawled in his best parade-ground voice. 'Come on! When do I mount?'

'Now!' some of the esquires called out.

'No! Think about the timing!' Tangnost ducked as the short-sighted old dragon nearly flew into him; she skimmed over the arena. 'Think!' he warned them as she came round for a second pass. 'If you mount too early, the dragon cannot raise her wings due to your added weight. At best she will be grounded and you will have to make an unassisted take-off, which wastes precious time. At worst she will rupture tendons and tear muscles, and you will have a lame dragon, easy meat for the hobgoblins. If you mount too late' – he looked at them – 'you miss the first vital winghold and your dragon leaves without you. Then you are easy meat for the hobgoblins!'

Then the dragon was past the dwarf and working hard to regain the roost. With a few flaps and a sideways hop she settled down to preen contentedly, her hooked beak teasing out another loose scale.

'Right.' Tangnost clapped his hands together. 'Let's see how you go with the real thing. On with your helmets and leg- and armguards. We don't want any broken limbs from wingstrikes!'

The esquires swiftly formed a line, each desperate to be the first to succeed and the first to impress Quenelda, whatever the dragonmaster's warnings. They soon discovered that theory and practice were two entirely different things.

The first to try was a gangly youth dressed in a fine grey

wool tunic and a heavy fur-lined cloak, which he refused to part with in the chill wind. Despite the slow progress of the elderly dragon, he was too hesitant, got a leg wrapped around his cloak and missed the wing completely, falling with a bone-jarring thud – to the catcalls and jeers of his friends. Quenelda laughed with them as he fussed about shaking the dust from his cloak. Hopeless!

Tangnost sighed. 'Next! Come on now, don't be shy!'

The second esquire fared marginally better. As the dragon swept slowly by, he leaped lightly onto her wing, but then his boots slipped. The rising tip of the leathery membrane caught him under the jaw and sent him tumbling to the ground, laying him out cold.

'Thor's Hammer!' Tangnost swore and strode over. He reached down to lift one of the hapless boy's boots, and let it go in disgust. 'How do you expect to be able to grip without proper boots on? Studs!' He lifted one of his own booted feet to reveal the short sharp spikes needed to grip the dragon's wing. 'Flying boots, boy,' he scolded, hauling the dizzy youth to his feet effortlessly with one huge hand. 'Flying boots with studs, or one slip and you're dead! Remember, the hobgoblins don't take any prisoners. If anyone else has forgotten theirs, go and sit on the bench. You'll not be trying today.'

There were some disappointed faces as four other esquires trudged disconsolately back to their seats.

One by one the remaining esquires tried their luck, their loud boasts coming to nothing until the freckle-faced esquire stepped forward. He had a quiet, confident air and a ready smile. Now he stood balanced perfectly on the balls of his feet and waited.

The bugle warbled. The dragon glided earthwards, closer and closer, before a gust of wind caught her and she rolled to one side. The esquire swiftly adjusted for her erratic flight path. Quenelda sat forward. This boy looked like he knew what he was doing.

Barely had the tip of the mare's left wing touched the ground when the boy leaped lightly up her leathery wing ridge. Gripping the pommel in one smooth movement, he swung himself up and into the saddle even as the dragon's wing rose. At the downward stroke he had the reins in his hands. To a chorus of cheers he turned the dragon in a slow circle to gain height, accepting the applause of his fellow esquires. Then he gently put her down on the roostpillar before nimbly descending.

Tangnost was delighted. 'Well done, Quester!' He thumped the boy heartily on his back, making him stumble as he headed towards his friends. Quenelda smiled and shook her head. The dwarf never knew his own strength.

'Let that be an example to you all!' the dragonmaster boomed, in high good humour. 'Quick now! Who's next?'

The instruction continued, using the second Dale. Wind vectors, body ratios and wing beat. Over and over, Tangnost drummed the lesson into them. One by one the esquires tested themselves. Some, like Quester, were doing well, but others, Quenelda thought, had no instinct for it. Two were packed off to the hospital barracks with minor injuries, followed shortly by a third with a broken leg. She shook her head. They were just hopeless! Only the one called Quester had caught her eye. She wondered if she could talk her father into making him her esquire instead of Root . . .

Quenelda let her mind drift, once more imagining herself racing up the wing of a battledragon, leaping into the air on some daring mission at her father's side. She sighed. There was not much chance of that happening. If only she could get a chance to show the dragonmaster what she could do. If only . . .

Tangnost cast a glance at Quenelda. Her eyes had a familiar faraway look. His lips twitched briefly. He had no doubt that in her imagination she was racing up a wing and soaring up into the sky . . . He nodded to himself. Time to test not just her ability, but her temperament. Time to see how she coped with being the centre of attention.

'Quenelda?'

She was in the saddle now and flying straight as an arrow towards her father . . .

'Quenelda?'

Quenelda blinked the daydream away and flushed when she realized everyone was staring at her. 'What?' She asked defensively.

Tangnost beckoned her forward from the benches. Some of the esquires cheered, but the low undercurrent of complaints that had begun when he first called her name grew in volume as she walked down the steps.

'Just because she's the Earl's daughter,' one muttered. 'She's far too young!'

Another scowled. 'Girls in the SDS! That'll be the day . . .'

'As if a girl could do better than us . . .'

Tangnost watched her come forward reluctantly. It was the first time he had included her in a lesson. And one way or another, this was going to be a hard lesson for her to learn.

She takes flying for granted – the Earl's words echoed in his head – she is young and thinks she knows it all. Nor does she understand that others have to learn to fly, have to overcome fear and stretch themselves to the limit to succeed. I want you to teach her to consider those about her, whoever they may be. Teach her to be more tolerant of their failures. And show her what it means to fail, because sometimes she will. We all do. She needs more discipline.

'I think you're ready, don't you?' Tangnost asked as the girl stood beside him.

Quenelda suddenly felt awkward. She spread her hands in protest. 'But . . . I've never tried . . . I've only practised on the wooden dragon,' she finished lamely, her face flushing. None of the esquires had practised on a dragon before and she had just been thinking how much better she could do. It was what she had wanted all along, so why was her heart pounding? She scanned the esquires' glowering faces on the benches.

Tangnost stood silently, letting her take her time.

Gritting her teeth, she nodded. She was ready!

'Take the Viper.'

'The . . . the Viper?'

'Aye, lass, if you think you're up to it?'

Quenelda looked up at the old battledragon. She could do it, she knew she could!

'Then, in your own time . . .'

As she instructed the groom to remove the Viper's hood, the murmuring swelled to a chorus of disbelief. Ignoring it, Quenelda checked the dragon over visually, then quested out to lightly touch his mind, immediately knowing his name.

Windswept Warrior, may the wind always sail under your wings. She greeted the Viper with respect, as was his due as a retired battledragon and Elder.

Dancing with Dragons, may you ride the stars for ever, the Viper acknowledged grumpily. *It is cold and my wing aches . . . When may I return to my roost?*

Your wing . . . ?

A fat Wingless One – he was careless.

When did this happen?

Before the last dark fell.

Yesterday, Quenelda thought, gritting her teeth with mounting frustration. One of the esquires hurt him yesterday! Ruining things for her! Just when she had a chance to show them all what she could do; that she was as good as them, if not better.

Disappointment curdled sourly in her mouth. But she was so light on her feet, she thought; light as thistledown! And she could do this, she knew she could. She would show them all. The trick was to leap as high as possible and step only on the leading edge of the wing and into the saddle, placing little or no weight on the membrane of the wing itself. Heavily armoured battledragons were different – you could mount the wing from any angle.

Can you fly for me, Windswept Warrior? Even as she said the words, Quenelda knew she should not be asking. She also knew that, as a battledragon, he would not refuse her. The Elders were a proud folk.

In answer, he spread his wings. A total hush fell around the arena. Tangnost was watching her keenly.

84

Taking a deep breath, Quenelda balanced herself as she had seen the dragonmaster do. She heard the mutters of derision and outrage but shut them out. Closing her eyes briefly, she prepared herself, unclenching her hands, relaxing her shoulders, swallowing away the lump in her throat. She tilted her head to one side and raised her eyes to watch the dragon. She gauged his wingspan to be as wide as she was tall, about five strides, and she knew that predators had a far faster wing beat so that they could catch their prey.

She raised her hand to signal that she was ready. Root raised the bugle to his lips, determined to get it right, if only this once. 'No!' Tangnost ordered quietly, indicating he was to put the bugle down. Let's see how well she can talk to him; what she can learn, he thought.

Baffled, the youth obediently lowered the instrument. A confused murmur ran around the arena.

Quenelda was oblivious to it. *Fly for me, Windswept Warrior . . .*

She was aware of nothing but the dragon. She was watching him intently. Watching as his still powerful hind legs gathered, then sprang twenty feet into the air. Watching as he circled around to gain height, noting that he could fly with only the slightest hesitation before gliding down.

He was fast despite his age, much faster than the Dale, faster than a heavy Sabretooth. Quenelda knew she would have only a matter of seconds in which to mount, and then he would be past and she would fail just as they all expected her to.

She began to calm herself, to do as she had so many

times in her head or on the wooden dragon.

One . . .

The dragon rolled forty-five degrees to the left so that his leathery wing talon was kicking up swirls of dust in the oval arena.

Two . . .

Then the dragon was there, the tip of his snout almost level with her, his large green eyes fixed on the arena wall ahead, leaving her to make the leap unhindered.

Three . . .

The wing was at its lowest point in the arc, the end talon almost touching the ground.

Four . . .

She willed herself to jump, to run the four steps up the ridge of the leathery wing that took her to the saddle just like she had in her daydream.

'Mount!' someone cried. 'Mount, or you'll miss your step!'

She lifted her foot, already hearing the applause in her mind, thinking of the tale she could tell her father at dinner that night. 'Papa, I—'

Then feelings of guilt stopped her abruptly. What was she thinking of? The air whispered as the dragon flew past and his wing began to rise again. In a moment it was too late. The dragon was already ten strides above the ground.

Quenelda was aghast. How could she even think of doing this? Hadn't she seen dragons being mistreated? Was she not angry when she saw careless cruelty and neglect? If she jumped up onto the Viper's wing, the damage might be permanent and the old battledragon might never be able to fly again.

She stopped in her tracks and turned anguished eyes to Tangnost. No longer concentrating properly, she was caught by the battledragon's tail and knocked off her feet.

'Ouff!' The air was punched out of her lungs as she landed heavily on her back.

Laughter rattled around the arena.

They were laughing at her! She could see them nodding their heads. Hear their self-satisfied words.

'I told you . . .'

'She's far too young . . .'

Furiously, fists clenched at her sides, she sprang to her feet and rounded on them. A hand fell on her shoulder and squeezed, just enough to make her pause.

'Steady, lass!' Tangnost warned in her ear. 'You're all right, aren't you? No harm done, is there?'

'No,' Quenelda answered sullenly. But then she saw his face. He was looking at her with keen approval and nodding.

She was still confused, not quite understanding what was happening.

'Well then,' he said quietly. 'Call him back, and let's take a look at that wing, shall we?'

So he knew! It had been a test!

Relief flooded through Quenelda, knowing now that she hadn't let Tangnost down, followed swiftly by shame that for a moment she nearly had, and for selfish glory.

'One of you lads fetch the dragonsmith,' Tangnost ordered. 'Who else noticed that he was carrying an injury? Can anyone tell me what's wrong?'

Careful not to provoke the old battledragon, the esquires gathered round while Quenelda replaced his hood. Tangnost waited while they examined his wings, belly and talons, then tail and snout.

'Anyone?' he prompted.

'Um . . .'

'Quenelda, why don't you tell them?'

He left her to explain. Soon the youths were looking at the Earl's daughter with surprised respect.

'I would never have spotted that.' An esquire shook his head as he looked at the slight swelling around the joint of the wing. 'Even with a close-up inspection I think I would have missed it. How could you tell?'

As Quenelda elaborated, Tangnost nodded to himself. She had not let him down. He had had no doubts about her ability to perform the manoeuvre – he'd seen her practise on the wooden dragon. But anyone who did not care for their dragon first had no place in the SDS. She had also tasted failure, frustration and prejudice. It was a start. She had passed a crucial test: her ambition did not outweigh her care for the dragons. And perhaps – he looked at Root sitting alone and miserable on the benches with his horn – just perhaps Quenelda might become more tolerant of the fears and failures of others; of those who, like herself, struggled against the odds. Well, these things took time, but it was a good beginning.

He sighed.

Getting Root back on his feet might take a lot longer.

Chapter Eight
Imagine . . .

That night after supper, following Tangnost's gentle but insistent urging, Root agreed to join the other esquires who often gathered in the dragonmaster's chambers to hear magical stories of great battles fought by the Bonecracker commandos, the SDS, and the Earl Rufus and his father before him.

'You're an esquire now,' he told the miserable gnome, 'and we are your family. Come and join us. This is no time for you to be on your own.'

It was no surprise for Root to find that Quenelda was sitting on the bench closest to the fire, her eyes closed and her scowl absent as she was drawn into the stories.

'What tale would you like to hear tonight?' Tangnost smiled, already guessing the answer as he cut a generous slice of black pudding and filled a pewter mug with ale from a keg.

'The Dragon Whisperer!' they choroused, huddling together as the wind whistled sharply outside and the moons rode the shredded clouds like galleons.

'The Dragon Whisperer?' Tangnost teased. 'But you heard that tale only two moons ago. Surely you want to hear another story . . . ?'

The fire was low. Taking an iron, the dwarf poked the hearth vigorously, sending sparks up the chimney. 'Right, lad, hand me a log or two.'

Root struggled to lift one. Tangnost took it effortlessly in a huge hand, then added a second. The heady smell of pine resin filled the air. Closing the pot-bellied stove door, he left the flue open so that the fire roared and threw back the shadows and the cold. The wet wood sang and hissed as it burned. Soon the stove glowed cherry-red, its flickering light reflected off the ring of faces and the undersides of the low beams above. The dwarf lit his pipe with a twig and drew on it, filling the air with the heavy sweet scent of tobacco.

'Imagine . . .' he began.

Quenelda closed her eyes as his hushed voice took on the soft hypnotic tones of a storyteller. The wind outside howled and hail rattled at the shutters, but it was cosy and companionable inside the dragonmaster's quarters.

'The First Hobgoblin War had dragged on for untold centuries,' Tangnost told them. 'Swarming in ever-increasing numbers, the hobgoblins had long since overwhelmed isolated settlements along the coastline. Then they moved inland along the banks of rivers and sea lochs to pillage and plunder. It was a dark time.'

Root anxiously fingered the carved amulets on leather strings around his neck. The flickering shadows suddenly seemed darker and the storm louder. He edged closer to Tangnost.

'It was a time of short days and long nights,' the dwarf continued, eye glinting in the firelight. 'Sometimes it seemed that the sun never shone at all, that all the land was bound beneath endless night.'

His audience shuddered deliciously as he pulled on his pipe. He dropped his voice to a hoarse whisper, making them draw closer.

'Every spring they swarmed onto the lowlands, killing anything that moved, stripping them of all life save those creatures that could fly, leaving the valleys and moors desolate with bleaching bones. Crops were destroyed. Cattle eaten. Merchant galleons pirated. Soon all the races and tribes of the lowlands took refuge in the great fortresses of the Sorcerer Lords, who alone of all the peoples of the Old Kingdoms, held out against the hobgoblin banners.

'Only in winter, when the hobgoblins returned to the sea to hibernate, were they safe from attack. But for those who survived, winter brought only famine and hardship. Then, come springtime, the hobgoblin tribes hurled themselves against the fortresses that still held out against them.

Finally, late in the Year of the Dancing Stoat, the Stone Citadel, the sorcerers' last great refuge, fell.

'As the citadel crumbled about them, the royal court and its citizens fled northwards, abandoning the lowlands forever. Lords and ladies, merchants and artisans, soldiers and servants; they all fled from the ravenous hobgoblins, taking only what they could carry. Ahead reared the forbidding peaks of the Storm Spike Mountains, and beyond them the uncharted frozen wastes of the highlands.

'The old and the young were the first to die. Those who survived fled north, away from the devastation, protecting the King, his young Queen and their infant son with their lives. But the endless cold sapped their strength, and with it their magic.'

The fire sparked and popped, making everyone jump and Root squeak. Quenelda sighed loudly and rolled her eyes in exasperation; the gnome's face burned with embarrassment. There was nervous laughter, then shuffling – the other youths were grateful it had not been them.

Tangnost resumed his story. 'That winter was bitter. Blizzards raged across the moorlands, As they stumbled, lost, through the featureless snow, thousands died of frostbite or starvation, but worse was to come. With no sun or moons to guide them, they unknowingly turned south, circling back the way they had come. In what has since been called the Weeping Glen they were trapped by the hobgoblin banners.

'There was a great battle that raged for many days. Before it was over, the King and many of his lords had died of their wounds. The women and children took refuge in the caves of the Five Wizards, but the hobgoblins found them. The Queen fled into the storm. After the battle they found her frozen body on the slopes, but the babe . . .'

Quenelda's skin tingled as she waited breathlessly.

'The babe was gone. All they found . . .' Tangnost waited for his audience to ask the familiar question.

'What did they find?' a wide-eyed esquire obliged.

'Dragon tracks, lad.' The dwarf nodded, resting his pipe on his knee. 'All they found were dragon tracks, and soon even they were gone, covered by drifting snow. They searched and searched the frozen wastes of the north from the Weeping Glen to the Midge Ridden Moors. No trace of the babe was ever found. Grieving, they abandoned the search.'

Tangnost took a deep draught of ale and burped with loud satisfaction. He wiped the froth from his moustache with his jerkin sleeve and prepared to resume his tale.

'So they had no King? No Queen to lead them?' a young

esquire next to Root piped up, his eyes wide. 'What did they do?'

Tangnost nodded. 'Bringing together the greatest of their scholars and their warlords, those remaining formed the Sorcerers Guild to rule in their King's stead until they could choose another to lead them. Then, with the hobgoblins in close pursuit, they continued their great trek north, where they were welcomed by my cousins, the mountain dwarfs. As the Century of the Stalking Wild Cat dawned, those who survived reached the glacial ice of the Sorcerers Glen.

'Thus it was here that the first great alliance between dwarfs and men was forged. Foreseeing the dark times to come, they built their greatest fortress: the Ice Citadel. The dwarf masters carved it out of the ice and milky stone, and the Sorcerer Lords bound it with High Magic. Only one part of that citadel remains standing to this day . . .'

'Dragonsdome's keep,' Quenelda finished for him.

Root sat up in wide-eyed surprise. The great milky-hued tower that reached up to the stars, so high that the observatory poked above the clouds, had always seemed other-worldly to him.

'It took nigh on a century to complete the great citadel. As it grew, so all the tribes and peoples of the Seven Sea Kingdoms sought sanctuary behind its growing ramparts from the marauding hobgoblins. But ever the ice retreated north. As the rivers and glaciers melted, so the hobgoblins advanced.

'Then, as the ice failed, a loch began to form in the deeps of this glen. Soon, all that remained was a black rocky island, the citadel's frozen ramparts rearing out of the cold waters. The ice that had once been their guardian now betrayed them. The hobgoblins came.

'All remaining peoples of the Sea Kingdoms gathered to face their foe one final time. Young and old, soldier and artisan, anyone who could lift a sword took their place on the ramparts of the Ice Citadel. And high, high above them, on the upper battlements of the great keep, stood the greatest Battle Mages amongst them, wielding their High Magic.

'A deep yellow haar shrouded the glen. The defenders could hear a great slithering sound and the deeper beat of dragonskull drums. All day the sound grew louder and louder till it broke against the ramparts like a wave, and the haar seemed alive.

'As the red sunset leached out behind dark clouds, seven black dragons were seen circling the keep. Alarmed and afraid, the sentries drew their bows and spears and called out to the Sorcerer Lords, who raised their staffs and stood ready to fight the great creatures.

'As the defenders gathered fearfully, the largest of the dragons landed on a high tower. His four companions settled on the ramparts about him. Smoke curled from their nostrils but they made no hostile move. Instead the great dragon moved towards them. In the darkness his scales shimmered brightly. His outline became fluid. The light was so intense that all were forced to shade their eyes or be blinded. As the light died away, a youth sheathed in the same black armour as the dragons stood before them, half man, half dragon. And this is the story he told them . . .'

The esquires grinned at each other. This was their

favourite part. Quenelda too was gripped by the magical tale as Tangnost's voice changed and he became the first Dragon Whisperer, explaining how he came to belong to the races of both dragons and men . . .

As the story unfolded, Quenelda pictured the tall young man with jet-black hair and the bright golden eyes of a dragon, clothed like the Elders in a living skin of dragonarmour. She imagined white-skinned Frost dragons flying through the raging blizzard, tracking hobgoblin war bands and hearing the cry of a babe. Turning back, they found him sheltered beneath his mother's frozen body. Understanding that the boy needed warmth and milk if he was to live, the dragons sought out the nearest roost amongst their fire-breathing kindred.

'The babe was taken deep into the dragoncoombs, where an Imperial Black nursed her brood in the warm heart of the stone,' Tangnost went on. 'She took the babe and fostered him along with her own four hatchlings.

'As the child grew, dragon magic flowed in his blood and built his bones. His heartbeat slowed and became two, and his lifespan lengthened to that of the Elders. His golden eyes glowed in the dark like his four brothers', and his senses grew keener than those of mere men. Small scales formed on his skin and membranes between his fingers. He spoke the dragon's language and knew the ways of the Elders who had walked the One Earth long before men or hobgoblins existed.

'When the boy came of age, he shed his soft juvenile skin for scales harder than diamonds. He shrugged off mortal form and became a dragon, with fire in his belly and hatred in his hearts for the hobgoblins, and the Elders

95

named him Son of the Morning Star.

'For the next hundred years the Elders and the peoples of the Seven Sea Kingdoms fought for their very survival against the rising menace of the hobgoblins, but none could stop them. During that time Son of the Morning Star earned great battle honours amongst his adopted people, for he had the strength and memories of two races in his veins, but it was not enough. As a second century drew to a close the dragons of the oceans and their landlocked brothers were almost extinct. Only those who could fly escaped the reach of the hobgoblin swarms, and they were injured and exhausted.

'From high on their mountain eyries to deep in their dragoncoombs, the Elders of all dragonkind gathered together and decided to return their brother to his own people, to forge a bond between all the races who fought the hated hobgoblins, so that together they might defeat them.

'And so it was that on the eve of the Final Battle their young prince was returned to the peoples of the Sea Kingdoms to offer them an alliance with the Elders. Knowing him to be their true King, they bowed before him and pledged their allegiance. In return the young King promised to summon the dragons in their defence. Turning once more into a mighty Imperial Black dragon, he disappeared into the night, escorted by his four brothers.

'Then the hobgoblins in their bone armour rose up out of the sea loch. The citadel was surrounded by a heaving, crawling mass. With blood-curdling cries and wild drumbeats, the hobgoblin banners whipped themselves up into a frenzy, then threw themselves into the battle, filled with blood lust.

'From the battlements great oak catapults lobbed chunks of ice that splintered into deadly shards, killing scores of hobgoblins on the black rock skirts of the island. The sorcerers cast hexes and detonations, spheres and pulses into their massed ranks. Arrows fell like a black rain, skewering their soft bodies to the sheets of ice that floated on the sea.'

Tangnost reached for his mug and took a gulp, then continued his tale.

'For two more days and two nights the Final Battle raged. After the first day there was no sunrise. Dark clouds spat lightning. Thunder boomed and echoed, and great hailstones rattled against the ice. By the dawn of the second day the hobgoblin banners had taken the outer moats and ramparts, and in an orgy of destruction slaughtered every living thing. Magic lay thick—'

Quenelda jerked violently, kicking Root. Images flickered through her mind – terrifying images, brilliant in their clarity. Tangnost's voice was not so much cut off as drowned beneath the sudden and terrifying clash of arms and the screams of the dying.

Weapons rose and fell, the sound of steel on bone making her flinch. The hobgoblins' ululating war cries were almost human, but the way in which they pierced her ears to explode white-hot behind her eyes was not. Their putrefying stench choked her throat. Explosions lit the suffocating darkness around her, revealing great battlements and spiralling towers of blue-hued ice . . . Spells broke overhead and spewed across the battlefield in blinding dandelions of colour. The loch below was hidden by the rising mist of spent magic that crept up the citadel walls.

Lightning cracked in the darkness as the heaving mass of hobgoblins crawled over the broken blood-streaked ramparts like maggots on a dying carcass. Pale hands reached up towards her; their clinging, sucking fingers made her skin crawl . . .

She cried out in revulsion.

'Quenelda?' Tangnost paused, frowning. 'Quenelda, lass?'

Turning, Root reached out a timid hand to touch hers, his hand pale against the deeper shadows of her cloak.

'Arghhh!' Quenelda screamed, striking his hand away hard. Then several things happened at once.

The shutters slammed open, letting in the ferocious wind. Freezing gusts blew through the room. Candles spluttered and went out. Outside, a tongue of lightning darted down, casting them all briefly in silver-blue. Several of the younger esquires shrieked. The room disintegrated into chaos.

Root fell over, banging his head, as Quenelda leaped to her feet, tumbling her stool to the floor.

'Quenelda?' Stepping over the dazed gnome, Tangnost reached her in two strides. Strong hands clasped hers. She was shaking violently. 'Quenelda . . .' he repeated gently, pitching his voice so that only she could hear. 'Look at me, lass.'

His quick intake of breath was stifled as the eyes that met his flared bright gold. And the pupils at their heart were not circular, but oval . . . oval like a dragon's. Then their glow faded and was gone, and the girl's terrified gaze came back into focus.

'T-Tangnost . . .' she breathed.

The dwarf turned and found Root's petrified eyes staring up at him. No one else was looking their way.

'Steady there, lad.' Tangnost squeezed the young gnome's shoulder. 'Nothing to worry about.' He found a smile.

He looked back at Quenelda. Her pulse jumped erratically in the dip of her throat and her eyes were pits of black. He had seen it countless times before on the battlefield – the glazed eyes, the shaking; battle fatigue. The hands he cradled were freezing. He rubbed them vigorously between his own. 'Lass, lass, you're all right now.'

'I must have fallen asleep.' Quenelda seemed dazed. 'It was a nightmare, just a n-nightmare . . .'

Tangnost nodded. This was not the time to discuss it.

'Lads,' he roared. 'Look lively! Get those shutters barred and the candles lit. There's a taper by the hearth. Now settle down, settle down. Just a strong gust of wind!'

Slowly the room was restored.

'You're cold, lass. Come sit by the fire.' Squeezing Quenelda's hand, Tangnost returned to his high-backed wooden seat, making a show of tamping down fresh tobacco and relighting his pipe, which gave him time to slow his own heart down and to watch the Earl's daughter. That was the first time – the first time since her birth – that he had seen her eyes like that. His heart thumped. Eyes of molten gold glowing in the dark, just like the Dragon Whisperer of his tale. And she spoke to the dragons . . . whispered to them in her mind. Could she possibly be . . . ?

Certainly since the death of the Earl's father the hobgoblins had swarmed in ever-increasing numbers . . .

'Now,' the dragonmaster said gruffly, satisfied at last that his voice would not betray his emotions. 'Where was I?'

'The Final Battle,' someone said.

'The Final Battle it is then . . .' he boomed. 'All through that third day they fought to halt the hobgoblin hordes, but finally the inner bailey fell.

'The fourth day dawned. The ice was awash with blood and dark with spent arrows and spears. The bodies of hobgoblins were piled so high they reached the inner curtain wall. Abandoning their weakened defences, the survivors retreated to the keep, where the babes, the injured and the very old were huddled.

'The thunder of the night fled, giving way to rinsed blue skies. For once the air was brilliantly clear, and as the sun rose, the hobgoblins fell back into the sea, affording the defenders a respite. Time to treat their wounded. To cast more wards.

'Then . . .' Tangnost paused, his grin fierce. A dozen eager faces leaned forward to catch his soft words. 'A storm blew up on the far horizon – a dark boiling cloud that spat forks of lightning.

'The hobgoblin banners cheered, rattling their weapons on their shields, believing that the Ice Citadel was at last doomed, that the victory would be theirs and the Dark was about to descend for ever. The defenders lost all hope and resigned themselves to a fight to the death, for still the dragons had not come to their aid.

But' – Tangnost's eye gleamed with fierce glee – 'this

darkness was not to the hobgoblins' liking . . . As the roiling cloud sped towards them, it seemed to grow and grow till it filled the sky. This was no ordinary storm. It was all the colours of the rainbow. This was a storm—'

'A storm of dragons,' Quenelda whispered.

Root sat up, a shiver of anticipation ghosting up his back, raising goose pimples. 'A storm of dragons,' he echoed, eyes wide. The thought was terrifying. He drew his knees up to his chin.

Tangnost nodded, and drew deeply on his pipe, sending out swirls of sweet tobacco-leaf smoke to thicken the air.

'Aye, a storm of dragons, summoned by Son of the Morning Star and his four brothers. Tens of thousands of them, forming an army vast beyond imagining, the like of which has never been seen since. Every conceivable colour, size and shape. So vast were their numbers that they blotted out the bright sunlight and the sound of their wings was louder than thunder.

'They swept down the Sorcerers Glen and fell upon the screaming hobgoblins, flying just out of range of their darts and spears. Their tongues spat down dragonfire – hotter than a furnace and slow to burn. Before long the very surface of the ice was on fire.

'The stench of burning filled the air. Ice was vaporized and the fog grew ever thicker. Dragons who could not flame swooped on their hated foe, raking heads and eyes and shoulders with their talons and tearing them limb from limb. Scores were seized up and away, to be dropped screaming through the air, their soft bodies popping and breaking like eggshells on the battlements.

'Filled with a wild joy, the defenders surged out of the

keep and attacked the hobgoblin banners. Trapped between them and the dragons, the enemy had nowhere to flee. By sunset it was finally over.'

Tangnost paused, his voice once more his own. He smiled round at them.

'Son of the Morning Star was the first to sit on the Dragonbone Throne of what became the Seven Sea Kingdoms, and his descendants rule us to this day. During his long reign a fortress was founded on Dragon Isle so that the best and greatest of each race could be brought together to fight their common foe. His own SDS regiment, the First Born, remains on Dragon Isle and here at Dragonsdome, and those of his four brothers still guard our kingdom's borders.'

'How did it end?' Root asked.

'One night at dusk, when the youth had become an old, old man and the fire in his eyes had dimmed to an ember glow, those four dragons were once again seen alighting on the battlements. As dark fell, a star flared brightly and shot across the night sky, fading into the inky dark. In the morning there was no trace of the King the common people called . . .' Tangnost paused, knowing that they all wanted to share the finish to his tale.

'The Dragon Whisperer!' they chanted in unison.

The dwarf nodded. 'Just so. The King they called the Dragon Whisperer! Legend says the lost Dragonsdome Chronicles speak of a time of great danger, when the hobgoblins swarm, when the seas boil and the Dark returns. Then they say a Dragon Whisperer will be born, a child who will walk two worlds: the world of dragons and the world of men.'

'And . . . and how shall we know who it is?' Root piped up, eyes wide.

'Ah . . .' Tangnost shook his head. 'Ah, lad . . . the legend does not tell. But when the time comes' – he nodded to himself – 'we will surely know . . . We will know . . .'

CHAPTER NINE
We Speak No Treason

The Inner Council of the Sorcerers Guild was in an uproar. And no wonder, the Grand Master thought. Never in living memory had such unwelcome news been received, here at the heart of the sorcerers' power. Some had heard of the attacks on brimstone mines, but none knew of the explosion that had nearly killed the Earl, nor of the attack on the fortress of the Howling Glen. Their shock was rising to the rafters.

'Order! Order!' Rising from his oak chair on the raised dais at the centre of the hall, the Grand Master struck the floor with his dragonbone staff of office, carved in the likeness of a seadragon.

'My Lord Earl' – he bowed formally – 'you wish to present proofs . . .' His voice was tinged with curiosity. Rufus had preferred to keep the nature of his proofs hidden until he could speak to the entire Council. It was a rare thing for the Grand Master to be excluded in this fashion, and it gave rise to a mild disquiet.

Moreover, a huge Imperial Black with almost one hundred fully armed Bonecrackers had materialized on the Guild landing pads barely an hour since. Shocked, he was as curious as the next man as to what they guarded. 'That there are signs the hobgoblins are being organized into an army?' he queried, his words tinged with doubt.

Nodding, the Earl calmly waited until the noise had subsided, showing no sign of his inner weariness. His wound throbbed. His skin crawled at the memory of the hobgoblin piercing through his weakened defences, teeth tearing through his damaged armour.

He beckoned to a Bonecracker in ceremonial armour. Nine carved bone necklaces were offered for guildsmen to examine. They took them with obvious distaste; some were hooked over wands or staffs so they didn't have to touch them. These, they had already been told, were the bones of their own dead troops, fallen in battle and taken as trophies.

'At least eight of the thirteen hobgoblin tribes have been united under a single warlord. A warlord we now believe to be named Galtekerion, of the Ramark tribe. Let me present you the proof.'

Used to commanding armies in the field, Earl Rufus projected his voice effortlessly to the furthest reaches of the vast inner guildhall, despite the uproar. 'Bring it in.'

His commandos leaped to obey. The carved doors swung open with a thump and two Bonecrackers entered. There was a gasp of horror as a bloodied and bound frog-like creature was dragged into the chamber, leaving a trail of mucus across the floor. As those nearest drew back at the smell of rotting offal, the fingers of the Grand Master's left hand, hidden beneath the long sleeve of his formal Guild robe, surreptitiously wove urgent symbols and runes of concealment and warding. Even as his fingers stilled, the squatting creature turned to look at him with its hooded green reptilian eyes, but its glance slid away without recognition. Its long pale tongue darted out nervously. The Grand Master took a long, shuddering breath.

The Earl nodded, misreading his concern. 'They are fearsome, Hugo, are they not?'

The Grand Master nodded wordlessly, his face pale.

The Earl Rufus smiled grimly. Most of these learned academics, wealthy merchants and artisans were probably seeing the face of their ancient foe for the first time; only seasoned veterans did not start back in repugnance. The stench was certainly revolting. Once they got over their shock, the guildsmen studied their frog-like captive with ghoulish interest.

The hobgoblin was mottled green and brown, its pallid skin dry and flaking from its imprisonment far from water. Blue tribal tattoos covered its body in complex knotted designs and whorls.

The SDS Commander pointed. 'See the strongly muscled thighs and huge webbed feet? They allow hobgoblins to leap great distances to ambush their prey. And they are, as you already know, powerful swimmers, at home in the water as on land, making them elusive enemies. When we pursue them, they slip into the sea lochs. In the winter they return to the pools of the Westering Isles to hibernate. Their numbers are so great that they are emptying the oceans of life. The fishing settlements around our coasts and islands are frequently attacked; our fishing boats come back empty, if they come back at all.'

'And our galleons too, my Lord Earl,' said another merchant. 'Since early spring a growing number have been pirated. Their empty hulks are found drifting at sea.'

All eyes slid back to the prisoner.

The hobgoblin's white bone armour was chipped and broken where a dwarf axe had found its mark, and its chain mail was weeping red rust. Ragged bandages oozed green slime from half a dozen wounds.

'We found this creature and its fellows skulking in the Never Ending Glen, five miles from the old castle that lies ruined since the last war.'

The Grand Master's eyes flickered at that news, but the Earl was not looking at him.

'They had recently feasted on dragonmeat and were so full they couldn't flee into the loch. You know we don't usually take prisoners – they are treacherous creatures that will kill at the first opportunity. But we needed intelligence, so we fed their warriors to our battledragons one by one until this one decided to talk to us.

'Our scouts have identified its tribal tattoos as those of the Chankit tribe. And these' – the entire chamber leaned forward in ghoulish fascination as the Earl pointed to three knotted circles – 'these tattoos, this hobgoblin boasts, belong to the new warlord Galtekerion's personal bodyguard. Other hobgoblins with the same tattoo were identified from three other tribes from the same war band. As I said, there can be no doubt. The tribes have united.'

There were cries of dismay, immediately cut short as the Earl went on.

'And there is more, this creature claims, my lords. Much more. Tell them,' he growled.

'There isss,' the hobgoblin croaked, the hollow of its throat pulsing as it spoke. 'Water,' it croaked again, bone earrings and nose-bones jangling. 'I need water.'

Its guttural speech was hard to understand, but they gave it a flask of water. It drank greedily and poured some over its head to dampen its dry skin.

'There issss a traitor amongssssst you,' the hobgoblin hissed, tongue darting out.

107

'A traitor?'

'Unthinkable!'

'No!'

The protestations were fierce, unanimous. The Guild might be riven by political intrigue and faction fighting between rival leagues and guilds, but they were always united against their common threat, their ancient foe.

'No, this cannot be – the creature lies to save its own skin,' the Grand Master cried. 'We speak no treason! Surely it is merely boasting. Trying to save its own miserable life while seeking to sow distrust and dissension amongst us.'

'I do not lie,' the hobgoblin hissed threateningly. 'Thisss . . . traitor teachesss usss . . . how to fight . . . givesss usss weaponsss . . . dragonsss to eat . . . This traitor will give ussss dragonssss to f—'

Urgently the Grand Master lowered his hooded eyes to meet those of the hobgoblin. 'You lie to save your miserable skin!' He hawked and spat, knowing it was a provocation, an insult to a warrior that would not go unanswered. He deliberately turned his back to address the chamber. 'My lords, we—'

With a gurgle of hatred the hobgoblin leaped so fast and so far that the councillors had no time to cry out as the Grand Master crashed to the floor, his staff of office flying from his hand.

He struggled to breathe as monstrously strong webbed fingers closed around his throat. The weight of the hobgoblin on his back pinned him down; finger suckers stung and tore at his flesh. There was a loud roaring in his ears; red spots danced before his eyes. Chains clashed taut

108

as the Bonecrackers tried to drag the creature off his back.

The Earl Rufus raised his dragon-headed staff and there was a muted flash that flared orange through the Grand Master's closed eyes; suddenly the webbed fingers about his throat went limp. He sucked in a desperate breath. The hobgoblin sighed, its dying breath enveloping the Grand Master in a toxic fog. The sorcerer rolled away, bile rising like sour apples in his throat, choking, retching, trying to loosen the limp fingers still stuck to his neck.

Finally the dwarf commandos dragged the dead weight from him. With a reluctant pop the suckers tore free one by one, and the corpse rolled over with a wet slap. The Grand Master clenched his jaw against the pain and pushed his hair away from his face. He struggled to his knees as guards and servants retrieved hat and staff from where they had tumbled.

The body of the hobgoblin beside him lay smoking on the slate-flagged floor. A circle of councillors lay around him, blown outwards like the opening petals of a flower. Blinded by the flash of Battle Magic, many were blinking owlishly, unable to see or hear.

A strong hand clasped the Grand Master's shoulder and squeezed it in silent symathy. The Earl reached forward and pulled his friend effortlessly to his feet.

'Forgive me . . .' His fierce smile raked the chamber. 'Time was of the essence. Battle Magic is never tidy . . . I apologize for the . . . fallout . . .'

There was a ripple of nervous laughter as the councillors regained their dignity and their feet. A few of the elderly were assisted to their seats, where members of the Artful Apothecaries Association treated them for shock and minor injuries.

'Th-thank you,' the Grand Master choked huskily, his throat burning. He massaged the red whorls that marked his pale skin and flicked mucus from his doublet collar.

The Earl kicked the limp carcass. 'They smell even worse when they're dead.'

Shaky laughter from the councillors relieved the tension.

A servant stepped forward with a horn drinking cup. The Grand Master gulped the water down with shaking hands.

'No matter.' The Earl nodded to his men. 'Take it and burn it.'

He turned back to the chamber as the manacled body was dragged out. 'So, my lords, you have heard it from the creature's own mouth. Its claims, though far-fetched, are nonetheless worrying. Should they ever lay hands on our weapons—'

The Grand Master sat down heavily in his chair. 'Th-they cannot be trusted, my lord,' he croaked. 'It is foolish to listen to such lies. Most likely they have taken weapons from ships or caravans they have ambushed.'

'No doubt,' the Earl agreed. 'But I do believe that they have united under one leader. Since time began the hobgoblin tribes have fought each other. They have had no sense of organization before other than to swarm mindlessly over the land, destroying everything, leaving a wasteland behind. It has always been their way and their weakness.

'Now, it seems, they gather their strength. They are united under a single leader, with a sense of purpose never seen before. Attacks on settlements are co-ordinated, forcing us to divide our strength . . .' The Earl paused. 'United, they pose a new threat. We are few. They are many.'

'My lord . . .' The Grand Master spoke out through the shocked silence. 'Rufus. How does the SDS propose to meet this new hobgoblin threat? What can we do?'

'Soon snow will block the highland passes and storms will close the shipping lanes for many moons. Ice will freeze even the sea lochs. Cut off from their food supplies, the hobgoblins will return to the Westering Isles to slip into hibernation or they will starve. Normally, all seven regiments stand down over winter to rest and re-arm. But not this year. I intend to take to the field again over midwinter. We will strike at the heart of the hobgoblin heartlands in early spring, where the tribes spawn – their sanctuary in the Westering Isles. We will attack just as they are coming out of hibernation, when they are slow and lethargic. This warlord must die, and the tribal alliances with him, before they breed and swarm next spring.'

'The Westering Isles? But how, my lord?'

'Our greatest problem will be to locate and reach the islands in the dark of winter. As you know, they shift on the cold currents from the far north; they have been known to drift some five hundred leagues offshore, well beyond the range of even our greatest dragons. Finding them will not be an easy task; flying that far even harder. The risks are high but we have the bare bones of a strategy.

'I intend to take three fully operational regiments, leaving all six fortresses at half-strength. I will also take the First Born from Dragon Isle and Dragonsdome, where only light garrisons will be left. We urgently need to re-arm and re-supply and recruit amongst the northern clans. Dragon Isle needs your seasoned timber and shipwrights. That, my lords, falls to you.'

'My Lord Earl,' the Grand Master confirmed with a slight bow, 'the Guild is at your disposal.'

The Earl Rufus nodded. He knew his next request would shock them. 'And dragons. We have taken heavy losses; we lost over a hundred and fifty-six dragons over the course of our summer campaign, with five score nursing injuries.'

The councillors were aghast. One hundred and fifty-six dragons lost in one year?

'M-my L-Lord Earl,' a guildsman in the tall scaled hat of the Dragon Breeders Guild stuttered, wringing his hands. 'We c-cannot possibly replace such losses. Our stud – it is just not possible. W-we have already delivered fifty to Dragon Isle this year. There are other juveniles, perhaps ten . . .'

'Ah' – the Earl smiled grimly – 'at least in this respect I bear good tidings.'

The guildsmen leaned forward eagerly, desperate to hear better news. 'My dragonmaster has successfully treated a badly injured Sabretooth.'

A gasp went round the chamber. The Grand Master's eyes widened. Why had he not heard of this earlier? He must pay more attention to matters at home.

The Earl smiled at their wonder and appreciation. 'He is now fit to return to war. Henceforth injured battledragons will be returned to Dragonsdome for treatment. Several dragonmasters from Dragon Isle will return here to help Tangnost Bearhugger in his work.

I know I leave this difficult task in the best of hands. I leave immediately for Dragon Isle. We have a campaign to plan. I will provide the Guild with more details as soon as I am able.

'Lastly, as you all know, we need brimstone. With the destruction of one mine and attacks on a further three in the Brimstones, supplies are short. The high passes are already closed with snow so ore will have to be shipped. I know that storms are due, but we need that brimstone.'

An old bearded guildsman of the Merchant Leagues reluctantly stood, eyes cast downwards. 'I regret to be the bearer of bad news, but this now bears urgently upon the matter just raised.' He looked around at the worried faces. 'As my Lord Earl said, there have been several recent explosions in brimstone mines, but there is more. In the last week alone a half-dozen of our ore-bearing galleons have been pirated or have simply disappeared. Our brimstone stocks are low and getting lower. We barely have enough to see us through the winter, let alone supply the SDS for this campaign.'

CHAPTER TEN
A Long Day's Work

'Come on, Root,' Tangnost bellowed. 'You can't be tired already! Not a young lad like yourself!'

Puffing along behind the dwarf, trying to keep up with his tireless stride, Root wondered how he'd ever thought being an apprentice was hard work. The dragonmaster had given him no time to brood over his father's death, no time even to think. Instead, he had plunged him into a punishing training schedule to prepare him as the Lady Quenelda's esquire. At the end of his second week Root was exhausted.

Every morning, when everyone sensible, including Dragonsdome's cockerels, was still asleep, Tangnost was already out and about. His day always began at the battledragon and battlegriff roosts with his roostmasters and mistresses. Sometimes the dragonsmith or surgeon would join them to discuss injuries or problems with particular dragons and they would then agree a course of action.

As they progressed from roost to roost, Tangnost explained the key differences between Dragonsdome's battledragons: Vipers, Vampires, Wasps, Sabretooths and Imperial Blacks. He explained each dragon's characteristics and its role on the battlefield; how some, like Spitting Adders, had vestiges of wings but could no longer fly; how some were armoured while others had to wear armour just like men. Struggling to take it all in, Root had resorted to sketching battledragons to help him remember. Tangnost nodded with approval. The boy had

114

an undoubted talent – for art!

Then they would move on to the domestic hippogriff and griffin stables, and Root would find himself relaxing, only to face a barrage of questions.

'Now' – Tangnost tested the boy on basics – 'a griffin is . . . ?'

Root took a deep breath. 'A griffin is a cross between a lion and an eagle. It has the head and wings of the eagle but the body of a lion.'

'Why?'

'Um . . .'

'That is why griffins – battlegriffs, that is – are mostly used for ambushing ground troops. And a hippogriff?'

Root pulled his drawings out of the small satchel slung over his back. 'Is . . . a cross-breed between an eagle and a horse. It has the head, wings and talons of an eagle and the body of a horse.'

Tangnost nodded. 'Which is why, like dragons, they are formidable opponents in the air.'

Every few days they would stop by to check on Two Gulps' progress: the dragonmaster and Quenelda would examine his injuries, with Root in reluctant attendance. Pleased with his steady progress, Tangnost became more optimistic that they would succeed; that the battledragon would indeed pull through.

As the weeks passed, he and Root visited the training cage to watch Two Gulps being exercised by Quenelda, who had chosen Quester to help her while the dragonmaster was training Root.

During the day they nearly always called at the hospital surgery, where Tangnost would consult with Professor

Willowfellow, the Earl's chief dragon surgeon, and Root would wander around looking at the bottles and vials of oils and pastes, the bundles of stalks and roots and bark. Then, after a hurried lunch – or worse, no lunch at all – they would move to the jousting lists or training arenas, where Tangnost would supervise battle training and exercises with the Dragonsdome esquires. Root followed, carrying a heavy dragon tri-horn.

Sometimes Tangnost would leave him in the care of the esquire hallmaster, where he was introduced to the many different saddles and bridles for dragons, hippogriffs and griffins. He had to learn what the different parts of the harness were called, how to mend them, how they were cleaned, and how a dragon or a hippogriff or a griffin was saddled. The gnome began to learn about their diets, the great scuttles of coal, oil, brimstone, oats and heather – and additionally for the carnivores, great haunches of elk, highland cattle, bison, bear and beaver.

At other times, when he was busy, Tangnost would leave more experienced and trusted esquires like Quester to instruct Root on the important differences between carnivores and herbivores, to explain how dragons that flamed needed brimstone ore to do so, and had three stomachs, not two, and how all had two hearts. Quester had welcomed Root from the first, and a close friendship was developing between the two. They shared a bunk in the esquires' dormitory, and the cheery snub-nosed lad was teaching Root about the ways of court.

'The Seven Sea Kingdoms are governed by the Queen, with the help of the Sorcerers Guild, who are sworn to her service,' he explained. 'She is protected and guided by the nobles and lords, and greatest amongst them is the Earl DeWinter, who is also the Commander of the SDS and Queen's Champion, as his father was before him.'

'And your father? Is he also wealthy and famous?'

Quester smiled. 'My father is a lesser lord, and I but the youngest of four sons.'

'So you have gold and castles of your own?'

'No!' Quester laughed. 'I have barely enough silver to buy an old suit of armour and an aged bandy-legged mount. The eldest son inherits all the lands and wealth of his father. That is why I am here, just like the other esquires. To learn the craft and art of warfare so that I may enter the SDS and earn fame and gold and castles of my own on the battlefield.'

'But w-why must I learn this?' Root protested. 'W-what have I to do with great lords and ladies?'

'As the Lady Quenelda's esquire, you will sometimes attend court with her,' Quester repeated gently. 'And so you must know the order of things and your place in it.'

'But I'm just a commoner.'

'No!' Quester slapped him on the back. 'No, friend Root, you're not. You are now the Lady Quenelda's esquire, and so equal amongst us!'

'But I don't want to be her esquire!' Root looked stricken. 'And she most certainly doesn't want me! She's made that perfectly clear.'

And she was not the only one.

'This place is really going to the dogs,' a loud voice declared when Root had first entered the esquires' hall with his meagre belongings. His heart sank. He knew who

117

it was before he turned round; this boy had been furious to find Root elevated to the position of Quenelda's esquire.

The voice belonged to Felix DeLancy, youngest son of the royal treasurer, a sour-tempered weasel of a youth who resented the fact that he would never inherit his father's titles. He took out his resentment on the apprentices at every opportunity. A shrewd opportunist, Felix capitalized on anyone else's misfortune and took credit for their successes; anything to catch Tangnost's attention and praise.

'I mean,' the pale, snooty boy drawled, 'allowing commoners to become apprentices was bad enough, but an esquire? Some people just don't know their proper place.' He sneered as Root edged past, desperately seeking a bunk as far away from him as possible.

'He's not going to last a day.' The voice dogged his footsteps. 'The Lady Quenelda will chew him up and spit him out for breakfast.'

'Or else one of the dragons will,' a companion offered – to hoots of derision.

'Just wait till you kiss the wooden dragon,' Felix called out. 'Then you'll realize . . . You don't belong in the esquires' hall!'

Root walked on, biting down on his lower lip to stop it from trembling. He had no idea what the wooden dragon was, but it obviously wasn't going to be fun – at least for him. Every time he thought he'd spotted an empty bunk, the esquires would gather around it, crowding him out.

'Here,' a voice said quietly. 'There's room here to bunk with me.'

Root looked round at the vaguely familiar voice to see

the young esquire with freckles grinning down at him. 'I'm Quester.' He held out a hand. 'I've seen you at the training arena with Tangnost. Is it true then?' His eyes sparkled as he jumped down. 'You've been made esquire to the Lady Quenelda? You're going to be flying with her, on her dragon, her battledragon?'

Root nodded miserably.

Quester whistled. 'I don't know whether to envy you or pity you. You must be very good with dragons.'

'Why?' Root felt faint. His heart was leapfrogging, slamming against his ribcage in an attempt to break free.

'Well, they say she can out-fly anyone her age and wants to join the SDS. In fact she's already good enough to enter the Battle Academy – only she's too young. And she's a girl. It's too embarrassing when esquires can't keep up with her. She's a natural, like her father. She's flown with him on battledragons since she was three! And rumour has it she helped the Bearhugger nurse a battledragon back to health . . .'

'That's true.' Root's voice quavered at the memory. He looked down at the burn on his hand; it had almost healed. He flexed it. 'I was there too.'

'Lucky you! I wish I had been!' Quester said wistfully. 'Come on,' he suggested as Felix's voice rose up in complaint again. 'Let's get something to eat and leave them to their childish bickering.'

There was loud taunting laughter as they left the hall.

'Ignore him,' Quester advised. 'He's just jealous.'

'Jealous?' Root found that hard to believe. 'Jealous of what?'

Quester turned keen ice-blue eyes on Root to see if he

was teasing. 'You really don't understand, do you? Being esquire to the Lady Quenelda: it's not a punishment, friend Root. It's a privilege, and one that's normally given to the most promising esquire each year. If you succeed in sticking with her, then your future and fortune are made!'

He slapped Root on the back as they entered the vast food hall crowded with Bonecrackers. 'Listen, let's have some honey mead and celebrate your good fortune and the Earl's safe homecoming!'

CHAPTER ELEVEN
Darcy's Devils

The sun was barely breaking through the early morning haze as Tangnost, followed by Quenelda, strode towards the outer paddocks. Behind them Two Gulps followed eagerly on his hind legs, his joy at being out in the frosty air evident in the red flames that licked around his raised muzzle.

Today he and Quenelda would find out whether he was ready to fly again. With barely five weeks until the royal joust Quenelda was desperate to take to the skies on her battledragon. Surely she would be the talk of the joust, the talk of the court! The derisive mockery of the other young ladies would be silenced and her dream of Dragon Isle would come one step closer. She tried to still the fluttering in her chest as she wondered whether that would be enough time to train Root.

It had been touch and go. The cast had been removed barely two weeks since and the last scale successfully grafted on a mere five days ago. As each scale rooted and hardened, its colour gradually changed hue to yellow or flaming orange or red to match the dragon's natural pigmentation.

Every morning Quenelda had assisted the training cage master and his esquires in taking the dragon through increasingly difficult exercises to tone his wing muscles and rebuild the suppleness and strength of his injured tail. She was amazed by how much she had learned in such a short time; how much she hadn't known before. Every afternoon she joined the senior esquires at their studies, often bringing the Sabretooth, who was always the centre of attention. Then, as another week came to a close and early frost froze the moat, the training cage master had finally turned to her to say the magic words:

'We can do no more here, lady. I believe he is fit for Open Sky. I will inform the dragonmaster.'

For the last few days Quenelda had been polishing Two Gulps' scales, paying special attention to the grafted ones, until her arms ached and they shone like mirrors. She had also carefully monitored his diet, selecting only the best giant elk and bear carcasses and finest grade brimstone, along with the oats and molasses to build up his strength, so that he could flame further than any other battledragon. Now it was up to him.

Up ahead, mounted Sabretooths darted through the air above the paddocks as juveniles were put through their paces. Soon they would moult their skin and a new diamond-hard coat of scales would appear. Then, as fully armoured adults, they would be ready for battle training on Dragon Isle.

The senior esquires made way for Quenelda as she approached, chatting excitedly amongst themselves, some of them smiling their encouragement and reaching out to touch her shoulder, some cheering. Their growing acceptance of her and her veteran battledragon bolstered her confidence.

She looked at Two Gulps proudly. The Sabretooth was the result of centuries of breeding. One day he would be put out to stud, but not yet. For now he was a battledragon – her battledragon! She had no doubts. Whatever it took . . . whatever it took – she glowered at Root, who was cowering at Tangnost's side – she would be flying him to the winter jousts!

'Take his hood off, lass,' Tangnost told her, frowning at her hostile stare and Root's evident misery, wondering if he had made a misjudgement throwing them together.

But Quenelda grinned; Root was already forgotten. Heart thumping, she reached up and unbuckled the leather hood. Was his tail mended? she wondered. Was he strong enough for her to fly? She stood back and signalled. *Fly for me, Two Gulps and You're Gone!*

Bunching up the muscles of his hind legs, the battledragon sprang fifteen feet into the air and slowly rose skywards on his stubby wings . . .

No one looked up as three magnificent hippogriffs swept overhead to alight in front of Dragonsdome, their glossy feathers shimmering blue and gold and red, their beaks polished and gleaming. Like their harnesses, their talon-sheaths were engraved and inlaid with silver and semi-precious stones. Heraldic banners attached to their saddles fluttered out behind them, declaring which aristocratic house they belonged to.

Three youths in racing leathers that matched their mounts' plumage dismounted swiftly, casually throwing the reins to the grooms. 'Darcy's Devils', they called themselves after Quenelda's elder brother, Darcy, relishing their reputation for the racing, drinking and outrageous behaviour that had caused so many rows between father and son. Today was Darcy's birthday. On leave from the Royal Household Cavalry (the II Unicorn regiment), he and his friends were going hippogriff racing at the royal castle of Auchterness, two days' journey to the north-east of the Sorcerers Glen.

'What do you think?' A strikingly handsome boy strutted down the sweeping entrance steps to Dragonsdome. Tall and slim, Darcy was wearing racing leathers that matched his emerald eyes. An extravagant gold-hilted wand set with emeralds was sheathed at his side. There were appreciative whoops and whistles.

'Way to go, Darcy!'

'Battlestar racing leathers! Nothing but the best for you, Darcy!'

His friends gathered round admiringly.

'Professional racing leathers in my colours!' Darcy boasted. 'With integrated body armour and wand sheath . . .' He pirouetted, arms held high. 'Check it out. Dual-density spinal pad and embossed—'

'Reinforced shoulders, thighs and knees!' Guy DeBessert interrupted him enviously. Guy was wearing last year's Dragoneye racing leathers in DeBessert kingfisher-blue. 'And a level five defence spell woven into its armour.'

'And look at the helmet,' Rupert Grime breathed, tracing the flaming dragon artwork and the spread wings that moved beneath his hands. 'A Griffin and Gamblepiece! Individually made to order – I've been waiting for one for almost five months!'

'It's got a titanium core and wide racing visor.' Darcy was delighted with their reactions. 'Light as a feather and reinforced with energy impact spells!'

'Like the spurs!' Rupert bent down to have a look at the vicious dragonspurs with four-inch spikes. Rumour had it that the Racing Guild was thinking of making them illegal.

'Dragonspurs?' Simon Woodville grinned. 'Does that mean you've finally got your own dragon again, Darcy? About time!'

'Yes.' Darcy smiled, pleased that their significance had been noticed. He would have to take them off again before he mounted his hippogriff. 'My own dragon, not one of Father's. I'll take you to see him. The Grand Master himself has given me an Arabic stallion from his stables for my birthday,' he boasted. 'He's called Desert Sandstorm. He's—'

'A dragon?' Though one year younger, Guy was even taller than Darcy, with long hair battle-braided on either side of his handsome face in the fashion of the SDS. He intended to apply to the SDS Battle Academy the following autumn on his seventeenth birthday the moment he passed his knighthood ceremony. 'You can fly a dragon?' he challenged. 'But I thought your father had banned you from flying anything but griffins or hippogriffs after you killed . . .' He hesitated, but the damage was already done. 'After Highland Moonshine died at the midwinter races—'

'My father isn't here!' Darcy was furious at being reminded. 'And this dragon is not his, it's mine!'

The public humiliation of that day, of being stripped of his winner's cup for taking his father's much-loved mare without permission, was still raw in his memory. It didn't seem to matter what he did, he never seemed to gain his father's approval! He'd won the race, hadn't he? What did it matter that the mare had died afterwards of exhaustion and blood loss? It was just a dumb animal after all. Surely, as in battle, it was winning that mattered? Not the cost of it!

Darcy's face twisted into an ugly snarl. Even when his father was at war he somehow managed to ruin things, he thought. 'One day he won't come home.' His lip curled bitterly. 'Sooner or later they don't. Then I'll be Earl Darcy DeWinter! And I'll be able to do whatever I please. I could even fly a battledragon if I wanted.'

'A battledragon?' Simon was unconvinced. 'No way, Darcy! No one can just fly one of those things! It takes six months of training at the Battle Academy before they even let you near one, let alone fly one. They're deadly! You could never handle one of them. Stick to unicorns,' he added scornfully. 'Leave the battledragons to the SDS.'

That was the final straw. Pumped up and angry, Darcy recklessly rose to the challenge to his authority. His friend Simon had been making a lot of pointed comments about Darcy's decision to stay with the Household Cavalry rather than join the SDS. He was even beginning to sound like his father.

'I could too – if I wanted,' he blurted, his new dragon already forgotten. But the enormity of the lie was already giving him second thoughts. 'But today I'm going to take a battlegriff instead.'

'Come on, then!' Guy grinned. 'Let's just pick a mount and we're out of here. I've heard Reginald is racing his new stallion this afternoon. You could pit your battlegriff against him. Then we'll see which mount is the better trained.'

They headed down the great tree-lined avenue towards the battlegriff roosts. In front of them a number of Bonecrackers were drifting over towards the paddocks, their rough voices raised in excitement. Darcy had never troubled to learn Dwarfish, so he had no idea what they were saying.

'Look . . .' Rupert paused. 'Look at that Sabretooth over there!'

'So?' Darcy shrugged. 'They're training battledragons. It happens all the time here,' he added casually.

'But it's a Sabretooth! That might be the battledragon that Tangnost Bearhugger nursed back to health.' Guy was suddenly excited. He cocked his head to listen to the dwarfs. He had already mastered the basics of their difficult language.

'No.' Darcy shook his head in denial. How had Guy heard that tale? 'It doesn't look injured to me. It can't be the same one.'

'It might be!' Guy held up a hand to silence Darcy while he listened. 'I think it is. They're talking about "the injured dragon". Why else would Bonecrackers be watching? They must know that's the one! Come on! Let's take a look!'

Without waiting for an answer Guy turned towards the arena, Rupert and Simon on his heels. Angry that attention was no longer on him, Darcy followed grudgingly behind them. The youths joined the small crowd gathering at the paddock walls just as the battledragon landed in front of Quenelda. Rearing up, he was beside her in two heavy strides, his weight hardly making a dent in the frozen ground. Folding away his stubby wings, he dipped his head to nuzzle her, long tongue rooting for honey tablets.

Quenelda slapped him away, her face flushing with embarrassment at being caught out. She had been spoiling her dragon, and Tangnost and his roostmasters would certainly not approve of Two Gulps' recently acquired sweet tooth. *No! Not in front of One-Eye! He will not like it . . .*

'There he is!' Simon pointed, craning to see round two red-hooded juvenile Imperial Blacks that were tethered close by. The dragonmaster's broad-shouldered stocky figure was unmistakable even without the double-headed axe strapped across his back.

'That's Tangnost Bearhugger all right.' Simon's tone was reverent. 'He's a legend in the Bonecrackers! He's with a couple of his roostmasters and esquires . . .' He suddenly paused. 'No . . . No, it can't be . . .' His tone changed to one of disbelief as Quenelda turned round to face them. 'Is that your sister beside him, Darcy? In breeches and buckled blue flying boots?' He stared at the small group. 'Yes, it's her. So she's still wearing boy's clothes! I thought she'd be in satin and lace by now like all the other young ladies at court.' He smiled fondly and shook his head. 'My sister thinks of nothing but clothes, diets and boys! She would never go near a big dragon, let along a battledragon!'

He watched Quenelda. 'She's in the arena with the battledragon too! So' – he turned to look quizzically at Darcy – 'the rumour that she's helped Tangnost nurse an injured battledragon is right, then? I didn't really believe it. No one's ever done that before, not even on Dragon Isle. And I've heard she's already flying solo on dragons!'

Darcy's face clouded with jealous anger. If it wasn't his father and the SDS, it was Tangnost and the Bonecrackers everyone talked about, and he was beginning to hear Quenelda's name with monotonous regularity. So she could already fly dragons when she was eleven, barely old enough to have her first wand, while he'd not managed till last year? So what!

'Dragonsdome dragons are the best-trained dragons in the world.' He shrugged casually. 'That's all. Anyone could fly one!'

Just because he wasn't eager to die under a hobgoblin cleaver, he thought bitterly, watching the Sabretooth take off a second time. No one seemed to care that he was a superb swordsman or that he could handle a temperamental unicorn. Sons were expected to follow their fathers. He shivered. The ancient dented and cloven suits of black armour that lined Dragonsdome's endless halls bore witness to the fact that his forefathers had rarely died in their beds.

For as long as Darcy could remember, everyone had expected the heir to Dragonsdome to excel at everything he turned his hand to, just as they had expected him to follow his famous father into the SDS. But that was not what he wanted. It had never been what he wanted.

'He's magnificent . . .' Simon was awestruck. 'I don't think I've ever seen such a huge Sabretooth. I've dreamed of flying one of them since I was knee-high. I wonder if Tangnost would le—'

'Look!' Guy interrupted, startled to see Quenelda step forward. A warbling bugle call beside her rang out, gradually gaining in strength. 'Look! Your sister is the one controlling the battledragon! And the roostmasters are listening to her!'

'Don't be ridiculous.' Darcy stuck out his jaw as the small group closed around his sister, evidently congratulating her. 'They can't be. What does a girl of eleven know that's worth listening to? She knows nothing about tactical training. She'll just be watching. It will be Tangnost or one of the roostmasters training the Sabretooth. Ignore—'

He suddenly realized that he was the one being ignored. All heads were turned skyward. He reluctantly followed his friends' gaze, feeling the familiar dizziness grip him. The dragon had become a dark speck against the glare of the sky . . . He put a hand out to steady himself.

'Lord Darcy!' A man's excited voice broke rudely into his thoughts. 'Lord Darcy . . .' The man-at-arms gripped his shoulder, his gap-toothed smile wide, breath stinking of stale beer and garlic. 'Is that the injured Sabretooth we 'eard about? He's flying again. Yer lord father's own battledragon!'

Darcy started, angrily shaking the man's hand away, noticing for the first time that they had been joined by a throng of men-at-arms. A large contingent of off-duty Bonecrackers were still gathering at the distant paddock walls, their guttural language carrying clearly as they pointed upwards and called to their fellows to hurry. Nearby, a returning Sabretooth patrol had landed; the tired troopers rested on their saddle pommels to watch Two Gulps. One of their dragons lifted her head, harness jingling, and called out a greeting as he flew past. 'Eeaaawaaak!'

Quenelda called out again, to be echoed by Root's bugle call. Up, up the circling Sabretooth slowly flew. Dozens of telescopes were now pointed skywards. For a moment the dragon hung in the air before folding his wings.

The crowd held their collective breath. No one moved.

'Drop Dead!' Simon's voice rose to an excited squeak. He coughed to cover his embarrassment. 'Drop Dead!' he repeated gruffly in imitation of the armoured men around him, who had now raised their weapons and were cheering hoarsely.

Quenelda looked up and saw her battledragon falling as swiftly as a flaming meteor. Trailing red flames haloed him. He swooped down with the sheer joy of flying in Open Sky once again. Now the battledragon and his mistress were showing off, choosing one of the hardest SDS manoeuvres to execute: Drop Dead.

Pride warred with doubt; adrenaline flooded Quenelda's bloodstream, making her legs weak. Have I pushed him too quickly? she wondered. She was suddenly scared. What if he's injured again? The growing crowd had encouraged her to show off. Nervously she jigged from side to side, setting her boot buckles jingling.

Two Gulps . . . She started to call out to the dragon, and then hesitated. Would he hear her thoughts through the roaring air as the ground hurtled towards him? What if she distracted him at a critical moment? What should she do? Feeling suddenly guilty, she chewed on her lip, realizing that she knew so very little about battledragons in combat.

Tangnost put a quiet hand out and nodded. Quenelda sighed with relief. If the dragonmaster was happy then she had nothing to worry about.

'Now . . .' he growled softly.

Now! Quenelda whispered fervently.

Her soft words were followed by the loud crack of sinew and tendon as the small wings unfolded. At the last possible moment the battledragon swung his hindquarters round and spread his wings, slowing his rate of descent. Would it be enough?

A gasp whispered around the paddocks. Flattening out, belly only inches above the ground, he hurtled forwards with a flick of his mended tail. Touching down, wings wide to balance, he bounded across the training arena, zigzagging around wooden posts, leaping over and around obstacles with his powerful back legs, smoking and setting dozens of straw-stuffed dummies alight in his wake.

Root stood horrified as this apparition from hell filled his vision and thundered towards him. And then, unbelievably, springing on his powerful hind legs, the battledragon somersaulted, to land with toes and talons outstretched, crushing three more dummies before flaming a further four. The wind roared and red smoke billowed across the paddocks as the dragon punched through, leaving a fiery trail like a comet. Inches from the arena wall, he skidded to a halt, his great hind claws furrowing the ground, sending clods of earth and a shower of pebbles raining over the stands.

Tangnost and Quenelda and the more experienced esquires ducked as stones flew overhead, striking a resonant note from the tri-horn and a squeal from Root. He crumpled to the ground, pale-faced and sweating, and promptly threw up – right into the bowl of his horn. No one noticed.

Cheers and shouts broke out around the paddocks. Then a groom was sent to the tack room: Quenelda was about to mount up.

'Drop Dead followed by Incinerator and a Single Twist Disembowel!' Guy coughed as he caught a lungful of smoke. Like all youths, Darcy's Devils followed the SDS's latest exploits closely, and their legendary manoeuvres were constantly debated on the racing circuits and at court.

'Amazing!' Rupert whispered, wide-eyed, having never been so close to a battledragon before.

Forgetting where he was, Simon stepped down from the paddock wall to whistle loudly and banged hand on helmet in approval, followed by Rupert and a tight-lipped Darcy.

'Come back!' Guy hissed at them. 'Get out of the paddock! Those are battledragons!'

'They're just juveniles,' Darcy scoffed at him as he clambered over behind Rupert and Simon. 'Scared?'

'Darcy . . .' Tangnost scowled in exasperation when he saw him. Darcy might be the Earl's son, but he and his spoiled aristocratic friends knew precious little about dragons, warfare and chivalry. They were disobedient, lazy and careless – dangerous traits around dragons, and almost certainly fatal around battledragons. They were going to get someone killed soon. Didn't they know that untrained juveniles were particularly dangerous? Surely everyone knew that red hoods were a warning sign.

The Earl had banned his son from the battlepaddocks and roosts last year, until Tangnost was satisfied he could behave more responsibly. Now he and his friends had climbed the far arena wall, perilously close to where two juvenile Imperials – Dangerous and Deadly, and Leave in Smoking Ruins – were tethered. Even hooded, the dragons could easily kill using their acute sense of smell and hearing.

'Have they no sense at all?' the dwarf growled.

'I'll send an esquire over to warn them.' Shaking her head in disbelief, Roostmistress Greybeard turned to one of the mounted esquires whose Sabretooth was licking Quenelda's hair in the hope of getting some of the honey tablets hidden in her pockets.

'Darmeed, over there at the double, please, and ask the young lords to stand down from the wall before they're injured.'

'Sir!' Dragon and rider bounded away with great leaps.

Then Tangnost noticed for the first time that Root wasn't beside him. 'Oh, lad . . .' He shook his head as he spotted the pale-faced gnome leaning against the stone wall, sweat running down his face and neck. 'Go and rinse your mouth out,' he said kindly. 'And I think you should rinse the tri-horn out too. In its four hundred years it's survived much worse, and so will you! Then go and muck out the empty roost stalls – you've done enough bugling for today.'

Root fled gratefully.

As if to give weight to the dragonmaster's words, Dangerous and Deadly's long neck snaked out sideways. The bells on the red leather hood jingled ominously as jaws snapped in irritable warning. There was an undignified scramble back over the wall as hot breath licked over Darcy and his friends. The rank blast showered the youths with saliva; gobbets of raw meat and bone smacked them in the face; a wisp of smoke curled from Darcy's hair. The soldiers around them guffawed at the boys' evident inexperience. Darcy looked thunderous.

'Ugh!' Rupert shook a stringy morsel off his leathers in disgust: it looked like a fleshy rope of intestines. 'That was a close shave!'

'See what I mean?' Guy looked defiantly at Darcy's high-coloured face. 'It doesn't do to go near them until you're trained. Otherwise you get bitten . . .' His voice trailed off as something caught his attention.

He and his friends watched in silence as Quenelda strode across to her battledragon and leaned up to scratch him behind his spiked ears. 'Your sister's certainly got a way with dragons,' he commented thoughtfully.

Aware of Darcy's hot eyes on him, Rupert closed his gawping mouth and tried to hide his admiration.

Darcy laughed. 'She's just a girl! Look at her in her scruffy boy's clothes and tangled hair. She's quite the scandal at court, a disgrace to the family name. No ladies of noble birth will be seen with her. She reeks of dragon—'

Simon wasn't listening. 'I wonder if it's true?' he said.

'What?' Darcy snapped, angry at being interrupted.

'The rumour that she wants to go to Dragon Isle too—'

'Dragon Isle! A girl?' Darcy laughed derisively. 'Forget her! Come on!' He stormed out of the arena towards the battleroosts. He'd show them that he could handle battlemounts too!

Striding past the huge stallions, Darcy stopped in front of a roost where a small silver-dappled female battlegriff lay curled up, asleep. The name on the stall was Ride the Rising Wind. Well, he could handle a battlegriff that size easily! The creatures were highly trained, weren't they? He had been flying hippogriffs since he was fourteen, so a battle-trained one couldn't be too different, could it? If his younger sister could handle a battledragon, then surely he could handle a battlegriff! He tried to remember Tangnost's tedious lessons on battle training and briefly wished he had paid more attention.

'Hey, you there, boy. Saddle her up,' he commanded Root, who had just arrived with bucket and mop to muck out the empty stalls. He'd show them all, he thought, especially Quenelda, their father's favourite. He was not going to be outdone by his younger sister.

'But . . . my l-lord,' Root stuttered, frozen to the spot. 'I'm not – I – I can't—'

'Yes, this one, saddle her up!' Darcy spat. 'And get a move on! Don't just stand there.'

The stablemaster on duty, an aged veteran who had lost an arm twenty years earlier, intervened cautiously: Darcy's short temper was well known. 'Ride the Rising Wind, my lord?' he queried uncertainly. Everyone knew that this little mare was fiery-tempered and required an experienced hand. 'But your fathe—'

His voice faltered in the face of Darcy's cold fury, but the old soldier stood his ground, gently guiding Root behind him with a shaking hand. Unsheathing his wand, Darcy angrily fired a casual magic that slammed the stablemaster into the stable wall. He groaned, head lolling on his chest.

Root turned and fled in panic, screaming, 'They've hurt the stablemaster!' as he stumbled, breathless, over the paddock wall, scraping the skin off his hands. 'Dragonmaster! Dragonmaster!' He threaded his way through the crowds to tug at Tangnost's battle-braid, his other hand pointing shakily towards the battleroosts.

'Steady, lad. Take a deep breath.' The dwarf bent down and put a comforting hand on the boy's shoulder. 'Slowly now – tell me what's happened.'

'The Lord Darcy has hurt the stablemaster because he wouldn't saddle up Rising Wind for him. He . . .' Root hesitated as more and more faces turned his way.

'What?' Tangnost was shocked. Only spoiled children who didn't know any better used magic to get their way with servants. 'Surely not?' Not even Darcy would be so foolish as to hurt a man who had fought in the SDS at his grandfather's side for thirty years.

'L-Lord Darcy,' the boy repeated, quailing beneath Tangnost's glare. 'He's intending to ride Rising Wind . . .'

The dragonmaster was furious. If the Earl's son was any judge of griffin flesh, he would know that the young mare was still half wild and very dangerous, not long broken to the saddle . He glanced at Quenelda, who was deep in discussion with one of his roost masters, Gromell Widgewort. They were examining the healed wounds on Two Gulps' hindquarters, surrounded by an enthusiastic group of esquires and Bonecrackers. They were about to saddle up the battledragon.

'You two,' Tangnost ordered Quester and Root. 'Come with me!'

CHAPTER TWELVE
Ride the Rising Wind

Inside the battlegriff roost, the stablemaster coughed and spat blood. Around him, half a dozen apprentices and several esquires stood rooted to the spot, each terrified of attracting Darcy's attention.

'Saddle her!' Darcy ordered as the old man tried to get to his feet. 'Now!'

'Immediately, my lord!' One of the esquires stepped forward to stand protectively between the stablemaster and Darcy's wand.

What luck! Felix DeLancy thought. What an opportunity to show up that little guttersnipe Root for the coward he was. It would do no harm to ingratiate himself with the young heir and appear to be protecting that stupid old man at the same time. Ride the Rising Wind was one of the youngest battlegriffs in the stable, so she should be easy to handle. This was his chance to prove that he was the best choice for the Lady Quenelda's new esquire, not that pathetic Root who had fled at the first sign of trouble.

'Immediately, my lord.' Felix raced for the tack room. 'You there,' he shouted at an apprentice polishing a spiked training bit used for breaking in difficult mounts. Vicious, Felix thought, but suitable for the young Lord Darcy. 'Bring that bit and a bridle,' he ordered. 'And you, a number three saddle. Move!'

'Hurry up and saddle her, damn you.' Darcy's fear had goaded him to foolishness and he knew it now. What if he made a mess of things? He couldn't bear the humiliation in front of his friends, who thought he was a daredevil like them. He knew he wasn't half the flyer that Guy was, and although he would never admit it to anyone, he was very afraid of heights. The Unicorn regiment suited him so much better.

Darcy's heart was racing as Felix threw a fleece over the small battlegriff. He turned his back on the stablemaster, who was finally struggling to his feet, and sheathed his wand. 'That'll teach him to question my orders,' he said coolly, pleased no tremor betrayed his rising panic.

'Go for it, Darcy!' His friends were laughing, clapping him on the back.

'Wow, she's a beauty, Darcy. You don't often see mountain hippogriffs these days.' Even Guy was wide-eyed with approval as Felix led her out.

The esquire was now regretting his bravado too. The powerful mare was more of a handful than he had judged, and Darcy's friends were only making things worse.

'Look at those golden eagle eyes and that blue beak! She could tear a man's head off with those talons!'

'My lord,' the stablemaster tried one final time, 'she is a wild creature!'

Wild? Felix swallowed, mouth suddenly dry with fear. He was now very close to those piercing eyes and that sharp beak!

'Think you can handle her?' Guy taunted Darcy. His rivalry with the Earl's son went back to the nursery.

'Of course!' Darcy snapped. 'I—'

'Keeaww! Keeaww!' Responding to the tense atmosphere, Rising Wind reared up. Her talons raked the air, forcing the boys backwards out of the stall.

'Watch out! She's a pedigree battlegriff,' Darcy boasted,

though his heart was galloping out of control now. 'One of my father's personal mounts. One day she'll be mine, just like all those others out in the paddocks. Bring her outside.'

'What are you doing?' Tangnost arrived, bristling with anger, and challenged Darcy as he emerged from the roosts. 'My lord, you're unsettling the battlegriffs.'

It was true. The roosts were now echoing with their cries and the flurry of wings. Darcy spun round.

'Settle them down,' the dragonmaster ordered the two esquires who had arrived breathless from the training arena. 'Now! Before they all get out of control.'

'How dare you! How dare you address me in this fashion! You, a mere commoner!' Darcy spat the last word.

Ignoring the insult, the dwarf held his ground, his expression steely. 'I merely obey your Lord Father's commands, my lord. As you should. You are expressly barred from the battleroosts.'

'My father is not here.' Darcy spoke coldly and deliberately. 'He is on Dragon Isle. So you answer to me now, not him. Stand down, or you lose your place at Dragonsdome.' He would show him; he would show them all what he could do! That he was fit for command.

'My lord.' Tangnost bowed mockingly. Well, he thought, the brat was about to learn a hard lesson in flying that he would not readily forget. The hippogriff would have him off in no time at all. He wouldn't even leave the ground. The Earl could deal with his son when he returned. He stepped back, a faint smile on his lips.

'Give me those!' Goaded to recklessness by the

dragonmaster's condescending tone, Darcy snatched the reins from Felix. 'Come on.' He jerked viciously as Rising Wind danced sideways and away from him, her hooves clattering on the cobbles. As he tried to mount, hopping awkwardly on one leg, his left boot slipped out of the stirrup and he nearly fell. Face flaming, he was rescued by Felix, who led the nervous creature towards the mounting block at the end of the stables.

'Stay still, damn you.' Darcy raised his arm and swallowed a cry as a wing struck him hard in the face. He spat blood and a feather. Highly trained though the young battlegriff was, she had no combat experience yet, and Darcy's unbridled panic was sending all the wrong signals. She had been trained to throw an inexperienced rider – a ploy to prevent an enemy from capturing a trained SDS battlegriff.

The Earl's son almost fell out of the saddle as he stepped off the mounting block, and his poor handling caused Rising Wind to step backwards, hooves striking sparks off the cobbles, knocking one of the esquires to the ground.

Fear made Darcy careless. Desperately gathering the reins, he unthinkingly dug the cruelly spiked dragonspurs hard into the hippogriff's unprotected flanks.

Rising Wind shrieked her outrage as blue blood ran from the deep puncture wounds in her silver flanks. As she reared, thwarting Tangnost's lunge for the bridle, Darcy realized too late what he had done. In danger of losing his seat, he instinctively yanked on the reins to keep himself in the saddle, digging the spiked training bit into the soft inner tissue of the hippogriff's beak. Blood-flecked foam sprayed the air, splattering Tangnost and Darcy's friends with blue droplets.

'Watch out!' the dragonmaster shouted.

Darcy's panicked movements were similar to the command to scythe on the battlefield: to clear the space around of all enemies.

'Stand back, you fools! Stand back!' Tangnost barked, pushing Darcy's friends away with a powerful thrust of his arms. 'Stand back if you want to live! My lord,' he warned Darcy, 'dismount! You have already lost control of her.'

The next second, with a powerful flap of her wings, the angry mare kicked out backwards with her hooves, while her beak and talons struck in the classic battlefield manoeuvre. The young apprentice next to Felix screamed and crumpled into a heap, clutching his stomach, his intestines drawn out like a string of pale sausages by a hooked talon. Meanwhile Guy's left hand was severed by the battlegriff's beak. The white-faced youths stood frozen in disbelief as blood sprayed into the air in a red fountain. Then Guy's knees buckled and he fell to the ground. Root fainted.

Sensing disaster as screams of panic filled the air, Darcy unsheathed his wand and fired a hasty subjugation spell. But his sloppy casting was poor through lack of practice and the weave was unravelling even as the spell settled on the battlegriff. The runes he chose were nowhere near powerful enough to dominate or bind a battlegriff to obey him. The effect was the opposite of what he had intended.

Certain now that Darcy should not be in the saddle, Rising Wind reared up, gathered her powerful haunches, and with a beat of her feathered wings, bolted upwards. The ascent was so steep that within moments Darcy was unseated. Held only by his left boot, which was snagged in the stirrup by his spur, he tumbled backwards with a scream.

Quenelda, halfway to the battlegriff roosts in pursuit of Tangnost, stopped in her tracks as she heard the screams ring out, then looked up in open-mouthed disbelief as Rising Wind climbed steeply overhead, her brother in his distinctive new racing leathers bumping against her flank like an unwanted piece of baggage.

'Darcy!'

She looked at the crowd milling around outside the roosts. She could hear Tangnost bellowing orders; panicked shouts carried on the wind. Looking up again, she knew it would take the esquires a while to saddle up, and there were no other dragons or hippogriffs in sight. There was no time to lose! Darcy's boot could slip any moment and it didn't look as if he had attached a flying harness. She turned back towards the training arena, where Two Gulps was still exercising.

Two Gulps and You're Gone . . . She wasn't sure if the dragon would hear her over such a great distance. She quested out towards him.

Dancing with Dragons? His whisper was at the edge of her hearing. But although they had not yet flown together, their bond was strong. Already the battledragon was responding to the confused jumble of Quenelda's unspoken thoughts and emotions. Knowing only that she needed urgent help, he flew swiftly over the paddock walls, leaving the confused roostmasters and esquires wondering what was happening.

In moments Two Gulps had reached Quenelda, his

right wing brushing the ground near the paddock walls where she stood anxiously on the cobbled path. It was clear what he was expecting her to do. She was his mistress now, and she needed to be airborne in a hurry.

Instinctively understanding his intentions, Quenelda ran up the rising wing and was seated at the dragon's shoulder as it dipped a second time. She braced her legs beneath the kuluck, the thick joint where wing and shoulder met, and lay along the length of his neck; then girl and dragon left the ground. With a powerful flick of his mended tail, Two Gulps rose steeply through the air.

Below Quenelda, turmoil had broken out. Guy had passed out, blood still pumping from his severed wrist. His companions stood frozen with shock. Cursing, Tangnost ordered two battlegriffs to be saddled immediately to go in pursuit of Darcy, and barked at Root, who was staggering to his feet. Best get the boy out of the way – he was as white as a ghost.

'Root, fetch the surgeon immediately. And where is the Lady Quenelda? We could do with her calming the roost.'

'Sir! Yes, sir!' Once again Root fled gratefully.

'Help me,' Tangnost ordered Rupert and Simon as he knelt beside Guy. 'Hold him down. We need to get a tourniquet on quickly or he'll bleed to death.' Cursing again, he whipped off his belt. 'Here . . .' he instructed Rupert. 'Strap it round his arm here and keep it tight.'

He went over to the apprentice. The young gnome lay gasping for air like a landed fish, his thrashing growing weaker by the second. Pink bubbles frothed around his lips. The dwarf knew there was nothing to be done for him now. 'Hush, lad, you're all right,' he said, gently cradling

144

his head. 'We'll get you to the hospital. Hold on, Grouse. Hold on, lad . . .'

The words were barely out of his mouth when the apprentice sighed and fell silent. Tangnost swore bitterly at the careless loss of life, not caring who heard him.

Reluctantly he turned his attention to the cause of all the mayhem. Darcy's own life was now in serious danger; somehow he needed to be rescued!

'Bearhugger! Look! Look!' Rupert was pointing upwards.

The dwarf's eye widened in amazement. Quenelda was already soaring up and up and closing fast on her brother. On Two Gulps and You're Gone!

'Mount up! Mount up!' he shouted to his esquires, who were finally leading out two mounts, tripping in their haste to get them saddled up. 'Mount up and help the Lady Quenelda to bring that battlegriff down before the Lord Darcy does any further mischief.'

'That was a combat takeoff! I swear it was.' Simon looked up from restraining Guy, who was moaning with pain. His blood loss had slowed to a trickle, but Tangnost could see that he was going into shock.

Still looking skywards, Rupert was open-mouthed. 'She's actually flying a battledragon!'

'When did she learn to do that?' Simon's eyes were wide as he looked at Tangnost. 'Wasn't that the Stoner Manoeuvre?'

Rupert lifted his telescope. 'It was,' he confirmed in disbelief. 'She's flying with no saddle or bridle—'

'What?' Even Tangnost looked up at that, frowning against the glare as if that would help him see the dwindling specks that soared above Dragonsdome.

A strong north-east wind was buffeting the battledragon. Quenelda clung on, fingers instinctively finding minute ridges between his scales. Two Gulps was much slower than the smaller battlegriff, but they had almost caught her when, folding her wings, Rising Wind suddenly dived, trying to rid herself of Darcy.

By now, Darcy's hoarse screams were growing faint. He was badly battered, and a sharp hoof had caught the side of his helmet, making his head ring. As the battlegriff plummeted towards the ground, he could barely breathe, let alone scream. Suddenly Rising Wind levelled out and he was dragged through the top branches of a chestnut tree, slapped and buffeted by branches. Rooks rose up all around him, screeching their outrage.

The Earl's son hadn't strapped on his new helmet properly. Striking a branch, it fell to the ground, along with the boy's wand, which detonated on impact, demolishing a tiled stable roof. The blow knocked Darcy out and he now swung limply beneath the battlegriff's belly like a clock pendulum, stoking her temper ever higher.

Quenelda was closing in. Two Gulps didn't need any guidance by bit or bridle; he identified the focus of her thoughts, and she wisely let him have his head. Having gained the advantage of height, he folded his wings and dived like bird of prey, swiftly catching Rising Wind.

The battlegriff passed low over the large paddocks, almost colliding with a juvenile Viper who was just getting airborne. On the pursuing battledragon, Quenelda had an impression of a white face, a fading scream and an explosion of feathers, and then they were sweeping over the paddocks.

'Keeaww! Keeaww!' the enraged hippogriff screamed, her beak snapping bad-temperedly. Darcy's stirrup was tearing a gaping wound in her side. Quenelda could hear her complaints: *How dare he? No Wings dishonours me! I am no fledgling to be broken with spur and bit!*

Your pardon, Ride the Rising Wind . . . Quenelda brought her dragon in as close as she dared. Any nearer and their wings might collide. The battlegriff was in a dangerous mood, spoiling for a fight. It would take a while to calm her. Meantime she might easily rake Darcy with her talons and beak, or kick him with her hooves.

Quenelda's mind raced, trying to dredge up every last piece of information she had heard from Tangnost about battles. What was it he had said to his esquires about combat landing?

If you become entangled in your mount's flying harness and your hippogriff lands, the impact alone might badly injure you. If that doesn't happen, then the odds are you will be crushed by your mount landing on you . . .

So persuading the battlegriff to land wasn't an option. What should she do?

No Wings does not know how to fly . . .

Quenelda tried to soothe the battlegriff while she searched for inspiration. *Forgive him – he is ignorant of our ways . . . Let me try and rid you of him . . .*

Perhaps the best thing to do was help her brother back into his saddle, then persuade the battlegriff to land.

'Darcy! Darcy!' she shouted as her brother swam back

to consciousness. 'Give me your hand! Darcy!'

As the trees and paddocks of Dragonsdome's outer training area swiftly passed beneath them, Quenelda rolled Two Gulps and You're Gone over through ninety degrees; then, moving forwards and hooking her right leg around the dragon's right kuluck, she leaned out to grab Darcy's hand; but her brother was rigid with fear, and didn't seem able to help himself.

Bringing Two Gulps and You're Gone to a hover, Quenelda tried frantically to think of a better idea. Remember – she heard Tangnost's words echoing in her head – battlemounts are trained to kill. That is their instinct. Never fly too close to another mount, and never fly directly beneath.

Flying alongside and running from wing to wing was also a highly skilled and dangerous battlefield manoeuvre, only practised by the SDS in extreme need. It required great discipline and long experience. She and Darcy clearly had neither. The risk of collision or of falling was too great, and Quenelda wasn't strong enough to lift her older brother up behind her.

Uncertain of Rising Wind's temper, she signalled the approaching battlegriffs to prevent her from taking off into Open Sky. Then the experienced battledragon made a suggestion of his own.

Shepherd . . .

Shepherd? For a moment Quenelda was confused. Then she realized what her dragon was saying. Yes! Yes!

Quenelda had never seen this tactic performed but had heard of it being used to protect an injured mount from enemy fire when landing. This was how many hippogriffs fledged their young, protecting their backs until they could defend themselves. But would Rising Wind allow herself to be shepherded down? Quenelda gave Two Gulps and You're Gone his head.

The battledragon climbed upwards but Quenelda sensed he was beginning to tire. It had been months since he had been battle-fit and flown in Open Sky. This would probably be their last chance before Two Gulps was exhausted. As the battlegriff passed below, Two Gulps moved into her slipstream.

Tangnost's words came once again into Quenelda's mind: Remember, you are always vulnerable to attack from above and behind. No matter how well trained, a battlemount is at its weakest when neither you nor your mount can see your approaching enemy.

Quenelda and Two Gulps glided down gently so as not to provoke Rising Wind. Then the battledragon spread his wings above the smaller battlegriff, forcing her down to where a sea of anxious upturned faces followed their every move. With every stroke of her wings the battlegriff was slowing and losing height. Thirty strides. . . twenty . . . ten . . .

All the while Quenelda was whispering to calm the mare: Slow down . . . I will rid you of him . . . Slow down . . .

Hands stretched up to gather Darcy, but he was just out of reach and the battlegriff was beginning to climb again. Quenelda had no choice. Move alongside, she commanded Two Gulps and You're Gone.

With a powerful beat of his stubby wings, the Sabretooth dragon edged out of the hippogriff's slipstream and moved swiftly alongside her. Once again, without Quenelda having to express a conscious thought, he rolled to the left so that she could reach her brother.

Grabbing him by his boot, cutting her wrist on his wicked dragonspurs, Quenelda reached forward and neatly sliced through Darcy's stirrup leather with her flying knife. Her brother fell half a dozen feet into some bracken and thistles. Seconds later, as Quenelda and the two battlemounts climbed steeply, she heard the cheers.

With the release of her tormentor, the battlegriff's flight immediately began to slow and her anger to cool. *Hush*, Quenelda whispered as they circled Dragonsdome for one final time. *Hush – he's gone . . .*

As they descended, she could feel the thud of her battledragon's two hearts matching her own rapid heartbeat, the elation of the chase stirring their blood, the exhilaration of having succeeded beyond her wildest dreams.

People were streaming towards the battlegriff roosts from all over Dragonsdome to join the vast throng of soldiers, stable hands and esquires already gathered there. Some of them were cheering; others looked stunned. Quenelda cautiously guided the battlegriff down over their heads to where Tangnost had ordered his esquires and men-at-arms to clear a wide landing space.

Strong hands reached up to take the battlegriff's harness. A red hood was quickly thrown over her head to calm her. 'Yer father will be right proud of ye,' the stablemaster said; a smile crinkled his face and brought a hint of colour back to his pale cheeks.

'Cool her down, then get her injuries seen to,' Tangnost

commanded as the battlegriff's esquire began to lead her away. 'That was magnificent, lass,' he said, turning to Quenelda and finding a rare smile just for her, despite his anger. 'I think we can safely say that Two Gulps is fit enough to fly!'

For the second time in one day, Quenelda flushed red with pleasure. Tangnost's compliments were few and far between, and all the more precious for that.

Darcy's two friends pushed to the front of the crowd, open admiration in their eyes. Simon held a hand out to help the Earl's daughter dismount. Unused to such gallantry, Quenelda wondered what he was doing before Tangnost tilted his head with an amused smile. Bemused, she took the offered hand and mumbled her thanks as she stepped down from her battledragon's wing.

'That was amazing.' Rupert elbowed Simon out of the way. 'No one will believe it! And without a saddle or bridle!'

'Where on the One Earth did you learn the Stoner Ma—'

'Bearhugger!' a new voice called out.

The dwarf moved away to greet an apothecary, who was already kneeling beside Guy. Beyond them, Quenelda saw that some apprentices were lifting a body half covered by a cloak. Then the cheering crowd closed in and her view was blocked.

'What happened?' she called out. 'What happened?'

A dozen voices began to answer her, but they tapered into silence. Then she saw Darcy pushing his way forward, brutally elbowing the crowd aside.

They gave way reluctantly, sullen muttering and muted

laughs hastily turning to coughs as he passed by.

Laughing! They're laughing at me! Darcy's glare raked the crowd for culprits, but their gaze remained firmly fixed on the battledragon and rider in their midst.

Rupert turned to him sympathetically. 'Darcy—' he began, then stopped mid sentence. Although his friend had two swollen black eyes where the battlegriff's wing had broken his nose, his armoured racing leathers had kept him from any serious harm. But it was the expression in his eyes that made Rupert falter.

'Guy's hand . . .' he began. 'It's—'

But Darcy did not so much as glance at his injured friend; he had eyes only for Quenelda.

Unaware, flushed with success, she stepped away from Simon to embrace her brother. 'Darcy! How a—'

But even as he bent to embrace her, his eyes were filled with such loathing that the words died in her throat.

'How dare you?' he hissed into her ear, his normally handsome features twisted and ugly, his grip on her upper arms painful. 'Little show-off! You did that deliberately! Embarrassing me in front of my friends – in front of half of Dragonsdome! You little upstart! You don't belong here. You've never belonged here. My mother died after Papa cast her aside. She was a noblewoman! Your mother was a nobody, a commoner, and so are you. Our father may have brought you to Dragonsdome and given you a title, but that means nothing. You should remember exactly what you are: a base-born bastard.'

Quenelda reeled back from him, hurt and bafflement on her face. Everyone knew her father had made a loveless, political marriage to Darcy's mother that had ended in bitterness and divorce. She had heard stories about Desdemona DeWinter: her dazzling beauty, her extravagant life at court, her shallow, selfish behaviour and her contempt for her husband. It was the fabled DeWinter wealth she had wanted, not the young heir to Dragonsdome. When she betrayed Quenelda's father, young Rufus DeWinter had no choice but to banish her from his life and from Dragonsdome. Was Darcy still so blind to her faults? Quenelda opened her mouth to protest, but the look of hatred was still burning in her half-brother's eyes.

'Papa isn't always going to be around to protect you . . . I'll get my own back,' he snarled.

'What—? What do you mean? What do you mean you'll get your own back?'

'One day,' he said softly as he turned towards the crowd with a smile on his lips that didn't reach his eyes. 'One day Papa's luck will run out. They all die, sooner or later. And then I'll become Earl, and you and your dragon will pay for today.'

CHAPTER THIRTEEN
Grounded

'You're grounded. The dragonmaster has been informed.'

'What?' Darcy was incredulous as he flung his helmet on the floor in a rage. 'He was just a stupid commoner! Just a gnome. What does it matter that he died?'

'Just a stupid commoner?' The Earl Rufus's voice was menacingly quiet. His eyes coldly considered his son. 'He was a young boy of ten. Last time it was just a dumb dragon you killed, never mind that she was one of our best breeding mares. Do you realize how vital pedigree battlemounts are in this war? And how about your friend, Guy? Does his injury not matter either? He was expected to take his place at his father's side on Dragon Isle.'

Darcy shifted uncomfortably.

'He will never fly with the SDS now.' The Earl shook his head. 'Or any frontline regiment. His father, the Commander of the Night Stalkers and one of my oldest friends, is furious, and rightly so. When are you going to learn, Darcy, that you have a duty of care to those around you?'

Darcy yawned. He had heard it all before. He would apologize, his father would return to the war, and life would go on as before. Simon and Rupert and a group of friends were waiting for him. They were going out to the local tavern for a night's drinking and gambling.

'And servants, Darcy, cannot be bullied and intimidated by inappropriate use of magic. Only undisciplined children behave that way. Magic may compel obedience, but it does not win hearts and minds. You must earn their respect and loyalty, both on and off the battlefield.'

The Earl's jaw hardened: he could tell Darcy's attention was drifting. 'Being an Earl's son is not just about having the best of everything, or having your own way all the time. I banned you from the battleroosts. You deliberately disobeyed me. There are many responsibilities that go with the title of Earl, and if you are ever to inherit the earldom, you are going to have to convince me that you merit it.' He paused, waiting to see if his son was even listening.

'What? Merit it?' Darcy echoed blankly as what his father had said sank in. 'If? If I ever?' He sprang to his feet. 'I'm your heir!'

'No, Darcy. Dragonsdome is no longer yours by right. You will have to earn it. I am tired of your irresponsible behaviour and your tantrums. Your little escapade with a battlegriff cost one life and put many others at risk, not least your sister's.'

'Half-sister!' Darcy spat, a lifetime of jealousy and resentment rearing up within the two words. 'No one apart from you even knows who her mother is! She could be anyone, even the lowliest servant! It's a disgrace to my mother's noble birthline. It's—'

Anger flared openly in the Earl's eyes. 'I have decided that you are to be enrolled at Battle Academy immediately, whether you wish to or not. They will teach you discipline and responsibility. They—'

'B-but I'm to be a captain in the Queen's Second Unicorn regiment!' Darcy pleaded, suddenly contrite. 'The Grand Master has promised me the best stallion in his stables on my promotion, a golden unicorn! I am to command a troop of my own: Darcy's Dragoons.'

'No,' the Earl said softly. 'No, Darcy. No son of mine is going to avoid active service by hiding behind pomp and ceremony. I had hoped that you would come to this view yourself, but since you have shown no sign of growing into your responsibilities, I have taken this decision. You will enrol with the SDS and enter as a lowly cadet. Artisan's son or Earl's son, you will all be equals on Dragon Isle. You will have to earn your promotion there, not buy it. If you disobey me in this, you will forfeit the earldom.'

'You can't do this!' Darcy shouted. 'I'm noble born! Command is mine by right! Only commoners and younger sons are cadets. You can't do this!'

'I think you will find,' his father said, 'that there is very little I can't do.'

Darcy turned and ran from the room in rage, barging past Tangnost, who was waiting outside.

'My Lord Earl?' the dwarf enquired, motioning after the departing boy.

The Earl Rufus smiled ruefully as his rain-soaked dragonmaster entered and accepted a welcome mug of mulled wine from a page. Tangnost nursed it gratefully. He was not as young as he used to be, and the endless cold was making his wounded thigh ache.

Like his lord, he had just returned from Dragon Isle, where he had seen for himself what the SDS were planning. He had spent five days conferring with other SDS dragonmasters from all over the Seven Sea Kingdoms, discussing tactics and training. It had given him a great deal to think about, and he had a few ideas. He had sketched them to Dragonsdome's foundry master, who had promised to have both equipment and arms for three troops ready by the week's end. The Earl let his dragonmaster settle comfortably, content to let him take his time.

'Can we do it?' he asked as Tangnost drew on his pipe. 'Will the recruits be ready in time? The task of replacing them would fall to you here at Dragonsdome. You have only two moons before they must go to Dragon Isle for full-scale exercises. The full resources of Dragonsdome will be at your disposal.'

Tangnost nodded, thinking of the wondrous things he had seen on Dragon Isle. Operation Crucible was bold and dangerous in the best tradition of the SDS. The Westering Ocean was a wild and dangerous place even in midsummer. But in winter none dared sail its storm-tossed seas, where rocky shoals and icebergs lurked in freezing fogs to sink unwary ships. But getting the SDS to the Westering Isles was a task that fell to others; his was to make the regiments up to full strength in a fraction of the time it normally took. Dragon Isle's imperial pilots and navigators had been training for weeks with battle-seasoned veterans drawn from all seven regiments. It was no easy task for them – but for raw recruits? It was a daunting undertaking, but what a challenge! He had been desperate to be involved, frustrated that his injury kept him from frontline operations. His instincts were no longer battle-honed – it was years since he had lifted his axe in anger. But . . .

The Earl saw the determined line of Tangnost's jaw and knew the answer even before he spoke. 'Yes, my lord. We can do it!'

Satisfied, Earl Rufus had one last thing on his mind.

'Bark Oakley's son. How is he doing?'

Tangnost paused, thinking. 'He is making progress, my lord. He is eager to please. But . . . he still fears dragons, and—'

'And my daughter is impatient to prove our choice of esquire wrong?'

Tangnost's answering smile was enough.

'Well' – the Earl nodded – 'the moment you are happy to relinquish his training into her care I want you to take overall charge of the Bonecrackers. Requisition whatever men, equipment and arms you need. In one moon you will begin night-time exercises with the Night Stalkers. Our winter campaign against the hobgoblins must be successful: the future of the Seven Sea Kingdoms depends upon it.'

CHAPTER FOURTEEN
Hobgoblins

It was a freezing night; cold white stars freckled the black sky, but the crescent moons had yet to rise. Darkness pooled in the Never Ending Glen below. A Vampire dragon dropped softly out of the darkness to land within the crumbling walls of a derelict old castle, ruined centuries ago in the Second Hobgoblin War. All but one of its escorts remained airborne, keeping watch for the SDS. It would not do to be found here.

'I will not be long.' The Vampire's rider dismounted, his breath blooming in the frigid air. 'Wait here, Knuckle. We must be back at the Guild by dawn.'

'My lord.' The man bowed as he took the Vampire's reins, holding his own mount in readiness.

Drawing his staff from his saddle holster, the black-cloaked figure moved confidently across the rotten drawbridge and into an inner courtyard, where he pressed a stone rune carved onto a wall, near invisible in the gloom. It flared briefly beneath his touch. Then, with a soft click, a stone door opened inwards to reveal steps descending into the castle depths. The man stepped through and the doorway closed behind him, leaving no trace.

He cast a small illumination spell with his fingers and the wall sconces flared into life. Then he made his way down the steep steps to the subterranean caverns.

The smell of salt grew sharper, and chains clanked in the shadows. His soft footsteps echoed as he reached a cavern where the sea sucked at the rocks.

The man smiled grimly and moved across to where a circular hole some five feet in diameter was sunk into the bedrock of the chamber. But this was no well. The water here slapped and gurgled in a steady rhythm as it slowly rose higher. The water here was tidal, connected to the distant sea by a maze of underwater caverns and tunnels that spread out into the deep loch nearby.

A strange curled horn with a long pipe was inset into the stone, its mouth many feet below the level of the sea. The man blew into it, sending eerie notes out across the sea, summoning hobgoblins to return . . .

Water frothed over the edges of the hole, heralding the arrival of the first guest. Bulbous webbed fingers reached up and effortlessly gripped the slimy rim with their suckers. The hobgoblin slithered out and flopped onto the floor before powerful thighs propelled it upright.

In the flickering light the hobgoblin's skin glowed with a faint sheen of phosphorescent green. It carried dented weapons recently stolen in battle, wearing them over a rusting hauberk of metal rings taken from a Bonecracker, and a helmet made from the skull of a juvenile Viper, encrusted with barnacles. A necklace of human finger bones and hanks of rotting hair, each one representing a kill in battle, rattled against his armour. Luminous eyes, used to the dark of the ocean, searched the cavern. Its thick lips drew back in a sibilant hiss, baring pale serrated teeth that caught the dull light. The bulbous air sack in the hobgoblin's throat bobbed. Its gills bubbled and dribbled as it expelled water and drew air into its lungs.

'SSSSorcerer Lord.' The creature squatted respectfully

on bended knees before raising itself up to its full height of over six feet, its eyes level with those of the figure who stood before it.

'You have a messsage for my massster, Galtekerion?'

The man nodded. 'Y-yes . . .' he croaked. He fingered his bruised and bandaged throat and tried again. It did not do to show weakness in front of hobgoblins, or let them scent blood. 'When the harvest moons are full, I will come to the Westering Isles. I will take the dragon you have been training for me. Tell your master to ready his warriors for battle before the frost moons wax.'

'Sssssssssssssss, it isss ssso? That isss good. Our food runsss low. The tribesss are restlessss for bone and blood before we sssleep. You promisssed usss a victory.' Its hiss died away. The tide sucked loudly in the cavern. 'In return for our allegiance.'

'And you shall have one. Be there at the Killing Caves at the full moons.'

'My lord, we shall be there.'

Hesitating, the creature licked its wet lips like a dog eager for a bone, its hunger naked in the darkness. 'You have dragonsss?' Its nostrils dilated. 'I can sssmell them.'

The Sorcerer Lord nodded. There were always dragons. 'A score.' He raised his hand and the flaming torch grew brighter, throwing back the shadows, glancing off the scales of the chained moor dragons. He was finished with his experiments – the hobgoblins could remove the evidence. 'But feast here. Do not remove the carcasses – leave them to rot. They will keep until you return.'

The hobgoblin dipped its head beneath the swell and called. A coarse, croaking cry rose and fell, echoing throughout the subterranean depths of the sea loch, carrying for miles and miles. The cry was taken up. In a matter of minutes the water churned and frothed as hobgoblins swarmed out by the dozen.

Sensing their approaching death, the dragons chained to the rocks screamed with terror and tried to throw off the iron chains that shackled them to the stone. But in moments they had disappeared beneath the heaving, boiling mass of ravenous hobgoblins.

CHAPTER FIFTEEN
The Wooden Dragon

The wooden practice dragon bucked and kicked. Suspended from the ceiling, it was rolling and yawing as Felix and his cronies pulled on the ropes, all eager to humiliate the upstart in their midst. They were putting their backs into the task with a vengeance.

As Root's helmet smashed into the dragon's head, his own head exploded yet again into bright stars. Next second he was swinging dizzily, his body slack in the safety harness, Quester's words echoing in his head.

'They call it kissing the dragon,' his friend had explained. 'Every esquire, every roostmaster, has kissed the dragon, so you'll be in good company. The fact that Tangnost has decided you're ready is good. He must be pleased with your progress.'

Ever since the dwarf had told him he was ready, Root had been tossing and turning at night, barely sleeping a wink. Neither had Quester, his bunk-mate.

'Here . . .' The cheery boy had rummaged in his trunk. 'Why don't you take my old tunic? I don't need it any more and it's about your size. It's well padded – and here, you can borrow my helmet and gloves for now. You'll need them.'

Just how much, Root had learned within moments of taking the saddle.

Now it felt as if he had kissed the wooden dragon more times in the last week than he could remember – he had a purple-blue bruise to show for each and every time. As the dragon pitched and tossed, he retched emptily, sweat soaking his padded tunic, making his skin itch and prickle. Unkind laughs and jeers greeted his failure to stay in the saddle for more than a minute at a time, but his feet were too small for the stirrups and the dragon too wide for him to grip with his thighs. All he could hang on to was the saddle's pommel. Every inch of his body was aching, battered, trembling, sweating . . . but he wasn't going to give in. He wasn't going to give them the satisfaction.

'Remember, friend Root,' Quester had warned him before heading for the training cage to work with Quenelda, 'Felix and his cronies want you to fail. He is bitter that you are the Lady Quenelda's esquire. They expect you to fail because you are a gnome, and not born to warfare.'

'And so does she,' Root muttered darkly as he headed for the wooden dragon. 'She wants me to fail . . .'

Well, he thought, sticking his jaw out determinedly, he wouldn't. He'd show them. He would be the first esquire that the Lady Quenelda would not be able to get rid of. He'd stick to her like a limpet. He'd make his father and Tangnost proud of him.

Fine words, the gnome thought sourly as he reached for the saddle's pommel rope to try again. He had already smacked into one of the roughly carved hinged wings and been caught by the tail when he tumbled backwards. If it wasn't for the flying harness and Quester's heavy padded tunic, he'd be in the hospital barracks. Root groaned.

This time he managed to last all of ten seconds before he was unseated. The dragon's tail clipped him in the air, spinning him like a sycamore seed. It was too much for him. Dizzy and sick, hanging limply in the air, he suddenly realized that no one was laughing any longer.

'Right, lad.' Strong hands reached up to steady him and unhook his harness. 'Down you come. Take a rest.' Tangnost glowered at the esquires, who avoided his eye. He didn't need to ask who the ringleader was.

'For a start,' he said to Root, 'let's get you a saddle that fits. Felix, you're senior esquire here, you should know better than to bully rookies. Pull another stunt like this and you'll be on mucking-out duty with the apprentices for a month. Fetch another saddle, and make sure the stirrups are adjusted to the correct length. Now jump to it!'

'Sir! Yes, sir!' Felix shot a vitriolic look at Root before darting into the tack room.

Root swilled his mouth out with a ladle of water and spat into the sawdust. He started as a heavy hand grasped him by the shoulder. 'Stick at it, lad,' the dragonmaster urged him quietly. 'Ain't no one could stay in a saddle three sizes too big. Don't lose heart now.'

Root nodded, unconvinced, and then winced, hand automatically reaching behind to the source of the pain – a tear in his padding.

'Splinter?' Tangnost enquired.

Root's face flushed. 'Right, lad' – the dwarf grinned at him – 'run along and see the surgeon. That's enough practice for today.'

Occasionally, Quenelda would come along and stare at the gnome and tap her foot impatiently. Whenever that happened, he would go to pieces and fail whatever exercise he had been set by Tangnost – then he heard her heavy sighs of exasperation and the other esquires' sniggers at his lack of progress. He began to hope that if he did badly enough, he would be demoted back to being an apprentice. Felix could have the job as far as Root was concerned. But then he thought of his father, and his last mission of exceptional bravery, and felt ashamed that he himself was so near to giving up.

Eventually Root began to feel better about himself. With the correct size of saddle and properly adjusted stirrups, he was actually making good progress. By the end of the second week he had managed to stay in the saddle without the other esquires being able to unseat him. His bottom and pride were still smarting from the indignity of his visit to the hospital barracks, where the apprentice undersurgeon had removed a nasty splinter. But he was beginning to believe he would actually pass the flight test, the first of many expected of an esquire.

After two intense weeks of training he felt ready to try his skills on the wooden dragon in front of an audience. Tangnost and his roostmasters and mistresses were seated in the small training ampitheatre: Roostmaster Windlewith, a whiskery goblin who always looked as if he had just sucked a lemon; Roostmistress Greybeard, the tough but fair dwarf in charge of the maternity roosts; Roostmistress Hammerbone, another small dark-haired dwarf with a booming voice and a ready smile; and Roostmaster Quintus, an elderly sorcerer who had retired from active service but still wore his old body armour and walked as though he were sitting astride a dragon. And behind these judges, in the whispery shadows, the other esquires were gathered. Root could hear them laying bets on the outcome.

'Root Oakley?' Roostmaster Windlewith lifted his beady black eyes.

'Sir! Yes, sir!'

'Saddle your mount!'

'Sir! Yes, sir!'

The sand timer was turned.

Hands trembling, Root ran to fetch his saddle. Even though it was smaller than average, it was still heavy, with a high cantle to enable the rider to stay seated through high-speed turns. Then he fetched the three-reined bridle with its delicate silver dragonbit that allowed for precise manoeuvring. He saddled the wooden dragon and stood stiffly to attention while Roostmaster Windlewith inspected his work, peering through his pince-nez spectacles.

'Hmm . . . not bad, not bad.' The goblin nodded. 'The windlet strap could do with tightening another notch.' He consulted the sand timer. 'Three minutes flat. Good, good. Now. Mount up! Mount up! Tail-end if you please.'

'Sir! Yes, sir!' Root ran up the tail plates of the wooden dragon and vaulted neatly into the saddle with a sigh of relief, trying to quash the memory of his distastrous first attempt at that manoeuvre. Taking comfort from Quester's ready grin, he nodded to show that he was ready.

Then, out of the corner of his eye, he saw Quenelda enter the training amphitheatre. He turned to acknowledge her.

'Sir! Yes, sir!' Felix sneered under his breath. 'Three bags full, sir!' He'd show them it was a mistake to make a guttersnipe into an esquire for the Lady Quenelda when it should have been his by right as senior esquire.

Distracted by Quenelda's arrival, Root failed to notice Felix pull down really hard on his rope without warning. It sang through the brass hauser. The wooden dragon dipped violently away beneath him and spun. He was thrown brutally sideways.

'Oouf!' he groaned as the saddle's pommel caught him in the midriff.

As the dragon righted itself, Root managed to brace his knees against the saddle and keep his seat, but then, as the dragon's head dipped and he leaned back in the saddle, the jointed rising tail smacked him hard from behind, pitching him forward.

'Hang on,' he thought he heard Quenelda's exasperated shout. 'Just hang on! Ride it out!' His head was ringing, so he couldn't be sure.

Dangling from the uncomfortable harness that was still two sizes too large, Root rolled his eyes as he scrambled back into the saddle. Hang on? Newt and toad! What on earth did she think he was trying to do? Why was she always such a bossy-boots? Why was she always so impatient with him?

The question barely had time to take shape before it was bounced out of his head. Next second the wooden dragon unexpectedly jinked sharply to the left. Somehow his right foot slipped out of the stirrup and he was unseated. Then gravity claimed him and he was falling, just as the pommel was rising and—

When he came to, he saw Quenelda standing over him. Her voice was fuzzy and distant as she asked him if he was hurt. He could hear the sniggers and guffaws of the other esquires. He had failed – yet again!

CHAPTER SIXTEEN
Fledgling Flight

With so much to do and so much to learn, the arrival of winter took Root quite by surprise. He woke up one day to find that four inches of snow had fallen overnight and the wells had frozen. A painful few days had passed since he'd failed his test on the wooden dragon. The news that Felix had been put on mucking-out duty for a month for his part in Root's humiliating failure was small comfort to him; he was simply dreading getting back in the saddle. Tangnost, full of patient understanding, was letting the gnome take his time. But Quenelda had plans of her own.

She had been counting down the days to the jousts impatiently. The previous six weeks confined to Dragonsdome had already seemed unbearably long. Four times since his return, her father had flown to the royal stud or the court without her. With Two Gulps now fit and flying, the only problem was Root. Well, Root had had plenty of time to learn the basics. It was clearly time for her to put theory into practice. The wretched gnome was going to learn flying the hard way. After all, the royal joust would take place in just under three weeks and she was most certainly not going to miss that!

The noon meal was over in the eating hall. A few esquires sat around playing dice games but most were studying. Root too was studying a barkscroll, struggling to learn the characteristics of Sabretooths. The Lady Quenelda had curtly told him he had better memorize them before she next spoke to him.

Root swallowed. He chewed mindlessly on a piece of bread, his fear of facing Quenelda and her battledragon making him queasy. Quester had gone through the points one by one with him the previous night; had even written them down for him. His friend's hand was clear and bold, but . . . Root shook his head. It was hopeless.

Sabretooths are flamers with a powerful reach that can kill at fifty strides. Their scale armour can deflect arrows, but not a direct sword or spear thrust, so they are often fitted with additional armour.

Sabretooths are used by the SDS for scouting in mountainous terrain and for driving hobgoblins out of their caverns and caves.

They . . .

Root sighed. These were just lifeless words – they didn't convey the breathtaking, heart-thumping reality of a battledragon.

He reached for his satchel and pulled out half a dozen barkscrolls, rolling out the largest and weighing it down with his plate and leather mug. The Sabretooth leaped at him out of the drawing: the power, the ferocity, the huge hind legs that made the ground shake, tipped by talons honed to a wicked edge, the great jaws . . .

A drop of sweat fell from Root's nose, smudging his charcoal sketch. In his mind he could see the yellowed teeth and smell the hot reeking breath that shrivelled the grass to a crisp. And as for the eyes, those bright inhuman eyes that skewered you at a glance—

'Root!'

He nearly jumped out of his skin. 'W-what?'

'Come with me,' Quenelda commanded briskly. She was dressed in heavy blue leathers and full flying harness. She threw a training helmet at him. Hands stinging with the impact, he just managed to catch it before it landed in his lunch. He looked up at her in confusion. Her next words spurred his heart into a terrified gallop.

'We're going flying.' She turned for the door without waiting to see if he was following. Root wished Quester was with him – his friend would have told him what to do, but he was in the training cage with the cage master. Out of the corner of his eye, Root could see Felix and his cronies watching with interest.

Hastily abandoning his scrolls, Root ran after Quenelda as she headed towards the battledragon roosts. 'But . . . but, Lady Quenelda, I – I haven't flown on a real dragon yet.' He heard his voice rise thinly in protest as he struggled to keep up with her. Quenelda could walk very fast for a young lady and he had shorter legs. 'I h-haven't even passed the wooden dragon.'

Behind him he could hear Felix and his friends speculating loudly on the outcome of his first flight.

'I know,' Quenelda replied over her shoulder. 'But at least you now know one end of a dragon from the other.' She suddenly stopped at the inner paddock wall. Root cannoned into her and rebounded.

'Ouf!' He felt his face colouring as he scrambled to his feet.

'Tangnost says you'll pass next time with no trouble.' Quenelda looked down at the gnome. 'That last time was just a . . . just an unfortunate accident. The other esquires, er' – she felt a passing pang of guilt but ruthlessly quashed it – 'took you by surprise?'

Root nodded cautiously.

'Well, then,' she said impatiently. 'That's all there is to it. Lean with the dragon and hang onto the pommel. The battledragon and I will do the rest.'

'The . . . the b-battledragon?' Root's heart now bolted completely out of control. He felt faint, spots swam in front of his eyes, his breath caught in his throat. He finally caught up with Quenelda in the tack room. A blast of hot air rolled out of the roosts, carrying the stench of sulphur. Root swayed on his feet. He thought he was going to faint.

'We're flying on a b-b-b-b—' He took a deep breath. 'B-battledragon?'

'Oh, you'll manage,' Quenelda said carelessly as she lifted a dual saddle down. Finally! She was heading for Open Sky and nothing was going to stop her. 'Flying's easy. You'll pick it up in no time at all. I want to be able to fly my own dragon to the royal jousts. And that means you have just under three weeks to become my esquire. So . . . let's see what you can do.' She handed the heavy saddle to the gnome, whose knees buckled under the weight. 'Now, mount up.'

It was too much. No one had ever once asked Root if being an esquire was what he wanted. Not Tangnost, not the Earl, and certainly not Quenelda. He stood there for a moment, emotions swirling around his head, fighting the tears that stung his eyes. His whole world had been turned upside down. His father was dead. The esquires constantly mocked him. Quenelda didn't want him – she was making that perfectly clear. He angrily wiped his tears away. Well, it couldn't get much worse, could it?

'No!' In a sudden fury he flung down the saddle. 'It's easy for you! But not everyone is like you, my lady. I don't want to fly dragons. I don't even like dragons. I hate them!' A tear trickled down his face, making him angrier. 'I hate them! Especially battledragons!'

Quenelda stared at him, open-mouthed. He gazed back, horrified that he'd said too much, certain that he would find himself dismissed, thrown out on the streets.

But Quenelda was stunned. No commoner had ever spoken to her like that before. As an earl's daughter, she was used to being obeyed without question. She stared at the pale-faced gnome as if he were a total stranger. This was a side of him she had not seen. With a guilty pang she realized she was stupid not to have acknowledged his acute fear of dragons; in her desperation to get back to Open Sky she had simply ignored it.

And she had to admit that he had made an effort. He had persisted in spite of provocation and prejudice, hers included. He had got back on the wooden dragon in the face of the humiliation and mockery – which, if she had not exactly encouraged, she certainly hadn't stopped. He had struggled against the odds despite his loneliness. Despite the fact he didn't fit in . . .

Quenelda paused. He didn't fit in. Just like she didn't fit in!

The sudden realization hit her like a hammer blow. How many times had she been mocked for her love of dragons, for her passion for flying? How often had she heard the snide gossip and unkind whispers speculating about the identity of her mother? Her own petulant words to her father came back to her: But I don't want to be a young lady! I'd hate it at court. I want to fly dragons!

She hated dresses and ceremony, the stifling formality of court. She flew dragons when no other girl did. And she wanted to apply to Dragon Isle. Some of her exercises with the senior squires had shown that some of them, if not all, didn't think girls could or should be allowed to.

And now that she took the time to look properly, she noticed that the gnome was as thin as a runner bean, all sharp elbows and knees, and his once chubby face had an unhealthy, gaunt look to it. He was still grieving for his father. She remembered her fear when her father had collapsed. What if he never came home? Fear suddenly made her knees weak. She sat down heavily on a bench.

Embarrassed, Quenelda closed her mouth, which was still hanging open, and opened it again to say something. She glanced up. Root was staring down at his scuffed boots. She followed his gaze and saw that the stitching was coming apart so that the toes on his left foot were sticking out. And he was shivering, whether from fear or cold she couldn't tell. Maybe both: his thin clothes were hopeless for anything but Lower Sky flying in summer.

Suddenly ashamed, she opened her mouth to say something. 'I—'

Root beat her to it. 'I'm sor—'

'No. I'm sorry,' Quenelda heard herself saying determinedly, her ears pink with shame at her arrogant behaviour. 'I'm sorry. Really.' She nodded, reaching a tentative hand out to touch his shoulder and pull him down on the bench beside her.

'I . . . er . . .' she continued awkwardly, biting her lower lip. She swallowed and sprang back up to pace restlessly across the tack room. This was a secret she had not revealed to anyone. 'I . . . I'm not used to having any companions . . . friends . . . apart from dragons.'

Quenelda sat down heavily on a bench opposite and stared at her blue-buckled flying boots, suddenly looking very young. Root stared at her. Was she going to cry? She raised her head and smiled oddly, torn between pride and bitterness.

'I'm different to other "young ladies" – other daughters of noble houses . . . I flew with my father almost before I could walk – on his battledragon Stormcracker Thundercloud – and I could talk to dragons almost before I could talk to people. I mean, I really can talk to dragons and they can talk to me. That's why I'm so good around them.'

The young gnome stared at her.

'When I was young, very young, no other children could fly with me. And . . . well, now,' she said, her lip trembling, 'no one my own age wants to be with me.'

Quenelda sighed. She had never divulged this to anyone – not that she had anyone to share secrets with except for her dragons – that was the point. But in the midst of the hustle and bustle of Dragonsdome, she was often lonely.

'None of the girls want to go anywhere near dragons – they think I'm peculiar. They're obsessed with clothes and court gossip. Sometimes gossip about me . . .' Quenelda paused, remembering how she had questioned her father about who her mother was.

'Ah, Goose,' he had sighed, 'many will ask why your mother's identity is a secret, and make their own judgement. Ignore them. Trust me when I say that I love and honour your mother and that one day, when the time is right, I will acknowledge her. But until that day comes, none must know who she is, not even you. Trust me, Goose. I have my reasons.'

'Nasty gossip about who my mother is. And as for boys' – Quenelda frowned – 'boys just don't like the fact that I'm better than them. Most boys my age are still flying griffins. A few manage to fly a hippogriff if they're lucky, but none of them can fly dragons, let alone battledragons. Not many people get to do that before they've even got their first wand!' She smiled bitterly. 'I was angry with you because I wanted to impress everyone at the winter jousts, to show them what I can do. And' – she bit her lower lip as she stared at the floor – 'I thought you were going to ruin my chances.'

Root shook his head. 'But how could I ruin that for you?' He shrugged his shoulders in confusion. 'I don't understand. What have I to do with it?'

'Papa told me I couldn't take to the Open Sky until I had taught you how to fly.' She coloured as Root's eyes widened with sudden understanding.

'With him being away at the war more and more, I'm just used to being on my own.' As she said the words, she remembered what her father had told her: that Root too was on his own. He really was on his own. A shiver of sadness ghosted over her skin.

'I don't always think of others . . .' She floundered for the right words. 'I'm sorry. I was just thinking of myself. I'll help you learn to fly. I really will. If you'd like me to.'

Root stared at her. Had she really apologized? His oak-dark eyes fixed on her in sudden hope.

'We won't fly on Two Gulps . . .' She nodded, thinking on her feet. 'At least not yet. I'll . . . I'll pick a dragon from the domestic roosts who'll be a really gentle ride, and we'll just fly around Dragonsdome, keeping low. No battledragons – I promise. And' – she hesitated, letting go of a lifetime of high society and court protocol – 'call me Quenelda. I'm happy with just Quenelda.'

Root managed a nod. His hands were shaking. He thought he might be sick.

'So,' Quenelda said briskly to cover the awkward moment, 'you'll need to get some warmer boots, of course, and a cloak. Just pick ones that fit . . .' She waved at the rows of flying equipment piled on racks and seats. 'It might seem warm outside, but when you're flying, the air is always colder. It's called the wind-chill factor,' she added helpfully. 'We won't go high, so you won't need a flying suit.'

Root nodded mindlessly and pulled a pair of boots two sizes too large and shrugged on a warm cloak.

They walked along the great tree-lined avenue between endless rows of paddocks, boot buckles cheerfully jingling. Past the unicorn stables and on to where the air was alive with glorious colours as griffins, hippogriffs and dragons wheeled and dived and swooped through the crisp afternoon air, roosting on trees and poles. The great hive-shaped roosts and terracotta-tiled stables stretched out in front of them. Every now and then Quenelda would stop to consider a dragon, pointing out its particular pedigree and characteristics to Root. He walked rigidly along beside her, eyes straight ahead, nodding automatically.

'Root?' Quenelda sighed and tried again. 'Root?'

She waved a hand in front of the gnome's face. Taking him by the shoulders, she turned him gently towards her. 'Listen, Root, there are as many breeds of dragon as there are of other animals. And each dragon is an individual. Just like dogs. Just like horses. Just like people.' She looked around for an example. 'Er . . . see those dragons over there?'

'Which?' Root's voice quavered. 'Th-th-those huge dragons with the h-h-huge back legs?'

Quenelda kicked herself mentally, but ploughed on. 'They're called Three-toed Windgoul dragons. Windgouls are stocky and powerful. See that mare? Her heavily muscled flanks?' She pointed. 'And those short wings? Two pairs? They are great over short distances; the wings aren't good for flying but they help them take great bounds. They're very, very powerful, and they don't spook easily. So they're mostly used for hunting. Those spurred forelegs can bring down a wild boar, even a great cave bear! The Queen breeds Windgouls.'

'Mmm.' Root remained unconvinced. A nerve in his jaw was twitching madly, giving him a demented look. One dragon looked pretty much like another to him; a variable assortment of claws, wings, scales and a double helping of teeth. He couldn't even always tell a herbivore from a carnivore. By the time he made his mind up, he would probably be dinner!

Unable to keep silent now that she'd opened up, Quenelda maintained a running commentary as they went.

'Look at that dark dragon over there roosting on the wall – no, not that one, look a little further back amongst the trees. That green dappled one with the triple wings? That's Whispering Wind. She's a three-year-old Spotted Cobblethwaite filly. A little too frisky for a first flight but gives a really smooth ride. And that dark blue dragon there, just coming in to land? She's a pedigree Tamworth Saddleback called Midsummer Murmur. Five-year-old mare. Very gentle and responsive – she's a possible. You might like her . . .'

Climbing over the paddock gate, Quenelda considered the dragons, dismissing first one breed, then another, trying to find one that might not frighten Root.

'That's the one for us,' she decided finally, pointing to a beautiful small dragon shaded from magenta through to blue, drinking from a water trough. 'Chasing the Stars. She's a Windglen Widdershanks; they're intelligent, quick to learn and very gentle. Smooth action in flight . . .'

She looked at Root's taut face and white knuckles where he gripped the gate.

'Sedate,' she threw in, watching him closely. 'Not easily spooked . . . very good natured . . . blunt teeth . . . vegetarian of course . . . Although she accidentally ate a gnome or two last week . . . gave her really bad indigestion.'

'Mm?' Root nodded mindlessly. He wasn't taking in a single word.

'Root!' Quenelda was mildly exasperated. She took hold of his shoulders. 'Listen. Chasing the Stars is a good choice. She's barely bigger than a shire horse, only nineteen hands at the shoulder. Strong back; strong enough to take two up. She's three years old and very well schooled.' She tried unsuccessfully to look modest. 'I raised her from the shell myself,' she said smugly. 'Slow wing beat too. She'll give you a smooth flight. We'll just fly around Dragonsdome really slowly, and we won't go too high this time. That will let you get the feel of being in the saddle and settle into the rhythm of her wings.'

Chasing the Stars . . . she whispered.

The small dragon immediately leaped across the intervening space in two wing-assisted bounds.

May the wind sing under your wings, Chasing the Stars. Quenelda smiled her welcome as Root instinctively stepped backwards. As she had promised, the dragon was no larger than a big horse, but to Root's eyes she was impossibly huge. A long climb up and an even longer fall – and, given his track record on the wooden dragon, the fall was a certainty.

And may the stars guide your path, Dancing with Dragons . . . The magenta-blue mare returned Quenelda's formal greeting. She turned her dark, intelligent eyes onto Root, who stuck out his chin and chest and tried to look unconcerned.

The young Wingless One is afraid of me, Chasing the Stars observed as she bent her slender neck to nuzzle the girl affectionately. *I can see his knees knocking.*

He's never flown before and he's afraid of dragons.

He's never flown with Dragonkind? Chasing the Stars was amused. *Then he hasn't lived. I can show him how to chase the clouds, to dance with the stars . . .*

In time perhaps, Quenelda conceded. *But not today. Today we must fly slow and low.*

As you say, Dancing with Dragons, so it shall be.

'Right, you wait here,' Quenelda told the petrified

gnome, as if there were any chance he'd be able to move one step. 'I'll go and get her harness. She's a size-three bridle and size-eight saddle. I'll show you again how to put them on, and then once we're done, I'll help you to clean them, and then groom her.'

Root nodded miserably. As Quenelda left, he tried to whistle but found he couldn't summon up a single peep; his mouth was too dry. Hooking his thumbs casually into his belt, he pretended to study a large stag beetle making its way through the grass, then glanced up at Chasing the Stars. 'N-nice d-dragon,' he ventured hopefully.

The mare considered Root with deep lavender eyes framed by long eyelashes, before turning to groom herself with her long delicate snout.

Root stood horrified as the dragon yawned luxuriously, baring her teeth and a long pink tongue that disappeared into her even longer throat. Seemingly ignoring him, she slowly stretched out her wings, then inspected her wing-thumb talons, all four of them. The gnome watched, swaying slightly, almost hypnotized by her languid movements. Then, with no warning at all, the dragon's head whipped down to where he stood.

Greetings, little Wingless One . . .

Root couldn't hear the dragon speak, but he felt the delicate whisper of her breath. She suddenly grinned at him, baring a row of large molars barely inches from his nose. Her breath bloomed hot and damp on his face. She fluttered her luxurious eyelashes invitingly at him, tickling his cheek.

Rigid with fear, Root quivered from head to toe. His own eyelashes fluttered for entirely different reasons. His eyes swam in their sockets. Then, with an almost inaudible squeak, he keeled over backwards.

Over on the other side of the paddocks, a group of esquires hooted and jeered.

'Fallen in love with a dragon, then?' Felix bellowed as the dragon licked Root's face. 'Fainting at her feet?' Their loud guffaws brought Quenelda hurrying out of the tack room.

'Oh, Chasing the Stars,' she rebuked the dragon. 'What have you done to him?' But she was grinning as she bent over the gnome.

'Root? Root?' She took his hand and tried to shoulder Chasing the Stars' solicitous muzzle aside.

'Ooohh . . .' Root's eyelids fluttered. Something wet, rough and heavy was rasping his skin. He opened one streaming eye. A lavender oval iris filled his sight. He put up his hands to fight it off, slapping at the long muzzle.

'Root, Root, it's all right.' Quenelda was feeling slightly alarmed at his ashen pallor. 'She's a herbivore, remember? Look, all her teeth are blunt. That means she's not going to eat you. She's not a battledragon. And their snouts are really sensitive. You could hurt her with your fist. You'd know that if you'd paid more attention to Tangnost.'

'Oh . . .' Root felt vaguely embarrassed. He couldn't imagine how he could hurt such a great creature. 'Sorry,' he said awkwardly, raising himself onto his elbows. He wasn't sure if he was apologizing to Quenelda or the dragon.

He allowed the girl to help him to his feet. She looked at him thoughtfully, keeping a firm grip of his hand.

'Wha—?'

'Trust me.' Quenelda took his reluctant hand and placed it firmly on the dragon's hide.

Root started with surprise. The skin was dry. Rough. Warm. 'It's . . . it's like wood,' he said wonderingly, stroking tentatively as Chasing the Stars shivered appreciatively. 'It's warm and grainy. I thought it would be cold and hard, or slimy. Or scaly like a snake.'

'They're not all the same' – Quenelda shrugged as she tried to find the right words – 'any more than we are. That's what I've been trying to tell you. Some dragons are armour-plated or ridged and pebbled like lizards or scaled like snakes. Others, like Chasing the Stars, are leathery or grainy-skinned like wood or even hard as stone. A few are feathered or furred like griffins and hippogriffs. Each breed is different.

'Here' – she took some round cakes out of a small satchel on her flying belt – 'give her some of these. Compressed dragon-food tablets,' she explained. 'The SDS use them in the field. They're made of molasses, brimstone, coal, oil, hay and brambles. High-energy food. Go on. They love them.'

Root hesitantly held out a couple in his shaking hand. The dragon's tongue snaked out and took them before he had time to grab it back. In a twitch the tablets were all gone and the long pink tongue was probing for more, its tickling forked tips curling around his fingers, searching up his sleeve then inside his cloak, seeking out pockets.

Root giggled then squirmed. He felt ridiculously pleased with himself. 'Do you have any more?'

With a smile, Quenelda slung him a small fodder-sack. Chasing the Stars munched contentedly and turned to nose at her. He is gurgling like a babe.

I know. Quenelda smothered her own grin at the broad smile plastered on Root's face. *Now let us both introduce him to flying.*

'Kneel,' she asked the dragon, signalling with her hand so that Root could see what to do. Mounting the dragon's bent foreleg, she threw the saddle over her back and swiftly buckled it up. She tightened the girth straps and beckoned Root over. 'You must always make sure the girths are tight,' she reminded him.

'What are—?' Root was too nervous to remember any of his training. He was feeling slightly sick again.

'Don't worry,' Quenelda reassured him. 'You'll settle down. A first flight is always nerve-racking.' At least, she thought, that's what everyone else said. She had loved it! 'Girths are the straps under the dragon's belly that secure the saddle. If they're too loose the saddle will slip. Here . . .' She put her hand behind the girth to show him. 'You need to be able to just slide a hand in behind the straps. Dragons will always try and outwit you. They have a wicked sense of humour. If you're inexperienced they always know. They'll test you. They fill their lungs and blow out their chests. Then, when you buckle up, you think it's a tight fit; only it's not. They relax and the saddle slips, and . . .'

'And I fall off and die,' Root completed her sentence gloomily.

'No,' Quenelda said with determined cheerfulness, 'you won't be high enough to die. And anyway, you always wear a flying harness. Give them a gentle punch in the ribs – that lets them know you're wise to their tricks. Here' – she bent down and picked up a wooden bowl – 'Tangnost thought this might be a good idea.'

Root took it and turned it over as if the base might give him a clue. 'What's this for?'

Quenelda looked at him thoughtfully. 'You'll work it out if you need to,' she said mysteriously. 'Just keep it on your lap. And now to mount . . .' She tapped the dragon on the knee. 'Remember, there are three types of signal you can give dragons: verbal, visual and touch. When you're flying, the wing and wind noise often drowns out verbal commands, so then it's touch through rein and stirrup, or hand signals. The SDS have integrated helmet comms – communication systems – so they can hear each other, but they also have a whole hand language to communicate, and in the heat of battle they use buglers. I know Tangnost started teaching you those signals; well, I'll teach you all the hand signals – that'll be far more useful if you're to be my esquire.'

Bending her front legs, Chasing the Stars half knelt down once again, head turned to watch the gnome's progress.

'But your brother . . .' Root was puzzled. 'He used a mounting block. Why . . . ?'

'Well' – Quenelda pulled a face – 'that's because he's such a bad flyer and he was scared of getting bitten. Mounting blocks are generally for children and the elderly.'

'And gnomes?'

Quenelda smiled. 'Well . . . yes, but I can teach you to be a better dragonrider than he is. Not,' she added half to herself, 'that that would be hard. Remember, you mount her like this' – she took Root through it step by step – 'and dismount like this. Your turn.' She smiled at him brightly. 'Up onto her front knee . . . Good. Now put your right foot in the girth stirrup and now your other foot in the saddle stirrup – no, your other one. Otherwise you, er – yes, you end up flying backwards! Now put your right hand on the pommel – remember the wooden dragon – and pull yourself into the saddle.'

The stirrup was too long, so standing on tiptoes, she gave the gnome a hearty shove which nearly had him out of the saddle on the other side. 'See? It's quite easy and not so different to the wooden dragon. Now, do it again, except this time sit in the pillion saddle.'

Root sat there, squirming, his short legs sticking out at ridiculous angles on the broad-backed dragon. The stirrups were so far out of sight he could barely see them.

Quenelda moved along the dragon's flanks. 'So now we need to adjust your stirrups,' she said as she pulled the strap up to its shortest hole. 'Comfortable?' She moved round to the other side and adjusted that. 'How does that feel?'

Root nodded cautiously, not trusting himself to speak. How was it supposed to feel? Mounting might be all right but, unlike its wooden counterpart, this dragon was breathing, its deep ribcage rising and falling beneath him. His heart felt as if it was about to burst, and his knees were knocking against the saddle.

Quenelda mounted and turned to speak to him. 'You just sit and relax. Hang onto the pommel or me – and don't look down. Look at the horizon. Look at the mountains, not up nor down. Ready? I'm going to take us on a slow circuit of Dragonsdome.'

She gathered up the reins. 'Remember there are three reins,' she told Root. 'The pitch bridle, the yaw bridle and the roll bridle. I'll teach you about them once you're ready to fly yourself. Meantime don't worry about them. Now, brace your legs . . . No, no – just grip lightly or the dragon will think you're giving an instruction . . . Lean forward slightly . . . relax. Chasing the Stars will do the rest.'

Root closed his eyes, feeling sick with fear. He could feel the dragon's hind legs gathering beneath him for take-off, the whisper of her wings as she spread them. This was something the lifeless wooden dragon couldn't prepare him for. He gripped the pommel with all his might, and then he felt the dragon launching herself into the air.

Quenelda kept her word. They flew so low that the dragon's wings brushed the wet bracken, her undulating tail powering her over fences, in between trees, braking, stalling, climbing, banking this way, then that. Root rapidly found out that height wasn't his main problem.

Up . . . down . . . the dragon's leathery wings flapped. Rising . . . falling . . . rising . . . falling . . . The world wouldn't stop moving. He bounced in the saddle. The upward and downward motion was making him decidedly travel sick. It was as if his entire body was aware of the dragon's wing beat and nothing else. Even his heart appeared to beat to that rhythm. He watched the tendons that supported the leathery wings ripple beneath smooth skin as they swept around the great metal ribs of the training cage.

'Root! Root!'

'Maiden flight, Root! Way to go!'

There were whoops of encouragement from inside the

great glass and iron cage as Quester and a group of esquires spotted their low-level flight. Root plastered a sickly grin on his face and tried to straighten up and wave, and then they were past and he sagged miserably in the saddle.

Unused to flying, he was already tiring with the effort of hanging on. His muscles were aching, burning. Sweat broke out on his forehead. His stomach was trying to tell him it wasn't happy. He burped. He felt clammy. Far from easing, his breathing grew ever more ragged. Eyes half closed, he swayed in the saddle. Up . . . down. His pallor changed from red to chalk with a faint hint of green. He burped and put a hand to his chest. Up . . . down . . .

He is burping like a babe – Chasing the Stars' laughter sounded in Quenelda's head. The dragon's ribcage vibrated beneath Root, making his toes tingle.

Up . . . down . . .

With a flood of self-pity, Root realized he was about to embarrass himself. Snatching up the bowl so thoughtfully provided by Tangnost, he surrendered his breakfast and his dignity.

CHAPTER SEVENTEEN
The Deadly Guild of Subtle and Cunning Assassins

Every city has its slums. On the Black Isle, in the city of the
Sorcerers Glen, they were called the Gutters; a ramshackle
warren of filthy dark alleyways, crowded hovels and
reeking factories down by the docks, where the
impoverished and the unfortunate battled to survive. Every
known race and creature in the Seven Sea Kingdoms was
represented here, and whispered rumours told of other
fearsome monsters that lurked in the overflowing sewers
beneath the apothecaries' factories – twisted creatures
created by the magical fallout that leaked out. Certainly,
those who ventured into the sewers that honeycombed the
island never returned to tell their tale. The City Watch
rarely ventured into these narrow streets and alleyways
where life was held so cheaply, and money could buy
anything, including murder.

In one anonymous street amongst many, where the
rickety five-storey buildings leaned so far over that they
almost kissed their neighbours, was a dark dirty doorway.
But unlike other doors here, this one was set about with
powerful wards and webs of concealment. For those who
passed beneath this portal entered a hidden world that lay
below the city: a labyrinth of secret corridors, rooms and
cellars.

In one such room, behind a desk, a dark-haired man sat
with treason on his mind. Over the last thirty years he had
perfected the business of murder – unofficially of course.
A rare talent for assassination had seen him rise quickly
from the slums of the Gutters through the ranks of the

Deadly Guild of Subtle and Cunning Assassins, a powerful and shadowy organization whose roots reached out like a canker into every aspect of life. His prodigious talent soon caught the eye of the Guild's Master of Assassins.

With the hidden but deadly hand of the Guild behind him, he had entered the Sorcerers Guild as a novice and his gift for sorcery immediately caught the attention of the Grand Master. Within the year he was the Grand Master's novice and friend to Rufus DeWinter, son of the greatest Earl in the kingdom, and the secrets of the SDS were his.

Then he found it: an ancient grimoire bound in dragonscales, in the distant recesses of Dragonsdome's great library, high in the ancient keep. All Guild novices were taught the dangers of forbidden Dark Magic. How Battle Mages who practised Maelstrom Magic in the Second Hobgoblin War, before its powers were truly understood, wreaked havoc and destruction. Initially wielding Dark Magic in defence of the kingdom, each in turn became corrupted by its all-consuming power, their minds eaten up till they became a danger to all and everything they had previously sworn to protect. It was the ultimate weapon of war – that was why it was named Maelstrom Magic, and those who practised it became warlocks.

Turned to utter madness, warlocks were hunted down and killed like rabid wolves. The cost of the Mage Wars that followed was catastrophic – the weakened SDS nearly fell prey to the hobgoblin hordes overrunning the Seven Sea Kingdoms.

But this did not deter young Hugo Mandrake: he opened the brittle pages of the grimoire and tasted the promise of true power.

His meteoric rise to Grand Master was marred by mishaps but these were, at least initially, put down to the impetuousness of youth. After that he was more . . . careful. He was charming, and his good looks opened every door. Soon he was being courted by high society. Women were spellbound by him. Men told him their secrets. Slowly, subtly, those who opposed him were discreetly threatened, bribed or removed. Within five years he had risen to the highest office of all, apart from the monarch. But he wanted more. Much more. His ambition knew no bounds.

He soon tired of the petty politics of the Guild and began to explore the dark side of sorcery. Not for him the weak inept magic practised by the enfeebled Guilds, but the raw, unfettered magic of creation itself: the forbidden Maelstrom Magic, the very crucible from which the One Earth itself was forged: powerful predatory magic, always seeking dominion . . . always seeking out susceptible minds. Like hobgoblin minds, empty of anything except the base urge to fight, to eat, to swarm like locusts across the land. Treacherous . . . greedy . . . susceptible hobgoblins . . .

And now, beneath the guise of friendship, he sowed dissent. Young Darcy was spoiled and inept: he would pose no threat once his father was dead. Indeed, the new Earl would owe him a debt of gratitude. The most powerful earldom in the Seven Sea Kingdoms and its magnificent dragonstud would be his!

The Grand Master of the Deadly Guild of Subtle and Cunning Assassins smiled. For once, the smile reached his dark intelligent eyes. He had nearly made a bad mistake, Galtekerion betraying too early that the hobgoblin tribes were now fighting as one. But it had turned out for the best. He now had two opportunities to destroy the Earl and the SDS.

It was time to fetch his new dragon from the Killing Caves of the Westering Isles. Come darkfall, on the turn of the tide, he would set sail.

CHAPTER EIGHTEEN
Flying High

Filling a small fodder bag with tablets, Root made his way along the great paddock avenues, scanning the dragons on both sides, finally spotting Chasing the Stars resting on a roost-pillar, wings fully spread, sun warming the delicate membranes of her wings.

Root quietly opened the paddock gate and crossed to where she was perched. 'I've . . .' The little gnome bit his lower lip and tried to stop his hand from shaking. 'I've brought you some tablets – dragon tablets, that is – dried thistle, molasses, um, and other tasty things . . . I mean, tasty to a vegetarian dragon. Er, I'm a vegetarian too.' Nerves made his tongue run away with him and he found himself burbling nonsense, but couldn't seem to stop. 'Er, all gnomes, ah, we're all vegetarians. Just like you!'

Approach slowly, head down, hands upturned, keeping eye contact to show you mean no harm. No sudden movements or noise. Then gently blow on their nostrils. They're very sensitive, Quenelda had told him. That way they'll learn to recognize you by smell. Then, if they like you, they'll rub against you, marking you with scent glands on their muzzles. It's their way of greeting you, of claiming you as a friend.

Looking Chasing the Stars firmly in the eye – not that he would have dared to look away – Root moved towards the dragon, hand held out, palm up.

'Steady there,' he said softly, as much to calm his own nerves as hers. 'S-steady, girl . . .'

His heart skittered and he squeaked as the dragon gave

a single flap of her wings and swooped down to consider him gravely with bright, piercing eyes. Stepping forward and taking a deep breath, Root very gently blew on her velvety nostrils. They flared as she breathed in his scent. Then she blew gently against his upturned palm in return. The warmth travelled up his arm, turning to goose pimples that shivered across his neck. Root wriggled, partly with nerves and partly with pleasure. The dragon's breath was sweet and musty, like new-mown hay. Feeling a little more confident, he blew again.

Chasing the Stars returned his blow, a little harder this time. Root blinked in surprise as a cloud of fine spray enveloped him. He blew again, harder, worried that he was not getting the message across.

Chasing the Stars blew once more. Root shook his head and blinked as gooey saliva dripped down his face. He was about to blow again when an amused voice intervened.

'You could be here all day just saying hello if you keep that up!'

Root jumped in the air. 'Quenelda!' He glared at her. 'What a fright you gave me.'

Quenelda grinned as she lounged against a paddock post. 'Every time you blow she's obliged to blow back. It's considered very discourteous if she doesn't.'

'Oh.' Root felt a little silly.

Quenelda snorted with laughter.

He looked at her. 'What?'

'Look at your boots. She's desperate for those tablets, but she can't take them until you invite her.'

Root looked down: the dragon was drooling all over his new flying boots. 'Oh! I'm sorry.' He thrust his other hand forward. 'Here!'

Chasing the Stars' tongue gratefully flicked out to scoop up all three tablets in one go. She crunched loudly and rolled her eyes, letting him know her appreciation. Her soft muzzle lipped at his hand. Root watched her, wide-eyed, until one of her stomachs began to rumble. Instinctively the gnome stepped away before remembering that Chasing the Stars was a herbivore.

'She's purring,' Quenelda said. 'She likes you.'

'She's what?' Root asked. 'Dragons purr? I thought that noise was indigestion . . . or . . . well, the battledragons make a noise like that when they're about to flame, don't they?'

'No, silly! Listen!' Quenelda told him. 'Just listen . . .'

Root stood motionless as the rhythmic rumble that began in the dragon's belly worked its way up to her throat, where he could see the pulse beating. The sound rose and fell as she breathed in and out.

Relaxing, Root smiled and shook his head in wonder as Chasing the Stars reached forward for more tablets. 'Dragons purr!'

The flying lessons continued.

Quenelda proved to be surprisingly patient, as if the gnome's success were the most important thing to her other than the time she spent with her father; and Root, once he got over his initial fear, found himself relaxing around dragons – at least around Chasing the Stars.

Tangnost watched with approval as Quenelda set about teaching Root. Rarely had she been so disciplined. Normally tempestuous and headstrong, she managed to replace impatience with patience, recklessness with care and consideration. For the first time in her life she had to think about flying, think about dragons, and in doing so, although she didn't know it, she was learning a good deal too.

Root quickly learned how to groom Chasing the Stars with coarse brushes that removed any parasites and sloughed off itchy loose skin. The mucking out, feeding and watering that he'd once thought of as chores had now become a source of pride as he began to compete with the other esquires.

He gradually learned that Chasing the Stars liked to be tickled and scratched, especially between her wings where she couldn't reach very easily. Quenelda taught him how to pare her dark blue talons and oil them to stop them cracking in the cold weather. He spent hours rubbing in special birch balm – an unguent made from honey, birch sap and stag-toad spittle – that stopped the mare from getting cold sores and kept her skin supple.

But his education didn't stop there. As an apprentice he'd already learned a little about tack – how to care for, clean and mend it – but he'd never actually had to put it on. And he'd learned the basics about husbandry – how to muck out and feed domestic dragons – but he'd never had to handle a dragon, had never even been close to one on his own. Now Quenelda introduced him to a whole new world.

Slowly Root learned about a bewildering array of bits, each for a specific purpose or a specific breed of dragon; about bridles and the different types of saddle that were used for training, flying, jousting or warfare; and about dragon armour. A crinet, Quenelda taught Root, was made from overlapping plates of steel that protected the dragon's neck. The peytral was a single huge piece of hammered armour that protected the dragon's chest, while the shaffron was a piece of armour moulded to protect a battledragon's or battlegriff's head. Each and every piece was tailored for a specific dragon, which was measured in the deep dragonarmour pits with great callipers and leather tapes.

Soon Root was lavishing all his spare time on the little dragon. On only their second week together, he was thrilled to find that when he called her, she came with eager bounds to nuzzle him affectionately, searching for titbits. He quickly learned that she had a passion for mushrooms and wandered through the woods with a sack slung over his shoulder. Best of all she liked nutsquash mushrooms, large thick chocolate-capped mushrooms with a nutty flavour that grew in the deep forest.

With each passing week, gnome and dragon forged a closer bond. Once, when she had a mild dose of colic, Root insisted on slinging up his hammock in the roost with her until she was well again. Soon Quester was teasing him about the amount of time he spent in the dragon roosts, and Tangnost, noticing the gnome begin to put some weight back on and gain some colour in his cheeks, was quietly satisfied. Unlikely though it had seemed, it was clear to anyone watching that the Earl's daughter and her esquire had found friendship where they had least expected it.

By now, whenever Quenelda wasn't studying with the esquires, they were flying out in the Sorcerers Glen; almost every day she and Chasing the Stars took Root a little higher and a little further from Dragonsdome.

'It feels strange.' Root had nervously shifted under the shoulder straps as Quenelda buckled his flying harness up for the first time.

She nodded. 'It will do to start with, but if we fly high in Open Sky you'll appreciate it. Right,' she said, tightening one last buckle, satisfied the harness was a good fit. 'Now your equipment. Flying knife . . .' She handed him a small sickle-shaped knife. 'It clips on here. Next, water bottle . . . Always make sure it's full: fill it up at the water pump, or get some myrtleberry juice from the kitchens. It clasps on there, like mine. Compass into one of those pouches; telescope, a distress flare, some dragon tablets.' She grinned, handing over a pouch. 'Make sure you hide them well from a certain dragon. And finally, I just raided the kitchens for some spiced scones – those are for you. And we'll need these . . .' She went over to where brightly coloured bundles hung from pegs.

'What are those?' Root had seen them slung on saddles but had never known what they contained.

'These are your dragonwings,' Quenelda explained, unpacking one and shaking out the crumpled contents. 'They're made from the shed skins of juvenile dragons – attached to a willow frame and bound with runes. You put them on like this, buckled up, and then you can clip this ring onto your saddle. So if you ever fall – although of course Chasing the Stars won't let you – your wings open automatically. Or you pull the cord yourself, like this.'

Root sprang back as the wings snapped into position, pulling the dragonskin taut. They made Quenelda look like an oversized fruit bat.

'But . . . but,' Quenelda repeated, seeing the gnome's horrified face, 'it won't happen. You won't need it. Honestly, you won't fall.'

It wasn't easy. Whenever the dragon dipped or turned – or, worse, when she suddenly climbed or banked – Root's instinct was still to lean the other way.

'Ride with her.' Quenelda leaned forward behind him and gripped him firmly by the shoulders. 'Always ride with your dragon. Lean into her. Trust her to find the right balance . . . relax. Find the rhythm so that you're moving with her, as if you are part of her. Right now you're getting thrown to and fro; you've no control. You're bumping around all the time. No wonder you've got saddle sores. And lean forward as her wings go down, back as they go up. She'll look after you.'

Root's other problem was travel sickness. He opened one eye. Bad idea. The world moved. Up, down . . . up, down . . . Sweat broke out on his brow. He swayed in the saddle as his stomach complained. 'I . . .' he panted, on the verge of panic. 'I . . .'

'Oh, you'll grow out of it, lad.' Tangnost grinned, slapping him heartily on the back after one particularly bad session. 'I was sick when I first flew too! Ain't natural to be in the air unless you've got wings! Dwarfs are used to having two feet firmly on the ground. In fact our natural inclination is to live underground. Tell you what, my third cousin on my sixth sister's side is medicine man for our clan. He brewed up something disgusting. It helped me.'

And so it did. The noxious brew was so disgusting that

Root had to concentrate hard on not being sick when he drank it: before he knew it, the queasiness had passed.

As the nights drew in, they sat in the hay lofts above the warm flatulence of the roosts, and Quenelda taught the gnome hand signals so that when they were flying they could 'talk' to other flyers. Root showed her his growing collection of sketches. Quenelda took some of Two Gulps for her chambers and decided to ask him to paint one of Stormcracker to give her father at the Yule festival. She in turn showed him her weather and star charts and taught him how to use the small brass compass. Then, as the month turned and the mountainsides were buried beneath another heavy snowfall, Quenelda decided Root was ready to take the pilot's seat.

The belfry struck half past the Hour of the Yawning Dormouse. Quester groaned and snuggled down beneath his quilt. The bed ropes creaked as Root bounded out of the bunk below. It was freezing, and with midwinter approaching, it was pitch-dark. The little pot-bellied stoves that kept the dormitories warm overnight had long since grown cold. Shivering, Root quickly pulled on a woollen overshirt, padded jerkin and leather breeches over his underclothes, then buckled up his flying boots.

Quester looked down at him, hair tousled, eyes blinking owlishly in the near dark. 'Root?' he hissed, putting his hand out blindly. 'What on the One Earth are you doing? It's still night time.'

'I'm flying today,' Root whispered. 'I just want to make sure everything is perfect—'

'Dragon's teeth!' Quester sat up, suddenly awake. 'Do

you want a hand?'

'No, I have to do this all by myself or I won't be much good to her as an esquire. But thanks.' Root took his friend's clasped hand.

'Good luck,' Quester offered. 'I know you'll do fine!'

'Ready?' Quenelda prompted him. It was late afternoon and the day had been gruelling for all three of them.

Root gripped the reins and kept his eyes screwed tight shut. He touched the carved wood and bead amulets he wore around his neck and kissed them for luck. It seemed like a dream. He, of all people, was in a dragon's saddle, in the pilot's seat! Esquire to Lady Quenelda! How proud his father would have been.

They were perched on a ridge, high on the Dragon's Spine Mountains, with a bitter wind whistling around them. Dark clouds were scudding across the sky, driving the sun towards the horizon. Below their perch, an underground river hurtled out before crashing down into the steep gorge below. Root knew that when he opened his eyes he would be looking westwards, down upon the fifteen miles of the Sorcerers Glen.

He touched his flying harness for reassurance, shifting the unaccustomed weight of the dragonwings, feeling the cord attached to his saddle that would automatically open them if he fell. Satisfied, he opened his eyes a fraction and scratched Chasing the Stars on the withers – the ridge behind her shoulder blades where neck and back were joined – just to feel her reassuring purr. He opened his eyes fully. The distant world below rushed up to greet him.

Scores of tiny galleons and tall clippers, sails plump in

the wind, rode the white caps of the sea loch thousands of feet below, their crew just tiny specks in the rigging, lanterns already lit against the coming night. A forest of flagged masts crowded the harbours that ringed the city. Tiny figures and wagons crammed the four causeways that linked the Black Isle to the glen.

Far to the west lay Dragon Isle and the endless great ocean that rolled to the horizon like a carpet of slate-blue. Root risked a glance upwards at the yawning expanse of Open Sky, at the scores of dragons to-ing and fro-ing across the glen and beyond, but the moving clouds made the world dip and he felt faint. He hurriedly looked down.

Quenelda's cough broke into his thoughts. 'Any time you're ready,' she suggested. 'It's a little cold to be sitting still up here. Remember, just a gentle kick and lean backwards as she swoops down. That way you won't feel like you're going to fall forwards out of the saddle.'

Root nodded wordlessly and swallowed down his fear. He could feel the power of Chasing the Stars' bunched muscles barely held in check against his knees; her eagerness to fly.

'Come on, girl,' he whispered. 'Don't let me down.' Then he gently flicked the reins and touched his boots to the dragon's shoulders; his other hand, hidden by his cloak, gripped the pommel.

With a terrifying suddenness that still took Root by surprise, Chasing the Stars sprang forwards and took to the air. His stomach rose into his throat as they dropped down for a heart-stopping five seconds into the spray-filled gorge. The water thundered around them. A million tiny droplets misted Root's visor, combining to drip off his nose.

Down . . . down . . . Root opened his mouth to scream.

'Ooouf!' Knees weak with nerves, he was winded as the dragon's wings swept down and the saddle rose up. He'd lost a stirrup. He was going to fail!

Wind whistled through his open visor and his eyes streamed with the cold. For the briefest moment of pure fear he hung there . . . Then the dragon's wings swept up and she dropped again before levelling out. He found the stirrup and took up the reins again.

There were a few moments of silence, then he leaned forwards and touched a hand to the dragon's shoulder; his heartbeat slowed and his vision cleared. The first stars were breaking through the indigo sky above. The crescent moons would soon be rising. Hugging the contours of the mountainside, the dragon swept down towards the loch, rudely scattering a flock of geese, heading for the lights of Dragonsdome. Root felt the joy of flight grip him; felt Chasing the Stars leap forward in response.

'I can fly!' he shouted as the wind thundered in his ears and his spirit soared. 'Chasing the Stars, I can fly!'

CHAPTER NINETEEN
The Killing Caves

The witching hour was approaching. As tattered rain clouds swept over the crescent moons, their light was extinguished, hiding the ships swiftly approaching a rocky island far, far out to sea in the Westering Isles.

Galtekerion, surrounded by his elite hobgoblin bodyguard, watched idly from the mouth of a great sea cavern as the two ships anchored in the bay: one was an ocean-going galleon, the other a swifter inshore cutter. His bone-armour breastplate was covered in the trophies of war – rotting skulls and hanks of hair. A necklace with a single huge dragontooth marked his lordship over the tribes.

Using a splinter of bone, Galtekerion was picking his teeth, chewing the last few stringy morsels of dwarf flesh. There was a lack of dragonmeat and his warriors were already complaining. Whale and squid were poor substitutes, and the hobgoblins needed sustenance if they were to survive hibernation and the coming winter. It was bitterly cold, still early in the month of the hunter's moons, yet some of his warriors were already slipping into the torpor of hibernation, their movements sluggish, their breath shallow. If there was to be a battle, it would have to be soon, before they ran out of food.

The deep sea sucked endlessly at the shingle shore, rattling pebbles as it drew out, only to return, its soft language as familiar to Galtekerion as the salt spray that cooled him. The whole island was a boiling, crawling mass of movement, busy as a termite mound, and with every moment more hobgoblins were hopping out of the sea to flop onto the seaweed-covered rocks. Several hundred were stripping two whales to the bone. There would soon only be skeletons left.

The ships' sails were furled and gangplanks crashed onto the rocks. A small group from the lead galleon disembarked, led by a dark-cloaked figure.

Shivering slightly – and not from the cold – Galtekerion wondered yet again who the approaching sorcerer was. The very air seemed to bend and warp around him; Galtekerion could sense a faint concealed emanation of Dark power – suppressed, hidden – which made his skin itch with foreboding. He knew what this sorcerer was: a warlock, a sorcerer who had turned to the blackest side of magic. A renegade with a single-minded purpose: to raise the Dark rule of Maelstrom over the world. A renegade who had helped him to rise from petty tribal leader to leader of all the hobgoblin banners, slowly shaping an undisciplined horde into an army. The thirteen tribes had pledged allegiance to him, but he in turn had pledged allegiance to this warlock. But who the warlock was he was no closer to learning.

'Welcome, SSSSorcerer Lord,' Galtekerion hissed, fist on chest in salute, in the manner of his tribe. 'Welcome to the Killing Cavesssss.'

'Galtekerion.' The Grand Master curtly acknowledged the hobgoblin with a brief bow of his hooded head. The sorcerer's clothes were all the shades of night, his face covered by a mask. The eyes behind were pools of darkness.

'You have news, lord?'

The figure nodded his assent. 'The time has come to prepare your warriors.' His voice was low and menacing.

Galtekerion nodded. 'Come then, lord . . .' He indicated the cavern behind them.

The entrance was dark, lit only by a few damp fires of heather and dried kelp, enough to see by but unable to banish the frigid air. Above their heads rusty cages strung overhead clanked and swayed in the offshore breeze.

'Perhaps,' the sorcerer suggested, once seated, 'attacking the fortress was too bold a step. The SDS now know that the tribes have united. They grow suspicious, and the Guild fear you as never before. The SDS intend to strike before the tribes swarm again in the spring when the snows melt. They are preparing to move against you in the depths of winter, when the land is locked by snow and the sea is freezing.'

'They will campaign over winter?' Galtekerion was surprised.

The Grand Master nodded. 'When your warriors hibernate in the cave pools.'

'Sssssssssssssssss . . .' Galtekerion's chilling hiss of displeasure was taken up by his bodyguard; it spread throughout the caverns. 'What strength will they throw against us?'

'Three full SDS regiments . . . and the First Born.'

'Sssssssssss.' Galtekerion sucked his lips. 'The First Born . . .'

'No one has ever campaigned over winter. With the storms and blizzards that close the shipping lanes and clog the glens, flying conditions will be extremely difficult. And these islands drift far from any of their support bases, so they believe they will catch you totally unprepared as your warriors emerge from hibernation; they will trap you in the caves and then hunt your army to extinction – or at least break the tribal alliance. But we will reverse the trap. You come out of the sea and surround them. I will bring Razorbacks to bear your warriors.'

'These dragonsss will bear usss?' Galtekerion's doubt was evident. The hatred between dragons and hobgoblins was as old as time itself.

'Yes, my magic has worked well. These Razorbacks . . . these dragons are part hobgoblin themselves.'

Galtekerion's tongue flicked out in nervous anticipation. 'But even with your dragons, they could still defeat us. My army is only uneasily united. The young warriors obey, but their discipline is poor. And the older warriors are slow to change their ways, slow to accept my leadership. Each tribe leader bargains hard, holds the greatest warriors back. The tribes have not fought enough battles together. If I am not present, each clan soon fights for itself, each warrior upholds his own honour.'

'That is true.' The Grand Master nodded. 'But the Dragon Lords took heavy losses during their last campaign. Our co-ordinated attacks stretched them thin. They need to rest, refit, re-armour and recruit to bring their regiments up to full strength. That is why we shall lure them out now, two moons before they are ready.'

'And how, lord, do we lure them here?'

'My plan is simple. We will give out that you have died of wounds taken in battle and that the thirteen tribes are fighting amongst themselves again. It will be the perfect time for the SDS to strike, ready or not. We shall ensure that their spies learn of this, but only a few will return to Dragon Isle to make the tale convincing. We will bait a trap the SDS commander cannot ignore. They will come to us when we are ready and they are not.'

'When will they come?' Galtekerion's cold bulbous eyes gleamed slightly in the dark. His bone necklaces clacked and rattled.

'When the moons have waned and full dark falls. They will deploy commandos – Sabretooths and Vipers to the centre of the island and the Imperials around the perimeter. They will use dragonfire and the Bonecrackers to drive your warriors out of the caves and into the maws of their cloaked dragons.'

'Sssssssssssssssssssssssss . . .' The hobgoblins hissed through their ragged teeth, the sound blending with the sucking of the sea. Fire – how the hobgoblins hated fire! Especially the dragonfire that burned slowly and ate them up.

'You will be ready and waiting, concealed deep in the cave pools,. I have camouflaged my Razorbacks. When they lie still, they look like rocks on the shoreline. Galtekerion, listen well. I want none to escape this trap. Make sure they all die. Sacrifice as many of your banners as it takes to obliterate the SDS. Let Dragon Isle wonder what has happened to it – the Guild and court will fear you all the more.

'When it is time, when I know when the strike will take place, when I know what they plan, I shall call your warriors as I always have, so that you may prepare. I may have weapons.'

'Weapons? Sssssorcerer weaponsss?'

The Grand Master nodded.

'My lord, they shall be there at your castle, awaiting your word.'

'And now' – the Grand Master turned his attention to another matter – 'you have had one of my dragons for three moons. Is it well trained?'

'Come, my lord . . .' Galtekerion beckoned. 'Let me ssshow you your dragon. We have kept sssome prisssoners for your entertainment.'

Boom . . . boom . . .

The tribal drums began, beating out a tattoo on their dragonskulls, their rhythms gradually blending into a single eerie and terrifying sound. All along the shoreline, the mass of hobgoblins was moving as one.

Boom . . . boom . . . boom . . .

Gradually warlord and warlock made their way to a viewing platform attached by rusting chains to the rock face; here a great pit darker than the night sky yawned before them. Its walls rose sheer to three hundred feet from the rocks below, up to where the hobgoblins jostled and pushed to see the entertainment in the Killing Caves. Brands soaked in pine resin and sheep fat flickered and smoked. Their fitful light barely illuminated the cages hanging from great iron hooks driven into the stone, and the rotten wooden platforms that jutted out from the pit walls.

The throbbing of drumbeats pounded out and echoed. Boom . . . boom . . . boom . . .

As he looked down, the Grand Master could see hands reaching out through the bars. Dwarfs. The hobgoblins' hated foes: Bonecracker commandos.

The drums beat to a frantic crescendo of sound, then abruptly stopped.

'Release the prisssonersss,' Galtekerion commanded. 'Make them walk the plank.'

'Walk the plank! Walk the plank!'

The Grand Master could smell the hobgoblins' blood lust growing, the mindless violence barely held in check. So much depended upon the tribes laying aside centuries of conflict and rivalry.

The cages were winched in. As their chains were loosed, one by one the dwarf prisoners were forced to the end of the plank by spears and bone flails. They were all wounded, some of them barely conscious. The dying fell with a silent thud to the floor. Those who survived the fall took up the shields and axes thrown down to them and stood back to back in a shield formation, protecting their injured comrades.

'Releassse the dragon!' Galtekerion cried.

A sudden hush fell. In the eerie silence, the Grand Master could hear heavy ragged breathing, the scraping of talons on rock, the clink of harness. Two great hobgoblin warriors started to crank a rusting iron handle. Chains rattled as an iron portcullis rose slowly, grating, grinding, setting the warlock's teeth on edge.

A sturdy black dragon the colour of midnight darted into the cave. A hobgoblin reined it in and walked it steadily around the dwarfs. Quietly, calmly, it circled them, ignoring them despite the smell of blood.

Good, the warlock thought. Good. It must have self-control. Must hold back until commanded . . .

'Attack!' The Grand Master's voice rang out. The

hobgoblin relaxed his hold.

Suddenly the dragon hurled itself into the pit. There was a scream as a dwarf's body was flung against the side of the arena. Then the dragon resumed its silent circling. It struck again, but the dwarfs fended it off, their shield wall holding.

The gathered hobgoblins began to shout, to jeer at their prisoners. The pounding of drums resumed. The warriors banged weapons – bone flails, long serrated swords and spiked spears – against their shields.

Boom . . . boom . . . boom. The rhythm reverberated through the air.

The dragon attacked, this time knocking a shield aside to pluck a wounded dwarf from inside the shield wall. With a war cry, a second dwarf broke ranks to attack the dragon, light glinting on his axe as it arced down to strike. The dragon did not flinch as the blade skittered across its hide but calmly beheaded its attacker with a single swipe of its talons.

This was repeated a dozen times. The dragon was stepping over bodies – joints cracked, skulls burst beneath its weight like dried seaweed. The shield wall dwindled. Finally the dragon was given free rein and one by one the remaining dwarfs met their grisly end.

Dawn was not far off and the tide was turning as the Grand Master boarded his ship. The dragon chained beneath in the hold was sleeping after being allowed to feast on its prey. Two decades of planning, waiting and experimentation were about to reap rewards.

'What's 'is name, yer lordship?' he heard a sailor ask as

he boarded.

'Midnight Madness . . . His name is Midnight Madness.'

CHAPTER TWENTY
The Lady and the Tramp

Root squawked as the decorative harness slipped down Two Gulps' flanks and engulfed him. For a moment he fought the weight of the trapping; then his legs gave way and he sat down hard.

'Stay still.'

Root could hear Tangnost's laughter as he lifted the heavy embroidered silk. He crawled out into sunlight.

'Let's try again, lad.' The dwarf raised his brows – though he was hugely pleased with the gnome's progress and his growing confidence around the battledragon. And the changes in Quenelda were startling. She seemed to have lost the bitter edge to her tongue.

Tangnost was no fool. He saw more with his one eye than many did with two. He knew how lonely Quenelda was, despite her dragons; how hungry she was for friendship. As she grew up it had only got worse. If dressing as a boy and riding dragons had ever been acceptable in a child, they were certainly not in a young lady. And the spiteful speculation about her mother dogged her footsteps. Young ladies openly shunned her, pouring scorn on her attempts to befriend them, on her dress, her hair, the way she strode about in flying boots. Quenelda pretended it didn't hurt, but he knew it did.

Well, Tangnost thought, it no longer mattered quite so much. Quenelda and Root had both found something unexpected in each other. He glanced over at her. She smiled briefly from the steps before returning to polish the already gleaming bit and buckles of the tooled leather tack.

They were working on one of Dragonsdome's smaller pads, permanently anchored near the sweeping stone steps of the east wing, so that the seamstress could be summoned if alterations were needed. The other pad was occupied by a gleaming carriage and three matching pairs of dragons. Half a dozen coachmen and footmen stood around chatting as they awaited their mistresses' return.

'Lady Armelia . . .' Quenelda had swiftly identified the DeBurgh coat of arms on the ornate carriage's door. 'Darcy's new sweetheart,' she explained to Root. 'She has only recently arrived at court. Young ladies' – her lip curled – 'attend court when they come of age. But all they do is dress up in petticoats and lace, dance, stitch tapestries, play music and catch a wealthy husband.' Her face showed what she thought of those shallow pursuits. Root smothered a smile. He could never imagine Quenelda trussed up in lacy skirts.

But her attention quickly turned back to more important matters. Earlier, she had been bouncing with joy when she returned from telling her father the wonderful news that Root could fly. 'Papa says I am to have my own coat of arms! We can caparison Two Gulps for the winter jousts!'

'Capa . . . ?' Root had had no idea what she was talking about.

'You know,' Quenelda burbled happily as he shook his head. 'When you see mounts dressed for festivals? You dress them in decorative trappings that match their lord's coats of arms?'

Root looked blank.

'Come on! I'll show you! Hurry! We don't have much

214

time!'

She had rushed him to the dragon armoury, where they borrowed great leather measuring tapes and dragon callipers from the forges. Two Gulps was measured from nose-tip to tail, wing to wing, and round his belly in a dozen places. The seamstresses of Dragonsdome had worked late into the night for half a moon to have the dragon's trappings finished in time for the winter jousts. Quenelda had chosen a gorse-yellow harness that matched the Sabretooth's scales, with small dragons picked out in flaming red. In time, she explained to Root, new devices would be added to her coat of arms that marked her passage to adulthood.

'Isn't it beautiful?' she declared now. 'He looks magnificent!'

Root grinned in agreement.

'Let's saddle him up and take him out. That way we'll see if there are any problems we're missing.'

Feeding Two Gulps the snaffle bit, Quenelda stood on the dragon's foreleg to slip the headstall on over his neck, then tightened the chin straps. Using the mounting block, Tangnost lifted the heavy double saddle and swung it over the battledragon's back, leaving Quenelda to tighten the girth straps.

'There!' She stood back to admire their handiwork. The polished brass harness shone like mellow gold and the battedragon's scales were oiled to a mirror sheen. Quenelda climbed into the saddle, her smile radiant as the Sabretooth reared up on his hind legs. The effect was brilliant in the sunlight. Root knew the pair would stand out long before the crowds realized that she was a girl, that the dragon was a battledragon.

'Yeeee-haaaa!'

Quenelda frowned, then groaned in recognition. 'Darcy!'

Heads turned towards Dragonsdome. There was a distant whoop as a green-feathered hippogriff stallion appeared scant feet above the slate-blue tiled roofs and hurtled towards them. Her brother left his reins slack – the mount was almost out of control. There were cries of consternation as everyone on the two landing pads scattered. At the very last moment Darcy, face flushed, heart thudding, stood in his stirrups and pulled with all his might to yank the headstrong young stallion out of its dive.

'Eeeaaakkkk!'

The hippogriff screeched as it levelled out between the two dragonpads, deafening Root and spooking the dragons harnessed to the carriage. The downdraught from its wings whipped Quenelda's hair into her eyes and drew a response from Two Gulps, who smoked warningly. Seconds later, whooping and cheering loudly, six other hippogriffs followed in Darcy's wake.

Only Tangnost stood his ground as their claws and hooves passed perilously low overhead, his mounting fury evident as he swore in Dwarfish. Darcy was supposed to be grounded and yet here he was defying his father's orders, doubtless showing off in front of his young lady and her friends, who were walking in the ornamental garden below.

Barely clearing the roof, the last mount's trailing hooves brought down several chimney pots; broken tiles rained down onto the courtyard below. As Rupert saw the battledragon smoking next to an infuriated Tangnost, he frantically pulled his hippogriff into a climb. Hot air buffeted the dragonpads as, at the last moment, he swerved and began to gain height.

Pandemonium broke out as the coachman and footmen tried to dive beneath their coach. The dragonpads shook. As Root regained his feet he saw that an eye-watering pile of dragon dung was steaming gently in the frosty air: the gilded carriage was part buried. Coachman and footmen were cursing and gasping for fresh air. Blue feathers wafted lazily down on them.

Root grimaced sympathetically as the smell hit him. Clearing up dragon dung was dirty work and the smell clung for days. Well, a dung cart would be along soon enough to dig them out. It was no longer one of his tasks.

'Right . . .' Tangnost rubbed his hands, putting aside his anger for later. 'You need to get ceremonial talon-sheaths on.'

Root moved over to examine the curved metal casings. He had wondered what they were. He counted them – eight large, and two smaller ones for the dew claws.

'You're going to be flying in very heavy air traffic,' Tangnost warned. 'We don't want any accidents if someone flies too close. Never forget' – he held Quenelda's eyes – 'that he is a trained battledragon. The moment you do, someone might die.'

Quenelda nodded, suddenly sober. It was a big responsibility. She reached for a talon-sheath, hefting its weight in her hands before passing it to Root to show him how to put it on. She ignored the smell. Anyone who worked in the battleroosts was used to it. Down in the gardens, raised voices trilled and tittered in excitement as the hippogriffs landed. With a quiet smile of satisfaction Quenelda got back to work.

The winter sun had sunk low on the horizon, casting long shadows, when the hippogriffs took off again, flying low over the paddocks towards the palace. Darcy was returning to court and his last days of duty before joining the SDS. The young ladies turned towards their carriage. Puffing and blowing, Root put down the soft mallet and looked at the two remaining sheaths. Soon they would be done, and not a moment too soon. He was starving.

Darcy's sweetheart, Lady Armelia, and a gaggle of friends reached the steps, their voices high and piping. Dressed in frothy lace, bright silks and pearls, they were followed by an elderly chaperone and a train of servants. A small fortune in gold and jewels glinted from hair and neck and fingers.

Root gawped at them, his glance darting to Quenelda and back, before bending to his task once more. A waft of heady perfume tickled his nose as they swept past him without a second glance.

'Eeuww . . .' A beautiful girl with dark ringlets wrinkled her nose. 'What is that dreadful smell?'

'It doesn't bear thinking upon,' one of her companions cried, frantically fanning her face.

They found out soon enough. There was a short silence as Tangnost thumped a talon-sheath home. Above them, the servants were doing their best to sweep the steps, but their small shovels had not yet cleared the steaming dung.

'You, boy,' the girl said haughtily to Quenelda, who

was lifting the final talon-sheath. 'Clear that . . . that . . .' She waved a fan in the general direction of the unmentionable obstacle.

Quenelda ignored her and picked up a file before kneeling to examine the ragged edge on Two Gulps' claw.

'This instant!' the young lady demanded, spots of colour rising in her cheeks. 'We are to attend court this afternoon. Boy!

'Me?' Quenelda turned slowly, eyebrows raised.

Root held his breath, aghast. Even Tangnost paused to watch with interest. Smoke curled warningly from Two Gulps' nostrils. The young ladies seemed oblivious to the battledragon. They're like me, Root thought. Like I used to be. They don't know one dragon from another!

Slowly, deliberately, Quenelda looked Armelia up and down, from the extravagant hat and golden furs to the high pointed heels that peeped out beneath layers of petticoats. 'And who are you to command me?' Her soft tone was deceptively silky. Despite her question, she clearly knew who the young lady was; just as it was clear to Root that the young lady had no idea whom she was addressing.

The girl's eyes widened in outrage. 'How dare you question me? I will see you punished for your impudence!' Nonetheless she answered, unable to keep the pride from her voice. 'I,' she announced, nose in the air, 'am the daughter of the Duke of Cawdor. My father is the Queen's treasurer,' she added for good measure.

'And I,' said Quenelda, smiling sweetly but with a knife-edge to her tone, 'am the daughter of the Earl Rufus, SDS Commander and Queen's Champion.'

219

There was a shocked silence. Smoke pooled across the landing pad, eddying around the young ladies' ankles.

'You're Darcy's half-sister?' Armelia's lip curled in disbelief even as her mind noted the aristocratic voice, the proud bearing. 'You can't be!' She laughed hysterically, then realized that no one else was joining in. They were all watching her with fascinated curiosity. She looked back to Quenelda, seeing past the patched jerkin and flying boots, the blonde hair tied back off her face, to the tawny eyes that now blazed with anger. Her eyes darted to the battledragon behind and widened as she recognized that this was no domestic dragon, despite its trappings. Darcy's half-sister?! She hadn't believed all the gossip at court. It was simply too outrageous to imagine a girl in boy's clothes flying dragons. But . . .

Root could see the exact moment when realization dawned, for the colour suddenly drained from her face.

'M-my lady,' the girl stammered as she sank into a hasty curtsy, followed by her companions. 'We' – she hesitated for a second, clearly not wanting to say what she really thought – 'did not recognize you.'

'No,' Quenelda said coldly, unforgivingly. 'Evidently you didn't.'

Sensing his mistress's anger, Two Gulps stretched his head over her shoulder. There was a crackle, and a purple flame rolled out to lick the young ladies' feet. It was weak, just a breathy warning, barely visible in the sunlight, all smoke and no fire, but it was enough.

Hysterical shrieks rang out. The girls stepped backwards, each trying to hide behind the other. There were squeals of dismay as one landed in the dung; two others slipped and fell down beside her. Quenelda's eyes shifted from them back to Armelia, whose dress was smouldering at the hem. Two horror-struck white-rimmed eyes looked out of a sooty face.

For a moment Quenelda was equally aghast. Then her shoulders heaved and a laugh took hold of her. Tangnost coughed to hide his own smile. Quenelda doubled up in laughter.

'You . . .' Armelia stamped her foot and then instantly regretted it. 'How can I attend court dressed like this? I didn't believe the stories, but you're just as they say! No wonder Darcy is ashamed of you! You're no lady! You're no better than a tramp! Like your mother!'

Quenelda's eyes flashed coldly. Two Gulps' neck snaked out. He opened his mouth, revealing his foot-long incisors. With a squeal, Armelia and her friends took to their high heels.

CHAPTER TWENTY-ONE
The Winter Joust

The Sorcerers Glen sped by, the air crisp enough to sear the back of the throat. Iron-coloured clouds hung low over the mountain peaks, heavy with the promise of snow. When Quenelda turned her muffled face to see how Root was doing, he saw that she was pink with cold. Harnessed in new brass and blue leather saddle and bridle, Chasing the Stars had positioned herself just above and behind Two Gulps. Root leaned forward to pat the dragon fondly before signalling back that they were both doing well. The freezing air made his eyes water, but he had to admit that the view was magnificent from this height.

Wherever you looked the air was full of dragons, hippogriffs and griffins, dressed like their riders and lords in bright carnival colours. Two- and four-, even some six-door carriages whisked by, drawn by teams of matching dragons, scales polished to a mirror finish, harness bells jingling. Glossy-feathered griffins and gloriously coloured hippogriffs dropped out of the sky, their keening calls carrying clearly in the crystalline air. And below, the loch was alive with large galleons and rowing boats ferrying both the privileged and the poor to the greatest jousting festival of the year.

Now that Quenelda was riding out as a young lady, her father had insisted she wear a dress. She had chosen the plainest and darkest possible and still looked uncomfortable. Only Root appeared to have noticed the heavy buckled flying boots that peeped out from beneath the layers of petticoats.

222

The Earl flew wing to wing with his daughter and marvelled at the changes he saw in her; the hint of the woman she would become. There was a sense of control about her, a new sense of calm. A year ago she would not have been so disciplined. She would have thrown her mount into a reckless race with her esquire, delighting in his failure. He glanced at the boy on Chasing the Stars and shook his head in wonder. That the two were friends was easy to see. That they was coming to the jousts at all was little short of a miracle. He had doubted whether Quenelda would master her impatience enough to be able to teach another what she knew instinctively.

Soon the storm of dragons was so dense that Two Gulps and You're Gone, Stormcracker and Chasing the Stars had to duck and dive to weave their way through the traffic, and Root started to feel uncomfortable. Dragons and carriages made way for the Earl's banner, but still their passage was turbulent. Once again the gnome's stomach was in danger of betraying him, and he wished he had not eaten quite such a large plate of haggis sausages and eggs before leaving. Trying desperately to think about something other than food – anything at all – Root lifted his new brass and leather telescope – a gift from Quenelda, along with a fully equipped flying suit and harness – and searched the distant loch for the royal castle of Crannock, home of the Queen.

The great mountain ridge of the Dragon's Spine sped by to the north, and the peaks of the Seven Wizards flanked the great sea loch to the south. There! On a high cliff on the southern shore of the loch beneath the great snow-capped peak of the White Sorcerer Mountain, the lofty towers and battlements of Crannock Castle swiftly grew larger. Root saw dozens of banners and the royal standard snapping in the wind. Rising out of the sheer cliffs, the castle looked as if it had simply grown out of the bedrock. He found it impossible to tell where cliff ended and castle began.

The paddocks and practice lists beyond were packed with dragons, their hot breath clouding the frosty air like billowing white sea haar. Raised wooden walkways that wound between tents, pavilions and pens were crowded; merchants, minor lords, soldiers, artisans and citizens streamed towards the arena that lay behind the castle's high curtain wall. Guards posted on the tower pads sat motionless on their blood-red Magma dragons, while dozens more patrolled the skies above.

Approaching from the north, the Earl's flight of six dragons swirled down around the inner bailey walls.

Quenelda's heart fluttered with fierce anticipation. She had attended court jousts along with her father for as long as she could remember, but the magnificence of the palace, the raw energy that tingled in the air, never ceased to thrill. Deftly weaving between the towers and turrets, she put Two Gulps down on one of the small dragonpads that crowned the tall spiralling Winter Tower. As Queen's Champion, the Earl DeWinter had many privileges; direct entry to the castle was only one of them.

There was a loud flapping of wings, followed by a thump as an overconfident Root angled down too steeply behind Two Gulps. With a hastily muffled squawk, the gnome was toppled from his mount to sprawl on the landing deck. Kindly pretending not to notice, the Earl and his daughter dismounted. Leaving the dragons to esquires of the Queen's household, the group made their way over to a stairwell that spiralled downwards into the bright bustling heart of the castle.

Root followed the Earl's retinue through corridors hung with paintings and costly mirrors, and down sweeping stairs into a huge colonnaded hall crowded with courtiers and knights and aristocrats.

'The knights' hall,' Quenelda told Root. A minstrel's gallery ran along its length, and bright heraldic banners and shields hung from the high rafters; white granite statues of previous kings and queens lined the walls. Great fires blazed at either end and the candelabra were so bright and numerous it was like an explosion of daylight. To Root, more used to the stinking tallow candles in the roosts, the effect was breathtaking.

The Earl motioned for Quenelda and Root to hurry off and take their places in the arena, then moved on up the hall, followed by his household knights.

Root looked around with a sense of bewildered excitement. 'Where's he going?' he asked.

'To wait upon the Queen, of course!' Quenelda could not keep the pride from her voice. 'As Queen's Champion, Papa will escort her to the joust.'

Root stood on tiptoe, trying to catch a glimpse of the young Queen, but his view was blocked by a group of well-fed merchants, who were discussing the coming jousts with enthusiasm.

'Oh, no!' one declared. 'DeWinter might be attending, but I assure you he won't be taking to the jousting lists. Take my word for it, he's been wounded. Badly, I heard say. Look! Look at that limp. Got it at the Battle of Howling Glen, a fine victory! Put your money on Lassiter instead. He's not been beaten this year.'

'I don't agree,' an elderly merchant protested. 'Lassiter took a tumble against the Black Prince at Tantallon Castle. Put your money on St John Belrack! That dragon of his, Marking Time – a fine filly if there ever was one . . .'

'I heard,' came a hushed voice, 'that our esteemed Grand Master has entered a dragon.' There were furtive looks towards the throne, where the Grand Master was bending down to listen to the Queen. 'Been down the paddocks to take a look at the black stallion of his that he's been boasting about. The one that won last week down in the Border Marches. Never seen a dragon like it.' The merchants leaned forward to hear. 'Ugly, mean-looking brute – looks like it's been in a fight or two with its roostmates. Always experimenting with breeding dragons, he is . . .'

'Well, I shall put my money on that beast,' a courtier declared. 'The Grand Master rarely loses. With the Earl injured, your money's safe with him.'

'Pssst,' Quenelda hissed, grabbing Root's jerkin, pulling him towards the door. 'What are you doing! Come on! We have to get there before the Queen. That's royal protocol. The Queen has her own private passages through the castle. It will take us much longer.'

Root allowed Quenelda to lead him along another crowded stone-flagged corridor and up a twisting staircase to the jousting arena. They stepped out onto a wide stone gallery, and Quenelda beckoned him forward. Standing on tiptoe, Root looked down onto the oval jousting arena, tier upon tier of seats falling steeply away below him. He had never seen anything like it. It was vast beyond imagining! The sounds and scents and sights were intoxicating!

'They call it "the Cauldron",' Quenelda said softly beside him.

'Newt and toad!' Root breathed, awestruck, blinking owlishly at the coloured brilliance all around him.

The crowd was now reaching capacity; many of the best seats had been filled even before dawn. Despite that, raucous crowds were still streaming in through the tiered white arches, pushing and shoving until the very last seat was taken.

Root whistled.

'Impressive, isn't it?' Quenelda grinned, pleased at his reaction.

At either end of the oval arena stood a great oak, taller than any Root had ever seen. At the top of each trunk the tree divided into a crown of many branches. Wooden platforms were set about the bole, and at the tops of branches.

Quenelda followed his gaze. 'Jousting lists for the dragons,' she explained. And far below stretched the great silver ropes of spiderdragon webbing, light as a feather yet stronger than steel, designed to catch the fallen and safely funnel them down to the sawdust floor.

Suddenly there were courtiers and knights of the Queen's retinue coming in behind them in twos and threes, chatting, discussing the merits of different dragons, exchanging bets. Quenelda pulled Root to one side, to stand behind her chair. Darcy accompanied by Armelia and two of his friends swaggered in; he was rebelliously still wearing the dashing uniform of the Unicorn Cavalry. They took one look at Quenelda, uncomfortably trussed up in her skirts, and broke into unkind laughter. When it seemed to Root as if the gallery could barely hold another person, two pages lifted great mammoth-horns to their lips. Their challenges boomed around the arena, the noise echoing, vibrating through the stone of the castle, making Quenelda's toes tingle.

There was movement behind, and then the Queen was there, with the Earl on her right, the Grand Master to her left, and her constable, Sir Gharad Mowbray, behind her; suddenly the courtiers were all bowing or sinking into graceful curtsies. Quenelda, unused to her dress, half bowed and half curtsied, raising muted laughter from the accomplished courtiers. Darcy and Armelia exchanged loud contemptuous remarks as Quenelda's face flamed hot with embarrassment. But one warning look from his father silenced Darcy, whose face flushed in turn.

As the Queen stepped forward to wave at the crowds, Root stole a glance at her. Her face was in profile, and although he had never seen her before, her determined look, the jut of her jaw, the elegant sweep of brows and high cheekbones seemed somehow familiar.

Everyone in the Seven Sea Kingdoms knew the story of how, when she was barely fifteen and a princess, the King, her father, her two brothers and the SDS Commander, the Earl Wilder DeWinter, had all died at the bloody Battle of the Salmon Trap on the Isle of Midges, wiped out by an overwhelming force of seven hobgoblin banners. With her mother long since dead, Caitlin became the youngest Queen in living memory, her inheritance guaranteed and guarded by the loyalty of the SDS and its new young commander, the Earl Rufus.

Dressed in cream brocade robes stitched with gold beneath a heavy fur-lined cloak, she wore her long blonde hair netted with fine threads of spun silver, inset with tiny diamonds. Waving one last time, she returned to her throne, wrapping her furs around her; the royal joust had begun.

The Earl, seated at the Queen's right shoulder, nodded to her high steward, who raised his staff.

At his signal a trumpet sounded. As Root watched, wide-eyed, three dozen dragons swooped down into the arena from all points of the compass, to a mass roar of approval. Flying around the stands, crisscrossing the vast bowl of the Cauldron in leisurely fashion, they then gave a great show of high-speed aerial manoeuvring to impress the crowds.

'If you want to see the dragons close up,' Quenelda shouted in Root's ear, 'then you can go to the parade paddock out by the practice lists. The esquires walk the dragons around before they're saddled and armoured so that everyone can judge them before gambling on the outcome. Though not all the dragons are here – some that are highly strung are only brought in when it's their turn at the lists.'

Root was riveted. The knights wore engraved jousting armour of many colours, beneath helmets crested with fantastical heraldic creatures. The dragons were also armoured, to protect them from injury by the jousting lances. On top of their armour they also wore brightly coloured caparisons stitched with the colours and coats of arms of their knights. Around the arena heralds in royal tabards called out all the jousters' names and titles, followed by the rules of the tournament. Then those dragons chosen to open the competition flew to the lower lists of the jousting trees, where their esquires waited for them, bearing shields and brightly garlanded jousting lances.

'And now,' the herald in the royal box declared, his voice sucked up by the mammoth-horn and expelled so that it boomed around the stadium, 'for your entertainment – in the blue list: Sir Winston Mowbray flying Thundering Tornado Talonthrust the Second. In the red list, challenging him: Sir Stelton Quandry flying Starstruck Highland Wanderer.'

Two dragons took off from the list trees. Slowly they flew once more around the arena, allowing the crowds a closer look at them before alighting on the small dragonpad in front of the royal gallery. Raising their gauntleted fists to their chest, the contestants saluted the Queen after the fashion of the SDS. One of the dragons stretched out her long neck to consider Quenelda with unblinking green eyes.

Greetings, Starstruck Highland Wanderer, Quenelda said. *May the wind always sail under your wings.*

Greetings, Dancing with Dragons, the dragon responded, her forked tongue flicking towards the girl. Abandoning any pretence at dignity, the courtiers tumbled backwards as one. Even the men-at-arms bent backwards as far as they could without falling over.

The Queen, with the Earl Rufus at her side, merely smiled, but the Grand Master's dark eyes turned thoughtfully to consider Quenelda. Observing the Queen's calm reaction, her embarrassed courtiers coughed, pretending their panic had merely been a jest.

You are not of Dragonkind – your skin is not scaled . . . you have no wings and no tail – yet you are not a Wingless One and you speak our language? The long red snout was softly blowing towards Quenelda like a warm spring breeze. By now Sir Stelton was red-faced and sweating with the effort of reining back his disobedient mount. Some courtiers were openly laughing.

Have you not yet shed your first skin? The dragon enquired solicitously as her tongue flicked out again, searching for the tasty food tablets in Quenelda's flying belt.

It has always been so, she responded, opening the pouch and stepping down to give the dragon a handful of tablets.

Ah, so that was why the dragon was so interested! A ripple of amusement went round the gallery as the dragon greedily took the offered treats. Losing interest, the Grand Master turned away.

And as you say, I have not shed my first skin. I only have eleven winters behind me.

Farewell, then. May the wind always blow under your wings . . .

Farewell, Starstruck Highland Wanderer, may you soar to the stars . . .

Then the silent conversation was blown to one side as the crowd roared impatiently and the embarrassed young knight finally succeeded in turning his mount away. Behind Quenelda, the courtiers had regained their courage

231

and were already placing bets in overloud voices.

'I'll wager twenty golden guineas on Starstruck Highland Wanderer.'

'Six to two on the red list!'

'Twenty silver shillings on Tornado Talonthrust!'

Root could hardly believe his ears. All around him small fortunes were changing hands – enough to keep a family for ten years or more. After listening for a moment, he leaned forward to whisper to Quenelda, 'Who do you think is going to win?'

Without hesitation, Quenelda pointed to the small but powerfully built dragon already alighting on the left lists,

'Sir Winston and Thundering Tornado Talonthrust. Sir Winston is a brave and accomplished jouster and his mare is also very experienced. They've fought in dozens of battles with the SDS. Sir Stelton is not so experienced – he's just seventeen – and Starstruck Highland Wanderer, as you saw, is young and headstrong and difficult to control.'

Swiftly, Starstruck Highland Wanderer alighted on the highest platform on the opposite list, her young rider anxious to prove himself.

'Each knight has three lances,' Quenelda explained to Root, whose mouth was still hanging open. 'Then, if both are still flying, they choose their own personal weapon. Papa always chooses a dragonmace.'

Root shivered and wrapped his cloak tightly around himself. 'Don't they get killed? Or horribly wounded?'

'They used to,' Quenelda admitted. 'Until recently they used battlefield weapons. But the Queen's father banned them because the SDS were losing too many young cadets before they even fought their first battle. The lances are blunt now, and both knights and dragons are heavily padded and armoured, so that rarely happens. The whole point is to test skills for the battlefield, to make them better fighters, so there's no honour in deliberately injuring an opponent. That's why the use of Battle Magic is banned too. It's too potent. It would cause casualties in the crowd. Wait . . . they're about to begin.'

The noise was becoming deafening. As it reached a crescendo, the high steward dropped the royal standard. A horn sounded and the dragons leaped out of the lists, coming together in the blink of an eye, brightly coloured lances catching on shields – and then they were past, throwing broken lances to the ground below. But to the crowd's disappointment, Sir Stelton was undragoned at the second tilt. Caught by the spiderdragon net, he bounced two or three times before being helped to his feet by stewards. His opponent landed and reached for his sword. But Sir Stelton's armour was badly dented. He tried lifting his sword but his arm was injured.

'I yield,' he said reluctantly.

The noisy crowd groaned; those who had betted on him reluctantly parted with their money. The herald blew a ringing note and announced the second combatants. Two fresh dragons flew around the arena.

The hazy sun was finally swallowed by heavy clouds. Instantly it grew darker; the braziers around the lip of the arena now shone brightly. Snow as light and puffy as thistledown began to drift lazily down.

'So' – Rufus DeWinter beckoned his daughter to his side as the two new combatants saluted the Queen – 'both knights are equally skilled at the lists. Which dragon would you put your money on, Goose?'

Quenelda could hear some of the courtiers laughing indulgently, whispering amongst themselves behind her. As if such a young girl could know anything about dragons! Their elders smiled knowingly and waited to place their bets. But the Grand Master stepped forward to listen.

'The Spotted Cobblethwaite' – Quenelda's eyes were narrowed with concentration – 'has good balance – strongly muscled – but he's carrying an old injury on the third finger of his right quipsom; it's healed but it's a weakness, and there's a hint of wing-droop too. Probably good for a quick knockout but I don't think he'd last a long contest, Papa.'

People were listening now as the two dragons pranced on the platform. The younger courtiers looked amazed.

'And the filly?'

'Beautiful bones and well muscled. But wait!' Quenelda sensed pain radiating from the young dragon and stepped forward to the balustrade.

A break? She asked the beautiful blue dragon who was turning away from the gallery.

A break, Dancing with Dragons, the young Arabian confirmed. *It is not yet mended . . .*

'A broken upper rib.' Quenelda turned towards her father. 'And it hasn't been given time to mend properly. One hit to her peytral and she'll be down. She's been treated badly.' She was indignant. 'See where she's scarred by spurs? And . . .'

There was a mass exodus from the royal box as

courtiers hastily changed their bets.

The morning wore on, an exhausting blur of wings and steel. Falling steadily now, the snow began to eddy and swirl in the rising wind. Quenelda raised the hood of her fur-lined flying cloak. Teeth chattering, Root thought longingly of a bowl of hot barley broth. Darcy cursed and called for more wine. Having loudly derided his sister's opinions, he and his friends had lost a great deal betting on the losers. The Earl cursed the injury that prevented him from taking to the lists. The Grand Master debated the finer points of dragonmanship with the Queen.

'I understand you have entered the young stallion we have heard so much about?' The Queen turned thoughtful eyes on him. 'They say he can't be beaten, Hugo; that you have bred yet another champion.'

'Your Most Gracious Majesty' – the Grand Master bowed – 'is too generous. Midnight Madness is certainly one of a kind. He takes to the lists now.'

The herald raised his voice. A hush fell. This was the battle the crowd had been waiting for. Quenelda, as curious as everyone else, raised her telescope towards the paddocks.

'In the red list, from the stables of the Grand Master, Sir Hugo Mandrake, comes Midnight Madness, ridden by Duke Roger Grenville.' A cheer went up from the crowd: the Grand Master's dragons were always exciting to watch.

Duke Grenville . . . ? Quenelda frowned. Then a memory clicked into place. Second in command of the SDS at the time of her grandfather's death, the Duke had expected to be made Commander, but her father had been appointed instead.

The Grand Master grinned wolfishly at his friend, the Earl. 'Care to place a wager, Rufus?'

The Earl smiled. 'Let's see his form first.'

The Grand Master's dragon entered the arena for the first time. Powerfully built, he was the colour of a wet stormy night. As he swept up to the podium to allow the Duke to salute the Queen and his patron, Quenelda knew she had never seen a dragon quite like him. A memory eons old that was not her own shied away. The hairs along her arms stood on end, and she shivered with sudden premonition.

The tall black-armoured Duke who rode Midnight Madness dipped his lance. His surcoat and his dragon's trapper were also black, on which the striking red adder of the Grand Master was quartered with the Grenville rampant lion, stitched in silver. The stallion wore only the lightest padded armour.

Quenelda continued to stare at the dragon and felt another prickle of unease. What was it about this dragon that was unsettling her? She cautiously quested out to greet him, but met with a violent rebuff.

Do not seek to play with me, little Wingless One. The angry dragon effortlessly batted her thoughts aside, as his talons struck the platform, gouging the wood. *I have no time . . . no time . . . the hunt is on . . .*

The hunt . . . ? She echoed.

'What is it?' Root whispered. Quenelda looked as if she had just been slapped in the face. 'What's wrong?'

'I don't know.' She frowned. 'That dragon's thoughts

are strange. It's as if he's in pain.' She lifted a hand and massaged her temples.

'And riding a stallion from Dragonsdome's stud, Greenstone Gemstar, is Sir William de la Timber, of the Earl's household guard!' Announced the herald.

A second smaller dragon was flying around the arena as the crowd roared their approval. She was a bottle-green Moss dragon with white spines, bred not only for her agility but because she perfectly matched the de la Timber coat of arms of a green dragon emblazoned on white.

'She's beautiful.' Root was open-mouthed as Greenstone Gemstar flew to her jousting platform.

Quenelda shook her head. 'Beauty is not what counts in the lists. She won't last a single lance against that brute if they collide. The weight of the dragon will add strength to the impact,' she explained, turning towards the red lists. 'He's more likely to be able to knock his opponent clean out of the saddle.' They both looked at the jousting platform, where the dark dragon now stood silently.

Quenelda stood up and studied him intently. The broad shoulders were typical of jousting dragons, as were the four powerfully framed wings, allowing for great speed over short distances. He looked like a Dale dragon. But his heavy-jawed head and pebbled hide were not typical. Not strictly against Guild jousting ordinances . . . but . . . but there was something else, something indefinable . . . It shimmered, tickling her senses like a cobweb. It was almost as if the dragon were going in and out of focus. She frowned, feeling a little dizzy, and blinked to clear her head.

'Are you unwell?' Root was concerned to see Quenelda

swaying on her feet. 'Perhaps you should take a seat?'

She sat back down heavily. 'No, it's just a headache coming on.'

There was something predatory about this strange dragon . . . as if this were a carnivore. But that wasn't possible. Battledragons were strictly forbidden at tournaments. They had been for fifty years. The risk of injury and death was too great, for once the excitement of the charge took hold, a battledragon could easily kill an opponent in a blood frenzy. If it were then loosed on the packed arena, there would be carnage.

Root followed her doubtful glance. Focusing his telescope, he agreed that Midnight Madness was the meanest, ugliest dragon he had ever seen. He gleamed like something that had crawled from out of a deep dark swamp. Nothing like his own beautiful, delicate Chasing the Stars.

Right from the start, even to Root's inexperienced eyes, it didn't seem a fair contest. The smaller dragon was agile and highly trained, her knight skilled, but the larger dragon wore her down. On the third lance the dragons collided; there was never any doubt as to the outcome. A broken wing put paid to Greenstone Gemstar's chance of winning and, disappointed by the unequal fight, some in the crowd booed.

The Grand Master's dragon beat his opponent effortlessly in each round, until there was just one left, which was swiftly dispatched; by now there were loud mutterings from almost everyone present: this had turned out to be the most predictable tournament in history.

Duke Grenville and Midnight Madness swooped down

to land in front of the royal box. The downdraught caught the edge of the tapestries and lifted the Queen's long hair beneath the slim circlet of gold that banded her head as she prepared to rise and congratulate the victor.

Instead of dismounting, the Duke pulled off a gauntlet and threw it into the royal box. It struck Root squarely, making him cry out and fall. In a daze he picked it up. The heavy segmented metal finger plates clinked in his hand.

'I challenge the Queen's Champion,' Duke Grenville roared.

The words fell into a well of silence.

'But, Papa . . .' Quenelda protested, jumping to her feet. 'You're still not well. Your leg!'

An outraged gasp swept around the arena as the Duke's words passed from mouth to mouth. The Queen stood, her fur-lined cloak falling from her shoulders as she did so.

'My lord' – her voice was as cold as the weather – 'such a challenge is unseemly. The Earl is but late come from battle, and his wounds are not yet fully healed. To challenge an injured man does you no honour.'

'Nonetheless, Your Most Gracious Majesty.' Grenville lifted his visor, contempt tingeing his words. 'As Tournament Champion, it is my right to challenge the Queen's Champion. He, of course, has the right to refuse, should he feel . . . unable to accept.'

'My Lord Duke' – stepping forward, the Grand Master also made an outraged protest to his liegeman – 'the Earl is injured!'

But Quenelda saw the faint smile playing around his lips, the strange glint in his dark eyes, and frowned. She turned to Darcy, imploring him to accept the challenge on her father's behalf.

There was a pause.

Quenelda watched with growing disbelief as her brother made no move.

'Your Most Gracious Majesty.' Looking at his son with bitter disappointment, Rufus DeWinter went down awkwardly on one knee, the other injured leg stretched out straight. 'As your Champion, I am sworn to take on all who challenge your authority.'

Quenelda knew then, with a sudden start of fear, that her father meant to fight – which for some reason was exactly what the Grand Master had always intended. She moved forward. 'Papa!'

But he held up a hand to stay her protest, softening it with a smile just for her. He turned back to the Queen, whose expression mirrored Quenelda's.

'However, I have no jousting mount, nor armour, nor weaponry.'

'If you insist on competing, then it is fitting that as the Queen's Champion you should wear the Queen's colours.' She turned to her constable, Sir Mowbray, and commanded him to ready Knight's Mace for the Earl.

The constable nodded with approval. 'And I shall serve as your esquire myself, my Lord Earl.'

The crowd roared its approval – the competition was on!

CHAPTER TWENTY-TWO
DeWinter! DeWinter!

Tension was reaching fever pitch. The crowd favoured the chances of the Queen's Champion, despite his injury, but the motionless black dragon unnerved them. Large wet feathery flakes of snow were still falling, clinging to everything they touched, soaking up the last of the light.

A midnight-blue dragon swept down through the snow from the castle roosts. Long-necked and broad-shouldered, with scalloped three-toed wings, Knight's Mace was decked out in the royal colours of russet and gold over heavily padded armour. The crowd roared its welcome for the Earl. Quenelda proudly joined in the applause as her father came to salute the Queen before flying to the blue lists. Looking at the Earl's gleaming armour, listening to the adulation of the crowd, Root wondered wistfully what it would be like to be the Queen's Champion, the greatest Dragon Lord in the Seven Sea Kingdoms.

Alighting on the lists, the Earl settled himself into the high-cantled jousting saddle and tried to ignore his throbbing thigh. He'd had to opt for light jousting armour as his leg still wouldn't take the weight of plate armour. That made him extremely vulnerable to further injury and he very much suspected that his unchivalrous opponent knew it.

'My Lord Earl?' Silver-blue beard bristling in the rising wind, Sir Mowbray offered up a heavy jousting lance, red twined with white. The old man could hardly lift it. The Earl Rufus dropped the reins, leaving his highly trained dragon to be guided by knee and spur, and hefted the lance to get the feel of its weight and balance. Positioning it under his armpit, he declared himself satisfied, then lifted the leather-covered wooden shield and allowed Sir Mowbray to tighten the straps. Satisfied with its balance, he dropped his visor, reducing his vision to a slit of daylight.

'Take care, Rufus.' Sir Mowbray relinquished the reins. 'The man has no honour, and remember how jealous he was of you when you beat him to become Commander of the SDS . . .'

Settling into the saddle, the Earl focused solely on his opponent on the opposite list. His heart slowed in readiness for battle.

The high steward dropped his flag. A horn rang out.

Neither dragon moved. The crowd began to murmur uneasily, the strange atmosphere making them shift nervously. Why didn't they charge?

The snow swirled more thickly, almost obscuring them. Duke Grenville sat motionless on his dragon. Midnight Madness raised his head, black harness jingling. Giving voice to his fury and pain, he opened his jaws to issue a shattering challenge that reverberated around the arena. 'Yyyaakkkaaaa!' The ear-splitting cry set everyone's teeth on edge. The Queen's Champion and Knight's Mace made no answer.

Quenelda cringed, sensing the creature's twisted pain.

Silence.

The air tingled.

The restless crowd held their breath. This was more than a joust. This was a battle of wills.

Up in the royal gallery, the Grand Master's jaw tightened. Darcy DeWinter smiled. Staring intently through her telescope, Quenelda focused closely on Midnight Madness, on the set of the dragon's head, the spread of his wings, the tension in his hindquarters that would give warning of sudden flight.

Pennants and standards snapped as the wind rose to a shriek. Snow curled beneath the pavilion to land on Quenelda's eyelashes and melted to blur her vision. Light was fading, winter-fast.

With a sudden explosion of power, both dragons launched themselves from the lists. The air thundered to the beat of their powerful wings. Within moments they were hurtling towards each other, blunt-headed jousting lances level. A blur of black and blue through a veil of white . . .

Closing fast . . .

Quenelda was out of her seat, white knuckles gripping the edge of the royal gallery. The Queen looked pale.

Closing . . .

Kill . . . A faint voice whispered in Quenelda's head. Startled, she gazed around but no one was looking at her.

Suddenly the two dragons came together; the Earl's lance found its mark and shattered his opponent's shield. The sound of splintering wood was lost in the crowd's roar. Even though he had deflected his opponent's thrust so that the lance slid harmlessly by, the Earl felt the shock, which slammed his shoulder back. The combatants swept down the length of the lists to their platforms, where their esquires waited with a second lance.

Kill . . .

They charged a second time, coming together in a bone-jarring impact that shivered through the air. The crowd groaned as the Champion's dragon was flung sideways above the crowds in a move that would have unseated most men. The Earl's shield shattered under the impact of the black dragon's shoulder; pieces fell down among the spectators, who fought for the prized keepsakes. Deftly turning his mount, shrugging off the broken shield's leather straps, the Earl reached for his third lance from Sir Mowbray. Not waiting for a new shield, he spurred Knight's Mace forward.

The crowd were on their feet now. 'DeWinter! DeWinter! DeWinter!'

The dragons closed. 'They're too fast!' someone cried. 'He has no shield!'

Kill . . . kill . . . kill . . . The insane whispers took form in Quenelda's mind. *Kill the Dragon Lord . . .* With a gasp of horror, she realized that this was no ordinary joust, no duel between rivals; the purpose of the challenge was to kill her injured father. She suddenly understood the murderous heart deep within the black dragon. He was a raptor! A wolf in sheep's clothing that would be drawn to blood, to her father's injury. At the edge of her vision she glimpsed her brother peering through the snow, beads of sweat on his forehead despite the freezing temperature; and in front she sensed rather than saw the Grand Master shift for a better view, saw the tension in the line of his jaw and the white knuckles that gripped his staff.

Once again the dragons flew down the tilting arena, but this time, hidden by the thickening snow, the black knight aimed his blunt lance deliberately low. The scream of raw pain cut through the noise of the crowd. The spectators nearest the duel gasped. Word swiftly passed from mouth to mouth. A steward murmured in the Queen's ear. The Queen's Champion was struggling to stay in the saddle as blood poured from the reopened war wound on his leg.

'End it,' the Queen commanded her high steward, who beckoned a mounted marshal forward. 'This is madness. The Earl has done more than enough to satisfy honour.'

As Earl Rufus reined in, sweat streamed into his eyes. His light jousting armour lay peeled back from his thigh like the silvered scales of a gutted fish. Rearing, Knight's Mace returned to the list platform, her spurred talons gouging the wood, her hot breath vaporizing the falling snow. Steam rose from her heaving flanks. She rolled her eyes at the scent of fresh blood. She was not trained for battle, and the musty scent of fear rose from her.

'End it.' The old constable caught the dragon's rein as a sickening gush ran red down the Earl's dented armour. 'My friend, Rufus, your wound is bleeding badly. You cannot go on. You risk your health—'

But even as the marshal sounded the trumpet to end the duel on the Queen's command, the black dragon had already left the lists.

Hearing the roar of the crowd, the Earl snatched up the mace the old man offered, gathered in his reins and spurred his mount forward to meet his opponent a fourth time. The crowds rose to their feet, sensing the end must be near. None could match the Earl in close combat, injured or not.

The wind swept back the curtain of white just as the two dragons clashed. Almost standing up in his stirrups, the black knight was using whip and spur, goading his dragon to recklessness. At the last moment the frenzied Midnight Madness rolled and lashed out with his talons, gouging a trough of flesh in the smaller dragon's unprotected flank. His tail lashed sideways as he swept past. The force broke the Earl's left arm and fractured his mount's thigh bone. The Queen's dragon screamed; a high-pitched shriek that made ears ring and Quenelda shiver with shared pain. Her father's cry was ripped away by the wind.

Knight's Mace tumbled in agony. Blue blood mingled with the red running down her flank. Numb from wrist to shoulder, the Earl's useless arm dropped his shattered shield.

'Papa!' It was so hard to see what was happening. Quenelda brushed hot stinging tears from her face that was already wet with snowmelt. 'Papa!' she screamed as his crippled dragon flapped helplessly in the gusting wind, blown this way and that.

The crowd roared, caught up by the frenzy of the fight. The Grand Master was looking as shocked as anyone; the Queen was on her feet, shouting to him: 'The stewards. Command your stewards forward! Now, man, before it's too late! The dragon's badly injured and may turn rogue!'

Quenelda turned back. The air was treacle-thick with suppressed magic. Everything around her slowed. The roar of the crowd faded to the edge of her awareness and she barely heard the bugle call. Through the swirling white she could see dozens of dragons swooping down from the small dragonpads that dotted the upper tier of the arena, their stewards armed with heavy spears and weighted nets. Dragons had gone mad with pain from a wound before.

246

'Forgive me, Madam.' Quenelda heard the Grand Master's voice as if it were a hazy dream. 'I cannot. I fear that a deathbolt fired at a moving target may bring down the dragon, but the fallout would cause many casualties in such a confined space, might even kill Rufus. I am no soldier, and the wind is unpredictable. Let the stewards do their job, Madam.' He laid a comforting hand reassuringly on her sleeve. 'They know how to deal with a rogue dragon. The Earl is in no real danger. My dragon must be wounded. Duke Grenville has clearly lost control.'

Far below, the Earl calmed his injured mount, halting their dizzying descent before she became trapped in the netting. Hefting his mace with his one good arm, he coaxed the trembling mare upwards by sheer force of will. Lifting his visor, he looked through the swirling white, searching for his opponent. The air suddenly gusted above him, and the Earl deftly manoeuvred Knight's Mace sideways just as the talons of the black dragon slashed through the air. The Duke's ruse almost worked, but years of experience on the battlefield had honed the Earl's instincts. Now, as Midnight Madness dropped down, he instinctively reached for his saddle holster and cursed as realization hit. He didn't have his staff! The wand, sheathed as ever on his hip, was useless against a dragon except at close quarters. He called to his household guard in the upper gallery.

'My staff! Get me my staff!' But his command was lost in the suffocating snow storm and the cries of the crowd.

'No use, DeWinter! They can't hear you,' his opponent mocked him. 'You're not afraid of a real fight, are you? You're surely not afraid to earn your spurs instead of having them handed to you on a plate by the Queen? Let's see if you truly deserve the command of the SDS!'

The Earl ducked as the wicked spikes of a dragonmace grazed the crest of his helmet, drawing an explosion of sparks. All at once he realized that his opponent was fully armoured for battle, not for a joust. His brutal treatment had deliberately driven his dragon rogue, provoked him to attack.

The Earl was now forced to use magic to counter this base lack of honour. Drawing his wand from its sheath on his left thigh in one swift movement, he threw a stunning spell straight into the unprotected maw of the attacking dragon. At such close quarters it was enough.

Jaws snapping shut only a couple of metres from his face, the unconscious dragon plummeted earthwards in a fading splash of red sparks, giving the Duke no time to react. He screamed as the vicious points of his left spur snagged in the stirrup and he was sucked down in his dragon's wake. Caught by the netting, both dragon and rider bounced and tumbled twice before falling senseless to the ground in a cloud of snow. Flung clear on impact, the Duke lay motionless, one leg bent at an awkward angle, snow rapidly turning his black armour white.

Moving in swiftly, the circling stewards fired their nets in a soft explosion. Expanding in the air, they settled on the downed dragon like layers of spiderweb. The crowd held their breath. In the unexpected silence nothing stirred. Sparks from braziers lit the gloom. A child cried out. Cautiously, the stewards put down beside the fallen dragon, raising mallets and banging in great iron pegs to pin down the net. Above them, the Earl finally allowed his exhausted dragon to spiral downwards.

Cheers ran around the arena, louder and louder. Feet stamped; hats were thrown in the air; strangers clapped each other like long-lost friends; money changed hands. Breathless, the Queen collapsed into her seat, cheeks flushed with colour. Darcy's face twisted with a mixture of disappointment and relief. The Grand Master's eyes narrowed with anticipation.

The crowd spilled out into the arena, racing recklessly past the stewards to greet their champion, confident that the black dragon was done for. The fight was surely over. But the Grand Master knew better. And Quenelda, hearing the rogue dragon's rambling thoughts as he struggled towards consciousness, also knew better. This dragon was not going to give up his single-minded purpose – to kill her father. She opened her mouth to say something; to warn the Queen. But who would believe her?.

Below, Midnight Madness stirred sluggishly, rising awkwardly to his feet beneath the weight of the webbing. Flexing powerful muscles, he shook his neck, throwing off the mesh like a dog shedding water. He had suffered a broken front leg on impact, but that hadn't dulled the red-eyed lust to kill. He leaped up, trailing a tangle of ropes and weights, catching the scent he had been trained to hunt. His damp nostrils flared and his tongue snaked out to taste the air. The prey was still close. Midnight Madness raised his head, red eyes watching as the Earl's dragon corkscrewed down through the mist of falling snow.

Kill . . . kill . . .

'No!' Quenelda's scream brought the Queen to her feet again. Courtiers peered through the driving snow, trying to see what had caused her to cry out. The Grand Master looked at her curiously as he went to peer down over the balustrade.

Springing upwards on his powerful haunches, the black dragon struck out with his thick neck; his bared teeth snapped towards the Earl. Then he lurched into the air, slowly gaining height despite the rents to his wings, his fractured foreleg hanging useless beneath him. Above, the Earl reined in Knight's Mace and frowned at the melee below as stewards circled warily around the riderless rogue dragon, trying to force him downwards by sheer weight of numbers.

Kill . . . kill . . . The mad whisper persisted in Quenelda's head. *Kill the Dragon Lord . . .* She was desperate. Her father did not know the danger he was in. The stewards didn't know. No one knew but her!

Break off . . . break off . . . Quenelda urgently instructed the raptor. *Break off your attack . . .* But in his blood frenzy and pain, Midnight Madness either did not hear her or did not heed her words. Baffled, heart hammering, she had no time to puzzle out why, no time to think. Anger boiled through her veins.

Break off your attack . . .

Nothing happened. Nothing! No dragon had ever disobeyed her before.

Break off your attack, she whispered.

The stewards crowded around the Earl, trying to coax his injured mount to take off to the safety of the list platforms, where archers waited.

Quenelda's head throbbed. Her eyes hurt. The slightest noise felt like a blow. Once again she concentrated on the dragon, trying to put her fear for her father out of her mind.

As she did so, strange runes formed in her mind. Words entwined themselves around her thoughts in a language long forgotten. She felt their power gather shape and a spell of binding and obedience take form. From somewhere between memory and imagination she cast the right words from the Elder Days and flung them silently at the midnight-black dragon. What happened next shocked her as much as anyone.

A freezing pulse of power radiated out from Quenelda, instantly turning snow to hail that rattled off the gallery. The wind shrieked, the force of its icy blast tearing at cloaks and ripping the damask awning loose.

All around the arena, men-at-arms staggered drunkenly where they stood, and those deep inside the palace lost their footing and fell. The screaming crowds on the far terraces shivered as goose pimples crawled up their spines and raised the hair on the back of their necks. Children cried out in fear and huddled close to parents.

As the pulse dissolved into nothingness, there was a deafening clap of thunder in the bowl of the arena, and the black dragon was flung upwards and sideways. Only just missing the Earl, he tumbled head over tail into the packed stands as if felled by a giant fist. His flailing body punched a ragged hole in the wooden struts. Oak beams and bones broke like matchsticks; stone imploded. The sound of protesting timbers filled the air, and then a whole section of the arena seating collapsed with a groan that carried to the Queen's pavilion.

Hindered by his broken leg, Midnight Madness

clumsily tried to regain his balance. Screaming spectators found themselves crushed like broken dolls by the thrashing tail. New shouts and screams of terror filled the air as the crowd panicked, trampling those around them in their haste to get away.

Head ringing with the effort, trembling with exhaustion, Quenelda felt her legs give way. Chilled to the bone, she sank through Root's outstretched arms and landed heavily. She felt faint and nauseous, the unfamiliar taste of raw magic bitter in her mouth. Despite the wailing wind she could hear the screams and cries and wondered what she had done.

Questions ran wildly through her mind, tumbling, incoherent. Who had caused the dragon to crash into the stands and reduce the royal gallery to a shambles? Was it really her? Clearly nobody else imagined it could be her. She opened her eyes. It was pandemonium.

She saw men trying to anchor the awning as severed pavilion ropes lashed out. Several of the Queen's ladies-in-waiting were on the floor, unconscious; others were being helped back into the castle. The Grand Master had taken off his heavy cloak to throw it around the shaking Queen's shoulders as she gazed down disbelievingly at the scene below. Of those still standing, only Root had noticed Quenelda's collapse and came to her assistance; the others were all riveted by the drama unfolding in the arena below.

'Archers,' the Queen commanded faintly. 'Kill it!'

'Kill it!' The Grand Master loudly conveyed the Queen's wish to the stewards over the howling wind. But not yet, he thought to himself. Not quite yet . . . You'll find your arrows will make no difference – he is armoured beneath that outer skin . . .

A bugle rang out. Archers! Archers!

Root's head went up as he recognized the call. 'They're going to shoot him, Quenelda,' he said, looking anxiously at her. She was pale and her eyes streamed with tears. He had never seen her cry before, and took her hand. 'It's going to be all right! Your father's safe. The archers are going to kill the dragon!'

Strung out around the lip of the arena, archers lifted their great yew dragonbows and took aim, eyes narrowed to gauge the range, compensating for the wild cross-winds. It was going to be difficult.

Thunk!

Some of the six-foot longbows found their mark. Arrowheads thudded into the dragon's heavy hide, pricking his body like a pincushion, rending holes in his wings. His scream of rage rang out, tearing through the air as if it were fabric, the noise sending shivers down Root's spine. Midnight Madness wildly snapped at the barbs that stung him, but then, unfolding his wings, he took to the air.

Shock and disbelief rippled around the crowd. No un-armoured dragon should be able to withstand the heavy punch of those barbed arrows.

'Break off!' In her frustration and fear, Quenelda screamed out loud; but as the dragon slowly gained height her voice was lost amongst the cries around her. 'Papa! Papa!'

It was no use. The effort of challenging the renegade dragon had left her dizzy and exhausted. Midnight Madness could no longer hear her weak commands and she could no longer hear his thoughts. This problem had never happened before, and she had no idea how to respond. She had always taken dragons' friendship and loyalty for granted. Desperately, she tried to see through the thickening snow. Now if this was a battle . . .

Of course! A battledragon! Her father needed a battledragon to fight the raptor, not a schooled jousting dragon.

'Two Gulps . . . Two Gulps!' she screamed without knowing she did so, but her words were stolen away by the swirling snow.

'He won't be able to hear you.' Root tried to reason with her.

Quenelda was frantic, her thoughts tumbling, almost incoherent. She cried in dragon tongue, flinging the mental cry for help with all her might to the Winter Tower hidden in the storm. Would it be enough?

Oh, Two Gulps! Papa is in danger . . . Two Gulps!

Dancing with Dragons . . . The brush of his mind against hers was light as a flake of snow. *I come . . .*

The battledragon was coming! He had answered her call! Relief made her weak at the knees and she collapsed back onto Root again. *Hurry*, she willed her dragon. *Hurry!*

Quenelda pulled herself up and leaned dangerously over the balustrade, whorls of snow wrapping her like a cloak of white. Suddenly Two Gulps swooped down like a blazing fire storm through the whirling snow, briefly blotting out the light. The downdraught of his wings blasted the royal gallery with freezing air and blew the snow into whirling coils. Quenelda leaped up onto the balustrade then bounded off onto the armour-scaled wing. As the wing rose up again, she threw herself into the saddle, and then, before any could draw breath, she was away.

'Quenelda! Wait!' She heard Root's cry receding into silence as the snow enveloped her. 'Wait for m—'

She's gone without me! The gnome was stunned as he knelt on the balustrade. I'm her esquire; I'm supposed to be protecting her!

CHAPTER TWENTY-THREE
The Cauldron

Darcy watched in slack-jawed amazement as Quenelda executed the difficult manoeuvre to perfection. Unease prickled up his spine. He knew his sister could fly battledragons, but even in his wildest dreams he hadn't realized she was this good. He had not been paying attention, dismissing her as an irritation, someone whose antics generated scandal and gossip at court. For the first time Darcy felt afraid, for Quenelda was now taking his place at their father's side in front of everyone.

The Queen was now at the balustrade, her courtiers beside her, commanding her lords and men-at-arms forward to protect the Earl and his young daughter. The Grand Master was also out of his seat at the edge of the box, unwilling to accept what he had just seen: a young girl leap onto one of her father's battledragons like a seasoned veteran, sweeping down to her father's aid. How had she known the dragon was coming? How had he been summoned? He shook his head. Well, much good it would do her. She would die with her father.

In the labyrinth of corridors and stairs, Root had twice taken a wrong turning. Now, crying with frustration, ignoring the stitch in his side, he finally reached the top of the Winter Tower.

'Chasing the Stars!'

The dragon lifted her delicate head as she heard Root's voice and turned to nuzzle him affectionately. Clutching a stirrup, he bent double to catch his breath.

'Untether . . . untether her . . .' he panted. 'Quickly!' The roosthands stared at him uncertainly. A sentry started moving towards the roost.

Desperately Root hurled himself into the saddle, gathering up the reins as if he were born to it. 'Hurry!' he commanded as he heard the great roar that greeted the arrival of Quenelda's battledragon in the arena. 'Hurry! The Lady Quenelda's life is in danger!'

That had the desired effect. One of the roosthands slashed the tether rope.

'Up! Up, Chasing the Stars!' Root urged, and she obeyed him instantly, rising up and disappearing into the storm.

Far below, the Earl dimly heard the cheers of the crowd and was puzzled. Had Darcy finally decided to act like a man? he wondered.

Black arrows arced through the air, falling like diving cormorants around the rogue dragon. As Quenelda's battledragon swept into the centre of the arena, two quarrels thumped into his armoured hide. Quenelda screamed with mingled fear and shock.

'Hold your fire!' the keen-eyed captain cried, squinting through the blizzard to identify the flame-red dragon enter the fray. 'Hold your fire. The wind is rising. We might hit the wrong mark!' Beside him the bugler rang out his command. Longbows were lowered. The flight of arrows ceased.

Root was flying, a blaze of magenta-blue flitting through the growing dark. Ducking and diving around the castle towers, gnome and dragon swept over the startled heads of soldiers patrolling the inner bailey battlements and up and over the side of the vast arena. The thundering boom of the crowd rose to greet them but Root hardly heard it as he searched for Quenelda. Banners cracked in the wind; braziers smoked wildly, making him cough as he landed briefly on the mid-landing of the list tree. As yet no one below had noticed him. All was muddle and turmoil. Shouts rose and fell on the wind. Shapes came and went in the murk. He squinted through the snow with his telescope . . .

The snow was falling thickly around Quenelda, muting all sound save the whumph of Two Gulps' wings and the frantic thump of her heart, loud in her ears. The wind had teased out her braids and her long hair swirled wildly around her face, whipping into her eyes; her heavy cloak tugged in the cross-winds, threatening to pull her from the saddle. With numb fingers, she fumbled at the clasp and let the storm seize it.

She saw dark shadows below scything through the snow; then, on the far side of the arena, she saw the wind suddenly buffet the injured Knight's Mace into the netting. The mare's shriek pierced the air like a dart. At the same time the snow parted to reveal Midnight Madness far below Quenelda. He was turning towards the sound.

Hold tight, Dancing with Dragons . . . ! Two Gulps and You're Gone folded his wings and dropped like a stone towards the dark dragon below. The sheer speed of their descent punched the breath out of Quenelda's lungs. The wind shrilled in her ears. Snow filled her nostrils and open mouth till she was choking. Intent on his prey, Midnight Madness didn't see them coming until Two Gulps smashed into him, locking his talons on harness and neck.

The shock of the impact nearly unseated Quenelda and rattled her teeth in her head. The metallic taste of blood flooded her mouth and spots danced in front of her eyes as her dragon drove his enemy relentlessly down towards the floor of the arena.

With Midnight Madness helpless in his grip, Two Gulps drew back his neck for the killing strike. Smoke was pouring from his nostrils, streaking Quenelda's face with soot. As the battledragon's opened his jaws and prepared to flame, Quenelda leaned forward, pulling back on his reins.

No! No! She choked. She had thought to rescue her father, not kill the black dragon, who, she realized, must have been trained to his task through no fault of his own. *Don't kill him, Two Gulps! Don't kill him!*

Dancing with Dragons? He was confused. *How can I defend your father . . . ?* As he questioned his mistress, his grip on his opponent slackened. Taking advantage, the black dragon rolled to free himself, leaving Two Gulps with a talon-full of saddle and tangled harness. On the far side of the arena, injured and faint from loss of blood, the Earl was still strapped beneath his injured mount. With a powerful flick of his tail, Midnight Madness headed into the storm towards the Earl.

Dancing with Dragons? Two Gulps was baffled. *I had him beneath my talons . . .*

'Oh, no!' Cupping her face in her hands in despair, Quenelda realized what she had just done. By preventing

Two Gulps from killing the rogue dragon, she had once more freed him to attack her father. What was she thinking? She had thought battle was glamorous, as if death played no part in it. She had been like a child playing games. To save her father the dragon had to die.

Oh, Two Gulps . . .

Letting the harness fall into the netting, Two Gulps and You're Gone turned in hot pursuit.

Root's eyes were streaming in the stinging snow as he scanned the arena. There was a sudden flicker of movement nearby. With his heart in his mouth, he saw Quenelda's cloak flit upwards like a demented bat.

'No!' Fearing she was already injured, maybe even dead, he cried out, fiercely brushing tears from his eyes. 'Go, girl! Go, Chasing the Stars! We're too late!'

Hearing the urgency in his voice, feeling it in the touch of his hands and knees, Chasing the Stars flew like she had never flown before, down and down into the swirling cauldron of snow, where the smell of blood rose up to greet her. A small dragon materialized in front of them, making Root's heart leap into his mouth.

'Get away! Get away you fool!' The steward tried to block his path but a gust of wind took him sideways. 'The dragon's gone rogue!' Dodging the man's outstretched arms, dragon and gnome flew on in pursuit of their friend.

Midnight Madness loomed over the stricken Earl, who had lost consciousness as they tried to pull his leg free from beneath his screaming mount. Half a dozen men-at-arms bravely stood over him, shields and spears raised.

260

Alighting on the netting, Midnight Madness killed Knight's Mace with a single slash to the throat. Then the scent of the Earl's blood reached him, and he raised his eyes to where Quenelda's father lay helpless. Now nothing stood between the rogue dragon and his prey.

Saliva and blood dripped from his jaws. *Kill . . . Kill . . .*

Quenelda and Two Gulps swept in above her father. *Two Gulps!* She choked as the dragon beneath them raised his head to strike. *Stop him! Stop him!*

Two Gulps' wings flapped frantically as he hovered above Midnight Madness. To attack now might also kill the Earl beneath him. With a sound that started in his stomachs and worked its way upwards through the bellows of his great lungs, Two Gulps and You're Gone opened his jaws wide instead and let out a rib-rattling battle challenge.

'Kwwwwaaaakkk!'

The arena vibrated. The Earl flinched at the familiar battlecry and stirred sluggishly back into consciousness.

Root's mare was not battle-hardened.

'Whoa! S-s-steady there, girl.' He tried to keep the wobble out of his own voice as he quietened Chasing the Stars: she was snorting and frothing at the mouth with fear. Her large, sensitive ears lay flat along her neck and her tail was curled in under her belly as she tried to hide in the storm.

'S-s-teady there. Steady, girl.' Root finally managed to bring her under control. 'It – it's going to be all right,' he repeated unconvincingly, as much to himself as to his mount. 'Come on, girl,' he said bravely, coaxing the little dragon forwards. 'We've got to help Quenelda.'

Suddenly Two Gulps' challenge boomed and reverberated around the arena. Unable to resist the primeval roar, Midnight Madness turned from his prey to face the other dragon and return his challenge. 'Yyyaaakkkaaa!'

With a few flaps of his four thickly muscled wings and a push of his powerful hind legs, the black dragon sprang up to attack. Quenelda screamed as Two Gulps feinted sideways, and the Earl looked up with disbelieving eyes.

'Quenelda?'

'Papa! We're coming to save you!'

As Two Gulps let the wind scoop him upwards and away from her father, Quenelda was jubilant. They had succeeded in luring Midnight Madness away! She could see her father's upturned face receding as two soldiers took his weight to help him down the netting towards his waiting household knights and safety.

'Quenelda!' The urgency of his voice stunned her. 'Goose! Look—'

Quenelda waved at him, but then she realized he was trying to tell her something, and slowly, reluctantly, she looked over her shoulder. A rank cloud of hot air buffeted her. Puzzled, she pushed back her hair. Bloodshot, smouldering eyes and an opening maw were almost upon her!

She tried to scream out, but only managed a croak. Panicked, frantically slapping at her battledragon's armoured hide in her frenzy to communicate, she finally found her voice: 'Two Gulps!' she screamed, hair streaming into her eyes. 'Fly! He's right behind us!'

Already sensing his foe's approach, Two Gulps leaped away, banking steeply down towards the floor of the arena, a manoeuvre that nearly unseated Quenelda. Then Midnight Madness was bearing down on them, the hot fetid stench of his breath vaporizing the snow as he came. Two Gulps rolled and swept backwards, wings beating frantically to pull away from danger, leaving Quenelda clinging precariously to his neck. Gobbets of tattered dragon flesh sprayed her, and then the rogue dragon thundered past, narrowly missing her with his talons. Suddenly her father's words came back to haunt her: *Quenelda, I know you can fly. But there is a great deal more to becoming an SDS pilot . . .*

She realized in a moment of clarity how foolish and childish she had been to think she could fight at his side simply because she could fly! But right now that was all she could do if they were to survive.

Fly, Two Gulps!

It was growing so dark she could hardly even make out the tiered seating around them. Braziers flickered briefly like marsh fireflies as they jinked to and fro, each dragon trying to win the advantage. Hampered by Quenelda's lack of battle experience or Battle Magic, Two Gulps knew he could not take the dragon on head to head or she might die in the fight. She wore no armour; her scales were soft.

Quenelda forgot to breathe. Never before had she felt so afraid of a dragon. For the first time she saw raptors through Root's and her brother's eyes: the reptilian mouth full of needle-like teeth; the powerful jaw that could crush a cow as if it were a soft-bellied grub; taloned claws reaching forward to seize and slice and tear . . . a predator.

'Fire!' the archers' captain shouted as Quenelda and Two Gulps flew past. 'Fire at will! Make sure of your target, lads! Make every arrow count!' As dragon and girl swept around the lip of the arena, a volley of black arrows rained down behind them. Quenelda heard the bellow of rage from Midnight Madness as many found their mark, then the faint screams from the crowd below as the lethal rain fell on them.

Leaning flat over Two Gulps' neck, she risked a look behind. She sat up. Where was the dragon? She frantically searched the driving snow – behind, above, below. The arrows must have killed him, she thought, and relaxed.

He's gone, Two Gulps. We've lost him. The archers will take care of him now—

Dancing with Dragons!

Wha-? Quenelda turned and realized that she had been looking the wrong way. There, hovering in front of them, was the black dragon, his armoured hide sprouting arrows like a monstrous pincushion.

I must fight, Dancing with Dragons . . . Jump. Jump into the netting and let me fight him alone. It is the only way – you have never before been in battle . . . Two Gulps feared for his mistress's life; why had she ordered him not to kill the rogue dragon? The battledragon pleaded for guidance: *Dancing with Dragons, what is your command? This dragon is crazed . . . His mind is brittle – fractured like broken ice. He must die . . . It would be a kindness to kill him . . .*

But then there was no time to do anything: Midnight Madness leaped at them and his open maw filled Quenelda's vision. She froze in sheer terror. She was going to die.

'Quenelda! Quenelda!'

At first Quenelda thought she must be imagining it, the familiar high-pitched cry. But how could it be Root out here?

'Queneldaaaaa!'

Then, out of a thick bank of snow, a tiny flash of violet-blue cut through the storm in front of her and then was gone, distracting the black dragon's attention away from her at a critical moment. Midnight Madness slashed out at Chasing the Stars. Taking advantage, Two Gulps slammed into his unprepared foe, tumbling him head over heels.

Stunned, Midnight Madness hit the netting hard and bounced back into the air once more. He was beginning to weaken from his many injuries, and the magic that bound him was finally beginning to unravel. He was slowly losing his mind. Hovering, he shook his head, trying to focus on the waiting battledragon. His tongue licked out to taste the air. Quenelda was not his prey, but she smelled like the man who was. Pain thundering through his veins, Midnight Madness leaped upwards.

But the little violet-blue dragon and her rider flashed across his path again and again. She darted to and fro like a sparrow attacking an eagle, forcing the raptor to strike out in increasing frustration, growing weaker with every strike.

His movements slowed and tremors shook him from snout to tail. The fire in his eyes dimmed. As he snapped weakly at Chasing the Stars, Two Gulps and You're Gone didn't hesitate: his mistress's life was in danger and the

SDS battledragon's training cut in to defend her. A vicious talon to the stomach and Midnight Madness died, his broken body falling out of the sky.

It was finally over! Wings spread wide, Two Gulps and You're Gone sank gently to the floor of the arena, where Quenelda's father stood surrounded by his household guard. The spectators, who had been streaming out, turned back to discover who had been flying the battledragon. In the swirling dark, the slim figure in flying boots, breeches and shredded dress was dimly silhouetted against the flickering light.

''Tis the Earl's son, the Lord Darcy.'

'It's a girl, Father!' a young boy cried. 'It's a girl!'

'Nae, lad.' His father shook his head. 'It can't be! That's a battledragon they've been commanding!'

'It is, Father! It's the Earl's daughter!'

'Quenelda! Goose!' The Earl shook off helping hands and limped over to embrace his daughter. As she dismounted, her dress shredded and spattered with blue blood, the Queen's men-at-arms thumped their swords on shields in acknowledgement of a warrior's success. The crowds took up the chant.

'DeWinter! DeWinter! DeWinter!'

The exhausted Earl asked one of his men for his sword. Taking the weapon, he wearily lifted his daughter's hand with his own, sword raised to the sky as they acknowledged the crowd's acclaim. Quenelda felt the persistent ache of fear drain from her, and with it all her strength. But somehow the crowd's adulation and her father's proud smile kept her on her feet.

'DeWinter! DeWinter! DeWinter!'

As the swirling snow shrouded them both in a veil of white, a deafening cheer erupted that roared around the arena faster than the storm. The very air vibrated. The stands shook beneath the stamping feet. The crowd recognized a gesture when they saw one. While the Earl's son had remained in the royal gallery, his younger sister had flown a dragon, an SDS battledragon no less, to her father's rescue!

'Quenelda DeWinter! Quenelda DeWinter! Quenelda DeWinter!'

'Easy, girl, easy.' Unnoticed by anyone, Root stroked his quivering dragon's neck as they watched the crowds below converge on the Earl and his daughter. He could barely hear their roar for his heart thumping in his ears. Chasing the Star's nostrils were still flared wide with fear. Her wings were caked with ice and snow, and her breathing clouded the air around her head in a sparkling halo. Root was in no better a state himself. 'Easy, girl,' he whispered. 'It's all over. They're safe now.' As a gust whipped gnome and dragon sideways and upwards from the list, he turned her towards the roosts; towards a warm stall and a rub down.

'And you can have as many honey tablets as you want!'

Pale with thwarted fury, the Grand Master found his veiled eyes meeting Darcy's cold, jealous ones, and a brief unguarded moment of recognition passed between them.

What on the One Earth had happened? They had all felt it, a sudden powerful gust of icy-cold air that buffeted the arena, throwing his unbeatable Midnight Madness into the packed stands with a clap of thunder. The tremor that followed a mere heartbeat later had shivered through the old stone bones of the castle.

In the ensuing chaos, only the Grand Master had recognized it for what it was; had recognized the underlying ripple of Elder Magic that had flared and died in the blink of an eye. He knew it from the unmistakable aftershock that had nothing to do with twenty tons of dragon smashing into the great arena; but it was a magic so strange, so uncanny, that he could not identify its source. The epicentre was close to where he stood, he was certain of it. It had the potency of Battle Magic, yet puzzlingly it was so carelessly cast that scores had died in the fallout, and much of its power had rolled over the lip of the arena to dissipate in the glen beyond. Yet none nearby had raised wand or staff, and anyway, only an Arch Mage or Battle Mage could cast such a spell. With the Earl and the Queen's constable down in the arena, there were no others in the royal gallery save himself. Magical signatures were unique, no two exactly the same. In the confusion the Grand Master had cast a subtle rune but it had revealed no telltale signature.

A small part of him was intrigued that someone was prepared to kill so many to save one man. It showed a single-minded ruthlessness akin to his own. But he was also incensed by his unaccustomed failure.

Whatever strange magic it was, it had crippled his dragon, diverting him from his true purpose so that Quenelda and her battledragon could sweep down and save the Earl's life. It had been hard to follow the battle through the curtain of snow but he had recognized the battledragon's challenge – and who would have thought that the brat – that gnome she called esquire – would have been so brave?

Conveniently, Sir Hugo's pale face, his trembling voice, his evident shock and rage would in fact protect him from blame or suspicion, had any been watching his little drama unfold.

'DeWinter! DeWinter! DeWinter!'

With a forced smile, Darcy also joined in the wild applause of the Queen and the royal court, keeping his thoughts to himself. All his efforts to make his sister an object of ridicule and derision had failed, undone by a single spectacular manoeuvre and the unbelievable sight of her controlling a battledragon in combat. What if Papa acknowledges her as his heir, here and now? He thought bitterly, panic rising like sour apples in his throat. Then I'm utterly lost.

'DeWinter! DeWinter! DeWinter!'

CHAPTER TWENTY-FOUR
Maelstrom Magic

The snow continued falling.

Quenelda had spent her childhood dreaming of a moment like this: the splendour and excitement of the battlefield; a great act of heroism; her father watching with pride. But now that it had finally happened, the reality of combat was worse than anything she had imagined. Somehow in her dreams she never heard the cries of the wounded or smelled the bitter stench of spilled guts and blood. She had never felt so exhausted or been so wretchedly sick. Without Root's brave intervention, she knew she would be dead; in her ignorance she had thought that somehow she could beat a rogue dragon simply because she could fly.

As the crowd engulfed them in a tidal wave of celebration, she was separated from her father. 'Papa! Papa!' she cried. but he was lost in the heaving, cheering mass. The Queen's men-at-arms tried desperately to keep the crowd back as the injured Earl was carried inside on a stretcher of shields. Suddenly remembering, Quenelda looked around frantically for Root, but could see no sign of him or Chasing the Stars. Then the blizzard had closed in again and she could barely see a yard in front of her face, making flying impossible.

Sending Two Gulps to search the Cauldron for Chasing the Stars, she had allowed herself to be carried along by the soldiers streaming into the inner bailey yards. Dazed and exhausted, chilled to the bone, she somehow found her way to the great keep. By now her head was throbbing, the taste of magic still bitter in her dry mouth. She was shaking from exertion and her close brush with death. Dizzily, she leaned against the cold stone of the battlements, before the swirling snow wrapped her in white and she slipped down . . . down . . . into a silent shrouded world . . .

In the teeming corridors conversation remained at fever pitch as rumour and counter-rumour swept its viaducts and high-vaulted halls. Grim-faced, the Queen's constable, Sir Mowbray, had gone to the Earl's quarters and then left without a word. Some said the Earl Rufus was near death, that the rogue dragon had nearly torn his leg off. Others claimed that, already weak from his war wound, he had broken his back and would be dead within the hour.

But another rumour was also rife: that it was the Earl's young daughter who had swept down to his rescue while his son looked on from the royal pavilion doing nothing. Only no one could find her . ..

'Quenelda!'

It had taken Root nigh on two hours to find his friend. Searching the heavily guarded rooms and corridors outside the Earl's apartments in the Winter Tower, he finally spotted a distinctive pair of size-six boots peeking out from beneath tattered skirts. No wonder she had been overlooked: none would take her for an Earl's daughter dressed like that, covered in gore, hair in knots. Quenelda was curled up on a stone window seat, almost completely hidden beneath a heap of snow that had drifted in through the arrow-slit. Bending over, Root had recoiled at the stench – the fetid smell of rotting meat that still clung to her clothes.

He struggled to wake her – he was close to panic when she finally opened her eyes, but her first words had chilled him even more.

'It was n-no accident, Root.' She was trembling, the words tumbling out in a torrent as he guided her through the press of soldiers and courtiers towards a burning brazier to warm her.

'What do you mean, it was no accident?' He helped her onto a wooden stool and looked at her anxiously.

'That d-d-dragon that attacked Papa, it was a r-raptor.' Her voice was barely above a whisper, throat raw from shouting, tight with fear.

'What? Wh—?'

'It w-was a r-raptor, inside.' Quenelda's elfin face was deathly pale and she was shaking as if she had a fever. Root took her hands in his and tried to warm her freezing fingers.

'It was magic of s-some kind. Really p-p-owerful magic, Root! It looked like an ordinary dragon, but it wasn't! The G-Grand Master's dragon was trying to kill Papa!'

'Sshh.' Root looked around anxiously at the press of courtiers and soldiers, noticing some wearing the Grand Master's livery. 'What are you saying?' he whispered.

Quenelda's voice was so quiet he could hardly hear her. He leaned down, his ear close to catch her words. 'The Grand M-Master was trying t-to kill Papa and make it l-look like a-an accident.'

Root was seriously alarmed. He had to warm her up; she was clearly delirious – she didn't know what she was saying. He put a hand to her head and yelped as if he had been stung. Her forehead was ice-cold! A flake of frost fell away in his hand.

'Wait here,' he told her, wrapping his heavy cloak around her shoulders. 'I'm going to see if I can find some help.' He ran off, but the castle was in uproar and no one paid a young esquire any attention.

Then he spotted a familiar face coming through the crowds. He jumped up with his hand in the air. 'Quester! Quester!'

'Root!' His friend hugged him. 'I've been looking everywhere for you! The Earl has been asking for the Lady Quenelda, and no one could find her. She was not in her chambers. He has half the palace guard looking for her – and for you. Is she . . . ?'

'No, no, she's not injured,' Root assured his friend. 'But she's . . .' He paused. 'She's ill. Exhausted, I think, and burning up with a chill. Let me show you . . .'

He led his friend over to where Quenelda lay. 'Can you stand?' Quester asked her anxiously. 'There is an apothecary in your father's chambers if you can reach them?'

Quenelda nodded. 'I th-think so.'

Between them they helped her to her feet. She seemed as light and fragile as thistledown. Quester had begun to push a way through the noisy throng when the whispering began. Heads began to turn their way.

'It's her!'

'I tell you,' a soldier wearing the Earl's livery insisted loudly. 'It's her; I've seen her at Dragonsdome a thousand times . . .'

273

Then someone whispered Quenelda's name and it carried like a warm breath of wind in front of her. The murmur of gruff voices rose around her, wrapping her warmly in their admiration. Quenelda stood a little straighter.

'Lady Quenelda . . .' A courtier bowed. A lady curtsied.

She looked up in wonder as they broke into a ripple of applause, all rising, the excitement of the day's feats fresh in their memory.

''Ere, yer ladyship,' a battle-scarred dwarf in the Queen's livery barked at his companions. 'Make way for 'er Ladyship Quenelda – make way . . .'

By the time she reached her father's antechamber, Quenelda had an escort of a dozen Bonecracker commandos. For the first time in her life, the guards came to attention for her and opened the doors. Trying not to stare, the crowd stood respectfully aside, calling out blessings on her and the Queen's Champion.

Quester hung back with them. 'You go on, friend Root. You're her esquire now. They'll let you in,' he told the gnome. 'And Root, no one can say that you do not deserve to be her esquire after what you did today. No one will care what Felix and his cronies think any more!'

'Papa!' Quenelda stumbled through the doorway, only her fear keeping her from collapsing. 'Papa! That dra—'

The words died in her throat. There were two figures sitting beside the fire. The bright light put them in silhouette. Quenelda raised a hand to shield her eyes. 'Papa . . . ?'

'Goose! Where have you been?' Her father rose to his feet and limped two steps towards her, then wrapped her

274

in a wordless embrace. Thank the Gods, he breathed silently.

'I'm proud of you, Goose,' he said fiercely, using the hem of his cloak to wipe the tears that trickled down his daughter's cheek. 'Stoner's Manoeuvre no less, I hear?' He stood back to look her in the eye. 'No father could be more proud of his daughter!'

Lifting his head, he searched the shadows and found Root hanging back near the door. 'And you, boy. Come forward. I have been told what you did this day. You took on a crazed dragon, and it was bravely done. Your father would have been proud. Name your reward.'

'M-my reward?' Root echoed, looking anxiously at Quenelda.

Despite his pain, the Earl smiled. 'Anything, boy. I shall formally raise you to esquire and appoint you to my daughter's household, with an annual income of ten gold sovereigns. But come, there must be something else a lad of your age longs for?'

Root sucked in a deep breath. 'I – I couldn't have done it w-without Chasing the Stars . . .' He glanced up anxiously to see how the Earl was reacting.

The Earl nodded. 'She's yours, boy. You earned her today! Tangnost will be informed.'

The other figure in front of the fire stepped forward into the candlelight. 'Thank the gods, Rufus,' the deep rich voice rang out. 'Your daughter is safe. I told you not to worry!'

Quenelda's heart leaped into her throat.

'This young lady can clearly take care of herself!' The Grand Master stood beside her father, hand on his

275

shoulder. His handsome face was smiling but his dark eyes weren't – they looked down at her thoughtfully.

'Dear child,' he said, teeth gleaming whitely. 'I never thought to see what I witnessed today. A wondrous thing indeed! You saved your father's life. You and your . . . young esquire here.' He barely glanced at Root. 'That Rufus's life should have been endangered by one of my own dragons . . .' He shook his head regretfully.

'Hugo' – the Earl turned to his friend and gave him a tired smile – 'don't punish yourself. The dragon must have taken an injury and the Duke drove it to madness. It has happened before. You were not to blame!'

'Nonetheless,' the Grand Master sighed, 'it was out of my stable and the Duke was my liegeman. I never knew the man was so twisted, so hell-bent on revenge. We could have lost you today. Well' – he glanced at the hour glass on the stone mantel – 'I must return to the Sorcerers Glen. Tonight's entertainments have been cancelled, but there is much to do if we are to get your men rearmed and supplied for the coming campaign. Tomorrow I go to my estates in the north to raise two regiments of Bonecrackers for you. Farewell. Take care of your injuries. I will send my personal physicians to restore you to full health.'

With a bow, he smiled and left the room.

CHAPTER TWENTY-FIVE
The Dragon Whisperer

'Papa,' Quenelda began hesitantly, looking to Root for support, 'it wasn't an accident. It—'

Her father frowned. 'What—?'

He was interrupted by a loud rap at the door. The guards opened it and the Queen's elderly constable, Sir Mowbray, came in, his armour clanking, his old joints creaking, his face grave.

'My Lord Earl' – he bowed respectfully, keen blue eyes quickly taking in the Earl's chalk-white face and newly splinted arm – 'the surgeon says you must not fly till midwinter, else you risk being lame for life.' He squeezed the Earl's good shoulder. 'And thank the gods your arm was broken cleanly and not crushed.' He said the words lightly, but held his friend's eye before turning to Quenelda. He bowed a second time, voice husky with emotion.

'Lady Quenelda.' He paused, noting the determined line of her jaw, the fierce tawny eyes that were so like her father's. He had not seen it before; but for those eyes she was the mirror image of her mother at the same age. If she were dressed in court clothes, others might also see it. They would have to be more careful. He searched for the right words and found inspiration. 'You are indeed your father's daughter. That was bravely done.'

Sir Gharad Mowbray had been one of the SDS's greatest commanders and had fought with the Earl's father. In other circumstances, praise from him would have been something to treasure. But now, anxiety gnawed at

277

Quenelda like toothache. She wiped away tears with the back of her hand and ventured a half-hearted smile. Swaying beside her, Root struggled not to give in to the exhaustion that made his legs wobble and his eyelids droop.

'Sit,' her father commanded. 'You're exhausted. And you too, lad, before you fall. Now, what do you mean it wasn't an accident?'

'Wasn't an accident . . . ?' Sir Mowbray looked from father to daughter. 'What wasn't an accident?'

'Midnight Madness . . .' Quenelda croaked, her voice still hoarse from shouting. Sir Mowbray moved to fetch her a goblet of water. 'It wasn't an accident, Papa. That dragon was trying to kill you.'

There, it was out. Would they believe her? She drank the water down gratefully, cleansing the bitter taste from her mouth, then handed the goblet to Root.

'I know,' her father said.

'You do?' Relief flooded her.

'Yes,' her father continued. 'It was crazed with pain. It happens on the battlefield. Even SDS dragons have been known to kill indiscriminately when badly wounded.'

'No! No, you don't understand!' Quenelda was desperate to convince her father. 'That dragon was trained to kill.'

'What?' The Earl stood back to stare into her anxious eyes. For a moment he thought he glimpsed a faint reptilian glow in their depths, but then it disappeared. He blinked and shook his head. He was so tired, in so much pain. He eased himself onto a bench by the fire. Quenelda looked anxiously at him.

'How do you know, Goose?' he asked, pulling her down beside him. 'How do you know it wasn't an accident? Surely the dragon was simply driven mad with pain.' His face held only curiosity; no alarm as yet. 'Certainly the Duke goaded it to recklessness. He wanted to win at any cost. If he hadn't died, he would be in prison for carrying battle arms into the jousting arena. It is forbidden!'

'His mind, Papa . . .' Quenelda frowned as she tried to explain what she had sensed. She held out her hand in appeal, begging them both to understand. 'He was mad, yes. And' – compassion touched her voice – 'he was in pain. Terrible pain. But not the way you mean. He wasn't injured – at least not to start with; he was mad from the first.'

She stood up again. How could she make them understand?

'His thoughts were twisted somehow, as if there were two different creatures inside one body, battling with each other all the time, one trapped within the other, trying to escape. He kept repeating, Kill him . . . kill him . . . kill him . . . kill the Dragon Lord—'

'What?'

'He had killed before, I swear it, Papa! He had been trained to kill. He wasn't a Dale dragon at all – well, he was, but only on the outside . . .' Quenelda suddenly realized how far-fetched it sounded, but her father and the constable were watching her intently.

'But there was a . . . a raptor trapped inside him. It was as if his shape went in and out of focus . . . the air rippled around him like it does on a hot day – did you not see it?'

Both men shook their heads, as did Root. Quenelda's shoulders slumped. They didn't believe her.

'Child' – Sir Mowbray was concerned – 'you are tired . . . overwrought after your exertions today, and naturally so. You ask us to believe that one of the greatest sorcerers of his generation is deliberately seeking your father's death? But why? Hugo is both a trusted friend and an ally. It is unthinkable!'

'Papa!' Quenelda appealed instead to her father. 'Midnight Madness had the mind of a battledragon. He was a raptor, and he was hunting you down.'

Her father frowned thoughtfully. 'That may be true. Even after the Duke fell, his dragon returned to attack me. Only a rogue dragon might behave thus; or . . . a raptor on the hunt.'

'But, Rufus,' Sir Mowbray protested. 'What you are suggesting is impossible. Domestic dragons and raptors' – he shrugged – 'are two distinct species. They cannot be interbred. Only Mael—'

Sir Mowbray faltered, horror etched on his face as the import of his words caught up with him. Maelstrom Magic: forbidden, dangerous, an extinct art, or so people thought . . . His mind raced.

'Maelstrom Magic . . .' he breathed. 'Only that has the power to twist nature from its true course, to bind one dragon within another . . .'

There was a sudden appalled silence.

'No!' Even to his own ears the Earl's denial carried no conviction as suspicion flared into sudden certainly. 'No!' He shook his head. 'Not Hugo! He is our Grand Master! He cannot be . . .'

But it might just be true.

As a young novice his childhood friend was always breaking Guild rules, and brilliant though he was, his appointment to Grand Master had been controversial. Since they parted company at the age of twelve, he to study at Dragon Isle and Hugo into the Guild, what had his friend risked in the pursuit of knowledge? Hugo's meteoric rise through the ranks of the Guild had matched his own through the SDS, but what if it was achieved by harnessing Dark Magic? Even if Hugo's motives were pure, it would eventually ensnare him. Even—

His horrified thoughts were interrupted.

'Maelstrom . . . ?' Quenelda's words trailed off in confusion as her father's words sank in. She swallowed; felt her heart thump against her ribs as Root stared at her. 'But . . .' She frowned uncertainly at her father. 'That's been outlawed by the Guild for centuries, hasn't it?'

'Ah.' Her father smiled unexpectedly. 'So you have paid a little attention to your classes, have you?'

'Papa!' she protested.

'Hush.' Her father laid a reassuring hand on her arm. 'I know it is no jest. Maelstrom Magic is deadly, its use justly punishable by death or exile.' He sighed, and seemed to come to a decision. Glancing at Sir Mowbray, he took his daughter's cold hand. 'That is why we must keep this knowledge secret.'

'Secret! But Papa, surely that is dangerous. Surely you—'

'No! No, Goose, we must stay silent. We are trapped for the time being. Regardless of his motives, to expose Hugo as a warlock would be folly. It would undermine the authority of the Guild to discover that the Grand Master, its greatest sorcerer, is corrupt. It would undermine centuries of rule and risk all that we hold dear. And Hugo is powerful. Perhaps with Maelstrom at his command he could beat us all. No.' He shook his head. 'To challenge him before we are certain of his purpose or his powers would be to squander a strategic advantage. What would it gain us? And how would we prove it? Who would believe us? Even I cannot believe he has knowingly practised Dark Magic. He must have unwittingly—'

'But the dragon!' Quenelda cried. 'It was a raptor. That is proof! It was—'

'Lady Quenelda,' the constable intervened. His voice was gentle. 'My men and I have already examined its carcass. The dragon looks like a Dale. There are no outward signs that it is a raptor, save that the arrows should have killed it. It was struck by four score yet did not die. But it would be impossible to prove what you claim.'

'Then . . . then I could tell my story; tell the Guild I heard the dragon's thoughts. Knew its intent.'

'No!'

Both Quenelda and Root were taken aback by the force of the Earl's denial. Only the constable seemed unsurprised.

'But . . . but, Papa, if you believe I can talk to dragons, why not let me tell my story?'

'Quenelda, you are young, very young; this would all simply appear a figment of an overactive child's imagination. None would believe you. But there is another reason why you must never repeat what you have said here to anyone else. You have a gift, Goose. A great gift.' The Earl tipped his daughter's pale face gently towards his, knowing that once the words were spoken out loud, nothing would ever be the same again. But the truth could no longer be denied. 'We believe you are a Dragon Whisperer,' he said softly, mind racing with the possibilities.

'A Dragon Whisperer?' Quenelda shook her head. 'But true Dragon Whisperers can do so much more, Papa! I have heard the old sagas and ballads since I was a babe. I can only talk to them. I cannot become a dragon.'

'Quenelda' – the Earl took her hand – 'have you never felt different to those around you? There must be countless times when you wondered why you could do things others could not, that Tangnost could not, that I could not, even though I command the SDS?'

'But' – confusion clouded Quenelda's face – 'but Tangnost . . .'

'Quenelda, you treated an injured battledragon. That's unheard of.'

'But Tangnost was there. He told me what to do. He is the one who calmed Two Gulps. He is always the one—'

'Tangnost has spoken to me. He believes the dragon would have killed him were it not for your presence. And you have clearly bonded with the Sabretooth. Such powers only come to those who have attained the rank of Mage.'

Sir Mowbray nodded in agreement. 'It's true, my dear. How else could you have done what you did today?'

'Others might think that it was Two Gulps and You're Gone,' her father continued. 'He was, after all, one of my battledragons, and they may think your rescue an SDS trick that I had taught you. But they would be wrong. Though he is loyal to me and loves me dearly, even Stormcracker would not have come to my rescue unless he could see the danger I was in. Yet Two Gulps came to you through the storm, just as you alone could hear that rogue dragon's twisted thoughts.'

'But . . . I can't become—'

'Goose,' the Earl protested, 'you are still young. You have not reached your thirteenth year. Do not look too soon for responsibilities and power. Believe me, they come at a price. Take the time to grow before you seek these things; they will come to you soon enough.

'In the meantime, we must be on our guard. Your heritage must remain our secret, and that means we cannot reveal the dragon as a raptor to anyone. Promise me. And you too, young gnome, you must also swear on my daughter's life you will tell no one.'

'My lord,' Root said proudly, puffing out his chest like a pigeon, 'as her esquire I am already sworn to protect Quenelda's life!'

The Earl looked at the constable, who returned his fleeting smile.

'But Tangnost . . . ?' Quenelda appealed as Root stood back. 'I mean – he already knows I talk to dragons, that I really talk to dragons.'

'Of course,' the Earl Rufus agreed. 'Tangnost has been sworn to secrecy since the day of your birth. But no others. If legends are to be believed, the power wielded by a Dragon Whisperer is greater than anything we know, far exceeding even that of an SDS Dragon Lord. Such power, if not schooled, could be very dangerous. Such power will attract envy and greed. I—'

The Earl's words struck a painful chord, reminding Quenelda of one thing that she had deliberately avoided asking. 'How many . . . ?' She took a deep breath. 'How many . . . ?'

'Died at the jousts?' her father queried. Quenelda nodded. He looked enquiringly at Sir Mowbray.

'Four score at the last count,' the constable confirmed, 'though more may die of their injuries. It was most unfortunate the beast was blown into the stands.'

'Eighty dead? No! It was all my fault!' Quenelda cried out despairingly. 'He wouldn't obey me!' Dwelling on the painful memory, she failed to notice her father's shocked expression. Sir Mowbray's jaw dropped.

'And I had to stop him somehow!' she went on. 'I—'

'What?' Her father interrupted and his eyes searched hers. 'That was you?'

Quenelda nodded her head tearfully. 'It was me. I didn't mean to hurt anyone. I was just trying to stop him attacking you . . . The runes – the spells just came into my head.' She bit her lower lip miserably. 'And I cast them . . .'

'I thought it was the storm. I sensed no High Magic.' Sir Mowbray frowned at the Earl.

'I too thought the storm had caught it.' There was a trace of something in her father's voice that Quenelda did not recognize.

There was a heavy silence punctuated by her sniffs; she wiped her eyes with the cuff of her sleeve.

So it has happened already, the Earl thought, stunned to learn how much power his daughter already wielded. I had hoped she would have many more years before she was burdened with such responsibility. A few more years to grow, to learn how to use and control this power growing within her . . . This changes everything . . . How now do I keep her powers hidden? How do I protect her? How do I protect those around her?

He chose his words carefully. 'Quenelda, what you did today takes great power. But power without learning and the wisdom to control it is dangerous, as you have learned. We must reconsider how best to teach you – for teach you we must, else you and those around you will be vulnerable. Your power already outstrips your control, as we witnessed today.'

'What will happen to me?'

'In truth,' her father admitted, 'I do not know. The Dragon Whisperers of old guarded their secrets well. A book is said to exist in the Great Library of the Sky Citadel, lost to us a thousand years since.'

'My lord . . .' Sir Mowbray drew the Earl towards the window and lowered his voice to a whisper. 'Rufus, if any should learn of Quenelda's powers they may wish to turn them to their own ends. If Hugo truly is a warlock, he may wish to draw upon it. If he cannot, then he may try to kill her before she becomes too strong, before she can defend herself.'

'He might try to kill me? Why?' Neither had noticed Quenelda approach silently.

'Elder Magic, the magic of the dragons. It is far older and more potent than the High Magic wielded by we Dragon Lords. And it is said to be the opposite of Maelstrom Magic, and just as powerful.'

'I think after all,' the Earl said slowly, 'that we shall

have to reconsider your education. The court is no place for you now.'

Once Quenelda would have whooped for joy. Now she was too exhausted to take in what her father had said.

'It is time you rested. A hot bath and fresh clothes will be laid out for you and the surgeon will be sent to your chambers. Go now.' He gently propelled his daughter towards the door.

'And I think, my Lord Earl,' Sir Mowbray suggested, glancing at the hourglass, 'that the Queen will be most anxious to learn how her Champion is.'

The Earl Rufus nodded, took a step forward and nearly fell as white-hot pain lanced through his thigh.

'Papa!' Quenelda reached out to take his elbow, gasping as fresh blood blossomed through his bandages. 'Papa, you are too ill!'

'No, Goose, I must attend the Queen. We have much to discuss.' Standing stiffly, he placed a kiss on his daughter's blonde head. 'And Goose?'

'Papa?'

'The Queen also wishes to see you and your young esquire. She will send for you later.'

'Us?' Quenelda's heart thumped. She looked at Root. 'Why?' she asked.

'Why?' For a moment the strong bearded face – the father she knew – grinned fiercely. 'To thank you, Goose, you and Root. To thank you for saving the life of her Champion.'

Chapter Twenty-Six
Dragon Isle

It was late into the night before Quenelda and Root were finally summoned to the Queen's presence.

The corridors of the vast castle were quiet now. The gossip and scandal of the day's events had stilled as exhausted courtiers ran out of steam and the castle brewery ran out of mead and ale. Those who could find no chamber were snoring in any niche or cushioned window seat they could find. Those of lesser rank found themselves a bed in the hay and rushes on the floor as best they could.

Candles smoked as the bitter cold outside crept in through cracks in the leaded glass. The castle's twelve-foot-thick walls and rich tapestries kept the worst of the cold at bay, but still Quenelda shivered.

Root looked at her pale face with concern. 'You're not well. You're still chilled, aren't you? Let me go back and get your warm cloak.'

'No, Root . . .' Quenelda began, but he was already running back to her father's chambers.

'Wait there,' he called over his shoulder, and then he was gone.

She shrugged. He was right. She just couldn't stop shivering, and she felt drained. She listened to his fading footsteps and rubbed her arms to keep herself warm.

Then suddenly the corridor ahead darkened and the hairs on the back of Quenelda's back prickled in sudden warning. The shadow grew, snuffing out the light from the lamps, sucking the warmth out of the air as if a door to the

winter outside had opened. Ice crusted about her. Frost
bloomed on the wall beside her . . . crept across the
flagstones . . . the air thickened.

'Well, well, my dear.' The Grand Master emerged from
the dark and greeted her, his voice soft. 'Well met. Quite
the heroine of the moment, hmm?' Danger and the threat
of it hung in the charged air like a thunderstorm.

It was the first time Sir Hugo had ever chosen to speak
to her alone. Sudden terror flushed through Quenelda's
veins, cold as ice. She felt her legs buckle. Struggling to
appear normal, to hide her suspicion and fear, she lifted
her eyes to look into his. The Grand Master's face was
hidden deep in the shadow of his hooded cloak, but she
could tell his dark eyes were studying her.

'Such a rare talent with dragons you have, my dear.
Wherever did you learn to fly a battledragon?'

'Oh, it was all the d-dragon,' Quenelda lied, angry at
the stutter that betrayed her growing sense of dread. 'He's
a Dragonsdome battledragon,' she said, trying to keep the
wobble from her voice. 'The best dragon in the Seven Sea
Kingdoms! I didn't have to do anything.'

'Mm . . . the Grand Master said thoughtfully. 'So
modest, my dear, and so like your dear father. But I'm sure
you must have had a hand in it . . . ?' He gave a smile, but
it didn't reach his eyes.

Alarmed, Quenelda stepped backwards till her
shoulders pressed against the cold stone.

'Come, my dear, no need to be afraid . . .' Sir Hugo's
voice was soft and insistent. He loomed over her, arms
outstretched like a bat so that his cloak enfolded her.

Quenelda felt a pressure in her head. Red and black

spots danced before her eyes. She was aware of an alien presence as something uncoiled within her mind and slithered forward, searching, searching . . .

The Grand Master's thin lips never moved, but she heard his voice clearly:

Tell me what happened today, the thought commanded. How did you command the dragon? Tell me . . .

The coils tightened. Her head pounded, the thump of her heart loud in her ears. Quenelda felt as if she were choking. Her body would not obey her mind. She ground her teeth as she tried to think of anything but dragons and dragon whispering.

The demand increased. The pressure was becoming unbearable . . . She could hardly breathe . . .

Tell me . . .

There was a roaring in her ears. She felt her control slipping away—

Suddenly, at the edges of her hearing, Quenelda recognized Root's voice.

The Grand Master had heard it too and cursed. She felt the presence in her mind release her and she slumped to the floor.

'Quenelda?' Root's high voice rang out from behind, the pounding of his feet drawing near.

Up ahead, a growing light flickered along the corridor. Hurrying footsteps and the hard sound of armour on stone approached. The Grand Master drew back a pace and dropped his arms. At his feet Quenelda coughed, struggling for air. Her body felt so heavy. Although sweat soaked her clothes, she felt frozen to the bone.

There was a brief flicker of movement and Sir Hugo was gone. The air thinned where he had stood, then returned to normal, allowing her to breathe. The light from the lamps returned. The frost beneath her shrivelled, leaving only a chill memory. Quenelda blinked and looked to her right and left. It was as if the Grand Master had vanished into thin air.

'Quenelda – here, I have it! I told you,' Root said accusingly, throwing the heavy cloak around her. 'You're not well. You must have fainted!' He took her white hands in his and rubbed them vigorously. 'You're freezing!'

They both looked up as two Bonecrackers rounded the far corner, followed by the tall, rangy figure of the Queen's constable. When he saw her on the ground, Sir Mowbray rushed forward. 'Lady Quenelda?' He laid a protective hand around her shoulders. 'Why, you are shaking, my dear!' His kindly eyes searched her pale face with concern. 'We feared for your health when you did not appear. My lady, are you still unwell? Should I send for the apothecary?'

Quenelda swallowed, sought for her voice and finally found it. 'No.' She was breathing heavily. 'No, thank you. I'm just a little dizzy . . .' She shook her head as her encounter slipped from her mind like a dream. 'I'm – I'm well.'

The constable nodded doubtfully and offered her his arm. Between them he and Root helped Quenelda to her feet.

'The Queen and your lord father await. I shall be pleased to escort you.'

Quenelda nodded, wincing. She felt unaccountably

reassured by the old knight's presence.

'Come, my dear,' he urged her. 'The hour grows late and you should have been in your bed long since.'

As he smothered a yawn, Root guessed he should also have been in his bed long ago.

They passed through carved and gilded oak doors and into the Queen's private chambers.

'Goodnight, my dear,' the constable said as he held Quenelda's hands. 'Do not fear for your father's or your own safety: no harm will come to you while you stay here.'

Root and Quenelda found themselves in a small cosy room with curtained diamond-paned windows, painted beams and dark wood panelling. The only light came from the dancing fire and two candles on the mantelpiece, which shed a soft amber glow. The smell of pine resin and scented candle wax filled the air. Two figures were seated on either side of the hearth. The Queen rose and moved towards Quenelda; she was dressed in a loose lavender robe edged with fur. The Earl Rufus sat in a tall backed chair. His bandaged thigh rested on a stool, his splinted arm across his lap. His face looked drawn with pain, although his eyes were alive and twinkling as he greeted his daughter.

Quenelda curtsied awkwardly. Root went down on one knee as he had seen the courtiers do in the royal gallery.

The Queen smiled. 'Rise, child,' she said, and took Quenelda's hand. 'Come, sit here beside me. And you, young lad. Come here also.' She patted the couch beside the fire. 'Now, how can I reward the daughter of my Champion for her bravery?' She looked down at Root. 'My Lord Earl tells me you have already claimed your reward. I know your father would have been proud of you today . . .' She hesitated a moment. 'I too know what it is to lose a father.' She held his eyes for a moment.

'All are talking of today's joust and rumours of your brave deeds are already sweeping the glen. The royal bard is at this very moment composing a ballad in your honour.' She turned to Quenelda. 'So how may we reward you?'

Quenelda looked stunned. 'Reward?' She hadn't expected this.

'I have long been aware of your special talent with dragons; the dragons watch over you, do they not? And now your father tells me you have also successfully treated a badly injured battledragon – indeed, the one you flew today. My dragonmasters confess themselves amazed. And for one so young to command a battledragon in combat is beyond anything I have ever seen or heard tell.'

Quenelda's blush of pleasure was lost in the firelight.

'Perhaps,' the Queen offered in the ensuing silence, 'I shall make you one of my ladies-in-waiting? A rare honour for one so young. How would a life at court suit you?'

There was a moment's hush as Quenelda's smile froze on her face and Root's jaw fell open. A log shifted on the fire. The silence stretched, and was then broken by a strange noise. Quenelda looked at the Queen, whose shoulders were shaking, a jewelled hand over her mouth. She turned to the Earl, who threw back his head and laughed out loud. Root shrugged and shook his head. He didn't understand either.

Baffled, Quenelda looked from her father to the Queen.

'Ah, no, I should not tease you so,' said the Queen. 'Your father tells me your dearest wish is to go to Dragon Isle. As you know, none but those destined for a life in the

SDS or those of royal blood have ever set foot there, home to the Dragon Lords.'

Quenelda's shoulders slumped. For a moment she had dared to believe . . .

'But' – a gentle smile played on the Queen's lips – 'today, you and Root have earned that right in front of all. I give you and your esquire permission to go to Dragon Isle with your father over the midwinter festivities. A fitting reward . . .' she said softly.

Reflected fire dancing in her eyes, Quenelda's smile lit up her drawn face. She clenched her fists in fierce delight. 'Dragon Isle . . .' she breathed, turning to Root, who was grinning from ear to ear. 'Root, we're going to Dragon Isle!'

Printed in Great Britain
by Amazon